# MAYBE I'M THE ONE

## ASPEN GOLD SERIES 17

### CHERYL ST.JOHN

Lyrics to songs *Maybe I'm the One, Baby We've Got This, One More Kiss, Long Time Comin'* and *Speaking of Mistakes* written and copyrighted by Cheryl St.John.

Cover image credit: majdansky via depositphoto

Cover and interior design by Cat & Doxie Author Services

**One More Kiss**
*~Audrey Knox*

The moon is high over the water
It's late and we should go
Yet here we are, still counting stars, still listenin' to the radio
In the magic of a summer night
there's nowhere I'd rather be, because...

Your eyes say one more kiss
What I want is one more kiss
Can we share just one more kiss
before we say goodnight?

My mama has the porchlight on
She's waitin' by the door
Yet here we are, still in your car, waves lappin' on the shore
Your hair smells like summer nights
and there's no one I'd rather hold, because...

Your eyes say one more kiss
What I want is one more kiss
Can we share just one more kiss
before we say goodnight?

# MAYBE I'M THE ONE

*Nashville* meets *Virgin River* when a beloved country singer returns to her roots and encounters the cowboy whose song she unknowingly stole.

*A woman with ambition*

Country singer Audrey Knox has traveled the world, followed her heart, and seen her dreams come true by becoming a worldwide fan favorite. Her face is on every magazine stand, and her songs are played all over the world. However, in achieving success, her world has become very small.

*A man who's been burned*

For Deputy Jericho Tanner, playing the guitar and singing was all about the music—and about spending time with the girl he secretly adored. His aspirations are to uphold the law and help run the family ranch he'll inherit. He learned early on that love is a weakness.

When Audrey returns to Spencer seeking acceptance, will Jericho allow pride to cost him happiness?

# CHAPTER ONE

*A*udrey stood in the wings, listening to Erik Bentley finish the last chorus of his song. The audience responded with whistles and applause. He had the crowd on their feet, which boded well for Audrey. Erik had been touring with her for the past five months on this US leg. He was a charismatic up-and-coming performer who knew how to work the audience, and booking him had been sheer genius on the part of her manager.

Gianna, her spiky blue-haired wardrobe assistant, attached the train of Audrey's dress quickly and efficiently as the calls from the crowd became a chant. *"Audrey! Audrey!"*

She glanced at her eight-year-old daughter beside her, and Hayden looked up with a smile. She gave Audrey a thumbs up, her usual encouragement for her mom to go out on stage and bring down the house. Audrey grinned and

hugged Hayden against her side. This date was one of the last
on her six-month tour. They'd sold out venues all over the
country, but everyone was ready for some well-deserved
down time.

Her make-up artist, Tam blended shimmery highlights on
Audrey's cheekbones and under the arch of her brows, then
added a last dab of color to her bottom lip. She handed
Audrey an open bottle of water with a straw. Willow
adjusted Audrey's already perfect pale-gold waves over her
shoulder.

"I think my hair's fine," Audrey told her stylist.

"Hair with its own Twitter feed has to be better than *fine*,"
Willow said with a quirk of her brow. She was in her thirties,
with straight dark hair to her shoulders and brown-framed
glasses.

Audrey rolled her eyes and stood patiently. She took a lot
of ribbing about that blasted Twitter fan account.

Absently, she noted her two bodyguards who accompanied her on tour, one on each side of the stage. Erik's song
ended and the crowd applauded. He took a bow and swept
an arm toward the band to thank them.

There was the usual synchronized change of instrumen-
talists and equipment as Audrey's guys took their positions.
She glanced down at the chunky beaded bodice of her dress
while Gianna fine-tuned the layers of pink and gold ruffles
on the train. Audrey loved this outfit. The top sparkled
under the lights and her pointed-toed cowboy boots were
comfortable and easy to walk in on stage. She was confident
and excited about tonight's show. Years of hard work and
sacrifice paid off every time she got to play to a sell-out
crowd.

Her introduction came over the sound system, and a
welcome tremor of nerves shot through her belly. A little
adrenaline was always good for her performance. She

exchanged a glance and a wave with Hayden and swept out onto the enormous stage.

The crowd cheered and phones were raised to snap photos. She waved to the fans filling the auditorium. "Hey, Atlantic City! It's exciting to be back here. Isn't Erik fantastic? Give him some love." She clapped along with the audience. "It's been so great having him with us on this tour. The Boardwalk is always one of our favorite places to play, and so many fans come out. I appreciate you, and I'm excited about this evenin'. Are ya'll ready for some more fun?"

The crowd roared, and the band played the first measures of Audrey's newest release, which had been in the top ten on the charts for the past three months. She took the microphone from its stand and smiled out across the ocean of upturned faces in the darkened arena.

*"'One two three four, don't try callin' me no more. Five six seven eight, I'm not your fool; I'm settin' it straight.'"*

A cheer rose from the audience; fans clapped and sang along. *"'Nine, ten, eleven, twelve, don't need you I'm doin' well.'"* It was a great crowd, responsive and loud. Audrey reached the chorus: *"'I'm not cryin' in the rain, and I'm not singing about the pain. But mister, I can't count on you.'"*

Audrey performed several of the songs from her new album before doing a costume change and getting a much-needed drink of water. Gianna fastened a dozen turquoise bracelets on Audrey's wrist and part way up her arm, then carefully arranged her necklace under her hair. She helped her into her turquoise boots while Willow adjusted the curls over her shoulders.

"Did Hayden and Everly take their seats out front?" Audrey asked Tam. Everly was their nanny and kept the girl at her side every moment.

"They were still here a minute ago." Tam dabbed gloss on Audrey's lips. "I think Hayden wanted to stay backstage a while longer. You know how she likes to be in the thick of things." She eyed Audrey's makeup and put the cap on the lip gloss. "What a fantastic crowd."

"I do love Atlantic City." Audrey spotted Hayden and Everly seated on a giant stack of equipment cases off stage right and smiled. Her daughter returned the smile and blew her a kiss.

Audrey swept back onto the stage in a body-hugging floral print dress that left her shoulders bare. After another song, she sprinkled her tried and true standby hits into the set. Fans loved those the best, and even though she'd sung them hundreds of times, it never got old knowing how well-received they were.

Audrey was halfway through *This Song* when a clanging metallic sound that was out of place caught her attention. She'd been performing for enough years to know there were occasional equipment failures and sound problems, and if she kept singing, the technicians would handle the issues before anyone knew what had happened. Behind her, the female backup singers stopped singing so, smile in place, Audrey glanced over her shoulder. The three young women had turned to observe whatever was happening off stage to their right. Shouts came from backstage.

"If your instruments are working, keep playing," she said to the band members nearest her.

Audrey followed their gazes and caught sight of the entire row of massive overhead lights listing to the left. In the wings, stage hands and musicians scrambled out of the way.

"Have to love a live concert, right?" Audrey said into the mic. "Please stay calm and in your seats while we figure out what's happening." Praying Hayden and Everly had taken their reserved seats out front, she placed her mic in the stand and took a few steps toward the band members. Her bodyguard, DeShawn, shadowed her.

As though in slow motion, the scaffolding that held an enormous row of lights plunged downward in a resounding clash of metal and broken glass, hitting stacks of black equipment cases. Exclamations and gasps flittered through the crowd as well as coming from the stage crew. Audrey's heart stopped and she stood with a hand splayed over her chest, panic rising in her breast. Where was her daughter?

Stage hands ran toward the pile of metal and gear. A couple of musicians on stage kept playing, but the song was a bust.

It wasn't easy to move quickly in the form-fitting dress, but she shot toward the place where Hayden had last been. Because of the tangle of steel framing and the crush of men moving away pieces, she couldn't get close.

A shrieking wail rose above the confusion, immediately recognizable as her daughter's. A shard of fear stabbed her.

"Hayden!" Panicked, she pushed her way through the throng of people. The scaffolding had fallen directly over the spot where her daughter and Everly had been seated on those black cases.

The stack of trunks had landed in a tumble, and her daughter lay in the debris of shattered lights and paint-chipped scaffolding heaped in a pile like pickup sticks.

"Hayden!"

Several feet from where her child lay, Everly pushed herself to a sitting position and swept her shoulder-length dark hair out of her face. She appeared dazed, but her dark gaze immediately searched her surroundings and landed on her young charge.

Workers sorted through too slowly, moving items away. DeShawn took Audrey's hand and assisted her over a piece of scaffold.

A helper shoved a trunk out of the way and helped Hayden to a sitting position. A rivulet of bright-red blood trickled from her forehead down her temple into her fair hair.

Audrey's heart hammered and she lunged over a pile of rubble.

Her daughter touched her forehead and looked at her fingers. Her eyes widened in fright, and her gaze darted from person to person.

"I'm here, Hayden!" Audrey called.

Her daughter's desperate gaze landed on Everly, and on hands and knees she scrambled to her nanny, flinging herself into her arms and sobbing.

Everly held her and smoothed her hair, uncaring of the blood that stained the front of her pink jacket.

At the sight of the two of them, a jab of pain thrust into Audrey's chest, adding another emotion to the fear already well-established. Hayden had immediately searched out Everly and turned to her for reassurance. Audrey hated the feelings carving a cavernous ache in her chest. Everly was like an extension of their little family; envy had no place.

Traversing the nearest rubble, Audrey knelt before the two of them. She met Everly's eyes, then reached to touch her child's head and reassure herself Hayden was all right. Her frightened daughter turned and gave her a weak smile. Blood still trickled from a cut on her forehead.

One of the stage hands tore off his shirt and handed it to Audrey to press against the wound.

"It's okay, baby." She glanced aside, spotting her manager hurrying toward them. "Where's the medical staff?"

"They're coming," Sidney Oliver assured her.

"What the hell happened?" Audrey asked.

"It all happened so fast," one of the crew answered. "But it looks like the scaffolding simply buckled. Maybe the bolts weren't fastened tight enough or there was a weak weld or something."

"We won't know until we sort through all this," Sidney said. "Right now, all that matters is that Hayden and Everly are all right."

Two medics arrived. One took the young girl's vitals and looked at her head. "That's going to need stitches, Miss Knox. And we'll want to make sure she doesn't have a concussion."

"What about Everly?" Audrey asked the other medic. "They were sitting together when this happened, and I don't know if they fell or the scaffolding hit them or what. Did anyone see what happened?"

Several crew members shook their heads.

"Do you hurt anywhere?" the EMT asked the nanny.

From her sitting position, Everly extended her arm and then her legs. "My arm hurts."

The uniformed young man tested that she could move and bend it. "You look fine, but to be safe we'll take you to get checked over. You both probably have contusions."

"Is my head hurt bad, Mama?" Hayden asked.

"You have a little cut and some bruises, darlin'," Audrey told her. "You're going to be fine. I promise."

Someone pushed a small bag of ice wrapped in a towel into Audrey's hand.

"The rig's ready to take you to the hospital." Cadence White was Audrey's publicist. "We'll play this down and bring Erik back out to do another set."

"She gave the audience half a show," Sidney said to Cadence. "I don't think we're obligated to issue free tickets or a partial refund."

Cadence pursed her lips in thought. "In the spirit of good will, and thinking like Audrey, maybe she can do an additional show. If we check the stadium's availability, she might be able do it before we leave town."

The two of them looked to Audrey.

"Handle it however you see fit while I go with my daughter," she told them. She wanted only to have Hayden checked over for injuries. They'd figure out the concert later.

Zane West, her lead guitarist, helped Audrey back to her feet and picked up Hayden. The girl wrapped her narrow arms around his neck. She appeared small and frightened in his hold, and she glanced apprehensively at all the people surrounding them, then toward the stage. The remaining band members were playing one of Audrey's songs. Hayden's horror was evident.

Imagining her confusion and what she must be thinking, Audrey's eyes stung. "Don't you worry about anything, sweetie. You and Everly are all that's important."

She felt sick about her daughter having been in direct line with a stage malfunction. It was a Thursday evening. Other children were at home doing homework with their families and their pets nearby. She dragged her daughter all over the country, ate in hotel rooms, traveled in a bus and offered band members as the kid's best friends.

It wasn't the first time she'd had cause to question the wisdom and security of their lifestyle. Her other choice had been to leave Hayden in their Nashville house with Everly and the tutor while she traveled, but Audrey had never been willing to do that.

The EMTs accompanied them down the corridor, Zane carrying Hayden, Cadence with her arm wrapped around Everly. Stadium security escorted them out a side delivery door and into a waiting emergency vehicle.

A couple of hours later, Audrey sat in a hospital room while her daughter slept. Everly slouched on another chair with a blanket over her and Sidney stood gazing out the window at the lights of the city.

"Were you able to arrange something with the stadium?" Audrey asked.

"They have Sunday afternoon available if you're willing to

stay in Atlantic City a couple more days," he replied. "Tonight's show was a sellout. I think fans would understand, but Cadence and I figured you'd want to give them the whole performance."

She nodded. "I do. Where do we go next?"

"Houston next week and then Tulsa. The last two dates on the tour."

"Let's stay here through Sunday then. After these bookings, I'm taking a hiatus from concert performances."

"Audrey, this could have happened at any time to anyone. It was an accident."

"I know that, but I need a break. Hayden and I need some time."

"You have the *Country Magazine* photo shoot scheduled at your Nashville home in late August and the Christmas television special filming early September."

"And I'll do both of those. I'll do everything that's already booked, but from here on out don't schedule any dates. Simply going light for a while like we planned isn't going to be enough."

She walked silently to the side of the bed where Hayden lay sleeping, her lashes against her pale cheeks. "I want to provide some normalcy for her," Audrey said softly. For both of them. Her daughter turning to her nanny in her state of panic still stung like salt in a thousand cuts. "She doesn't get to make friends or be in Girl Scouts or 4-H because she's always being tutored on the road or hanging out in a recording studio. We're together, but we're not *together*. I can't remember the last time I cooked for her. I feel like if I leave her home, I'll miss out on her life, but because I bring her with me, she doesn't get a life. Not a real kid's life. There's always someplace to be, something to do."

Sydney raised his gaze to Audrey's. His kids were older, but he'd been on the road for many years as well. He gave an understanding nod. "We can free up some time for you. You deserve it."

Relieved, she nodded. "I'm scheduled for the Rockwell County Fair for two weekends in September."

"You specifically asked for that engagement."

"I did. That's my hometown. And after Colorado, I don't want any dates." Her child was eight already, but there was still time to reestablish their relationship before her teen years. This time right now was imperative.

"You could stay with your mom through the holidays," he suggested.

She gave him a grateful smile. "Thank you for making it work, Sydney. Hayden and I need some quality time together."

Perhaps this had been the wakeup call she'd needed to breathe and take stock of her life, figure out what she was doing and where she wanted to go from here. She'd sacrificed to get to this point, and she still worked hard every day and night. She didn't want to miss her daughter's growing up years, all the formative moments. She wanted to give her a taste of normal life—whatever that was.

It was time to go home.

# CHAPTER TWO

*Spencer, Colorado*
*September*

Jericho glanced at the clock on the dash of the RCSD Chevy Tahoe, noting he had forty-five minutes left on his shift. His stomach grumbled. His phone rang, and he touched the blue tooth button on the steering wheel. The caller was Sheriff Joe Cavanaugh. "Tanner here."

"Hey, Jericho. Just finishing up paperwork and want to run something past you."

"Go ahead."

"You sure you're okay with both of those Saturday security details for the performers at the fair? Evans won't be cleared after his surgery until the following weekend, and Wick is waiting on a baby any day. I could take the shift if you'd rather. I don't mind."

"I'm good," Jericho replied at the same time his stomach

dipped. He was just hungry. "You take Chloe to the concert and enjoy yourself."

"So, you're good," Joe clarified.

"I'm good."

"All right then." In the background a phone rang. "I'll let you go."

Jericho disconnected the call.

He was thankful for the consideration, but he didn't need people tiptoeing around his feelings like he was still eighteen. He might have imagined Audrey Knox was his soulmate back then, but ten years later, his life and hers couldn't be further apart. His feet were solidly planted in this mountain county, helping run the family ranch and jockeying into position for Joe's job eventually. He didn't have time for grudges or pity parties.

The radio crackled. "Deputy Tanner, are you still in the vicinity of Big Augur Trail?"

Joe's voice again, this time official.

"Affirmative. On County Road Twelve."

"Female hiker on the trail reported a bear sighting. Fish and Game is on the way, but you're closer. Caller reports her can of bear spray malfunctioned. Sounds terrified. We grabbed coordinates from her phone. Texting them to you."

"She's alone?"

"Ten-four. Advised her to make a lot of noise, but she's petrified. She'll likely stay in place."

"Tell her I'm on my way." Jericho turned the SUV around on the shoulder and accelerated. Four minutes later, he slowed to a halt on a pull-off beside a small white car. "Ten twenty-three. Does the caller have a white Camry?"

"Affirmative," Joe replied.

"I'm grabbing gear and heading up the trail." From the rear of the Tahoe, he seized a backpack and inserted bottles of water, checked that the first aid kit was inside.

He opened a case and took out his Smith and Wesson 629. The conservation officers would be armed with Tele Dart guns that tranquilized large game, but he was first on the scene and in an emergency, this was his best defense.

Even the biggest and most powerful guns weren't guaranteed to stop a charging bear if the shooter didn't make a good shot. With accuracy and a little luck, his handgun could get the job done if need be. Hopefully, this bear didn't want any trouble and had already left the area.

There was probably only an hour of light remaining when he started up the trail. The path was well-worn, though narrow. With his shoulder radio, he kept in touch with Joe, who relayed the caller's distress. She was still hearing the bear nearby. Jericho paused and checked the coordinates on his phone. "I should be close," he spoke into the radio. "Tell her to call out."

"Ten four."

He listened. The drone of a small airplane in the distance was the only sound. "I'm not hearing anything."

"Caller is afraid to alert the bear to her location."

"That bear knows she's there," Jericho replied.

"You and I know that."

"What's her name?"

"Melinda."

"Melinda!" Jericho called repeatedly, still heading up the trail.

Finally, a thready voice called back, "I'm here! I'm up here!"

Figuring she was hiding, he called out as he approached. Rounding a curve in the trail, he spotted her crouched behind a thicket of Kinnikinic bushes, now reddish purple in September. Wearing a bright aqua-blue jacket and jeans with her hiking boots, she was huddled with her chin on her knees, but she got slowly to her feet. The twenty-something was obviously terrified.

"Hi, Melinda. I'm Deputy Tanner. I'm here to get you safely down the trail."

Her face was tanned, but there was no color in her lips. "The bear is still nearby. I can hear it in the dry leaves."

"Do you have any open food?"

"No, nothing. I have a couple granola bar wrappers in my bag."

"Are they sealed up?"

"No."

"Black or brown bear, did you see?"

"No, I only heard it." She'd been eyeing the landscape, but she turned her gaze on him. "I know what a bear sounds like."

"I believe you. Black bears are attracted to food, and brown bears usually see you as a threat."

"All I thought of was that saying about how if it's black, fight back, but if it's brown, lay down. I didn't know which was right, but I was too scared to do anything except hide."

"You do want to convince a black bear that you're not an easy meal, but you need to convince a brown bear that you're not a threat," he answered. "Usually, if you make enough noise, either one will simply leave. Come on with me, now. We'll head back down."

Melinda took a step on unsteady legs, her wary gaze darting into the wooded mountainside. "I've never been so glad to see anyone."

"Ah, all the girls say that," he teased.

She actually gave him a feeble smile. She wore her pale hair in a short ponytail, and she was fair-skinned with wide blue eyes. She moved in step right beside him.

"You always hike the trails alone?"

"Yes. I have a can of bear spray, but I tried it and nothing came out."

A rustling in the brush, followed by a low woofing sound and a grumbling moan had Jericho drawing his weapon with his right hand and pushing Melinda behind him with his left.

"It's there," she keened. "It's still there."

Twenty feet away, a brown bear ambled its way from a thicket and paused to look at them while sniffing the air. The beast's woofing sounds told Jericho it was as distressed as he was, but probably not as terrified as Melinda, or the animal would have been gone.

Jericho opened his mouth and sang at the top of his lungs, "'Boom clap! The sound of my heart, the beat goes on and on and on and on and—boom clap!'"

The animal didn't move forward, but it didn't turn around either.

"All right then." He fired the gun twice into a tree trunk a dozen yards away from the beast.

Behind him, Melinda yelped, covered her ears, and crouched down against the backs of his legs.

The bear turned and ran the opposite direction.

"Nothing personal, I hope," he called after it and watched for a few minutes. Finally, he leaned down and took the young woman's arm to help her to her feet.

Melinda stared at him, appearing dazed. "What just happened?"

"Playing loud music or singing loudly is supposed to scare off a bear. I sang loud, but it didn't work."

She pressed her hand over her heart and swallowed hard. "You don't look like a hip-hop guy to me. Why that song?"

He holstered his gun. "It was the first irritating song that came to mind. Do you want some water?"

"Yeah, thanks." With trembling fingers, she accepted the plastic bottle.

He made his way through the brush off the trail and took a photo of the two bullet holes in the trunk of the tall lodgepole pine. Easy way to account for his ammunition.

"Fish and Game heard shots," came a voice over his radio. "Are you all right, Deputy Tanner?"

He pressed the button. "Affirmative. The brown bear has left the area, and I have Melinda with me. She's fine."

They made their way down the trail, and as the sky grew dark, were joined by two green-uniformed Fish and Game officers, who led them down the mountainside with flashlights.

"Thank you, Deputy," the girl said as she opened her car door. "You're a pretty good singer, by the way."

The officers gave him a curious glance, but he got in the Tahoe and headed for Spencer. An hour later, he'd checked in his vehicle, security cam and radio, filled out a report, printed out the photos from his phone and turned his weapon over to the sheriff for routine inspection. Getting into his pickup, he was starving. Home was another half hour drive, so he called in an order to Pearl's, picked it up, and ate chicken sandwiches on the way. Once on the highway, he powered on the radio.

Clear as the stars shining in the night sky and every bit as mesmerizing, came a sultry voice that never failed to make his heart beat a little faster while it unearthed a hundred memories and raised two hundred questions.

*"'What we have now was a long time coming. Seems all I ever did was wait. But when you saw me, you really saw me, and our love is more than I could anticipate.'"*

As it always had, his entire body responded to her voice. Audrey Knox would be in Spencer in another week, and performing at the Rockwell County Fair soon after. And he'd be working security with her people.

He'd rather face another bear than be in close proximity to the woman who'd clawed his heart to shreds.

"Good morning," Audrey said to her sleepy-eyed daughter when she showed up in the kitchen of Audrey's childhood home. Her mother, Dorris, had been up early, cooking, and the smell of bacon had lured Audrey from the guest room bed. Everything looked pretty much as it always had, the same wood table and chairs, the same cupboards and counters. The appliances had been replaced a few years ago.

"I hope you're hungry, Hayden. I've made you breakfast," Dorris said to her granddaughter.

Hayden blinked at the bounty on the table. Dorris had prepared waffles, scrambled eggs, biscuits and set out pints of jam.

"This is like the Waffle House," Hayden said. "Everly took me there once."

"Oh, this is better than the Waffle House," Audrey told her. "Your Gramma knows how to make a breakfast for ranchers."

"The biscuits didn't rise the way they should have." Dorris put a waffle on Hayden's plate and set the other bowls nearby.

Audrey helped herself to bacon and eggs. "I'm sure they're good."

Hayden spread butter and jam on her waffle and cut into it. "We usually eat fruit and yogurt with granola."

*Uh oh.* Audrey steeled herself for Dorris' reaction.

Dorris raised her eyebrows. "That's no breakfast for a growing girl."

"We eat on the bus a lot, and Everly and I watch carbs," Audrey said. "But a special breakfast like this is a treat."

"Well, Hayden doesn't need to watch carbs," Dorris replied. "She's a little stick of a thing."

Audrey exchanged a glance with her daughter, and Hayden dug into her food. Audrey hadn't wanted to cloud Hayden's opinion of or relationship with her grandmother, so she'd said nothing to prepare her for Dorris' criticisms. It had always been clear that her mother adored Hayden, and that's the way Audrey wanted it to stay. She could hold her own.

She'd debated with herself over the decision of where to stay once they'd arrived in Spencer. Sidney Oliver had suggested that Aspen Gold Lodge was the most private and secure place, but she'd insisted she didn't feel the need for privacy in this town where she'd been born. She wanted Hayden to experience a different kind of life than one on the road, and how could they do that if they were always holed up away from people and normal living?

There was a hotel near the fairgrounds where they'd made reservations for staff members who wanted to be in Spencer during the county fair, and the band members would soon be arriving with her tour bus. The bus was luxurious and spacious enough for several people to stay comfortably. But having Hayden here with her grandmother was the best choice.

After finishing her breakfast, Audrey opened a cupboard. "I'll check expiration dates."

She emptied the contents of the cabinet, checking dates and tossing spices and baking soda into the wastebasket. She jotted down a couple of items on a lengthy grocery list on the counter.

"There was nothing wrong with that baking powder," her mother said from where she stood, loading the dishwasher.

"Both baking powder and baking soda lose their effectiveness, Mom. That's probably why the biscuits didn't rise the way you wanted them to."

Dorris said, "I can clean out my own cupboards."

"Of course, you can. But Hayden and I came to visit and help out, so let me help."

"At least pour that baking soda down the sink."

Audrey fished the box out of the trash and did as her mother asked. "We'll go to the market and buy fresh this afternoon. Hayden was five the last time we got to spend time in Spencer. Do you remember seeing the sights?"

Her daughter had finished eating and was reading yet another volume of *The Babysitters Club* on her iPad at the kitchen table. A barely-discernable pink line along her hairline, a nearly-healed wound sutured by a plastic surgeon, was the only visible evidence of the accident that had been Audrey's final incentive to take a hiatus. Within Hayden's reach lay a compartmentalized container filled with hundreds of colorful rubber bands for making bracelets. She wore three on her slender left wrist. Everly had made sure Hayden had a supply before they headed out.

Probably sensing her mom's perusal, Hayden glanced up. As it often did, her irrepressible smile reminded Audrey of her younger brother, and a twinge of sadness momentarily nicked her joy. Grief eventually lost its piercing edge, but the dull pain of missing the person never went away.

"What are the sights?" Hayden asked in her curious good-natured manner. She'd taken the accident in stride and seemed no worse for the experience. Audrey on the other hand, still bore the sting of her terrified child immediately turning to her nanny in her moment of crisis.

"Well, let's see," Audrey answered. "There's Brook Park, with a bandstand where Spencer High School band plays and the VFW band plays on the Fourth of July and Memorial Day." She glanced at her mother. "Do they still do that?"

"I suppose so. I don't go to those things."

"Well, there are drinking fountains and converted gas lamps. It's charming. We can take photos for Everly. There's a firehouse, the library. Pearl's Coffee Shop always had great breakfasts and lunches. Your grandpa used to take me there. Oh, and Curly's Cone Factory. Is that still there, Mom?"

"Better yet, we can haul out the ice cream freezer and make some of our own," Dorris suggested.

"You know how to make ice cream?" the girl asked her grandmother.

"I can figure it out."

Audrey's dad was the one who'd always made ice cream on summer evenings. Her heart constricted at the memory. They'd always been close. He'd made Audrey feel special. Wanted. Important. She glanced at her daughter, her wavy strawberry blond hair pulled into a ponytail, regretting Hayden would never have that kind of relationship. Hayden's father had been killed in a small plane crash six years ago, and even before that Tucker Frost hadn't been the fatherly sort.

With Audrey's demanding career and hectic schedule, it was becoming more and more difficult to be a mother as well as make up for lack of a father. She'd worked hard to keep stability in their lives, but months on the road wasn't conducive to a home life. Hayden's tutor and Everly traveled with them, and this was their first time without them in years. A short break from her studies wouldn't hurt Hayden's education.

"There are trail rides and go carts. And there's Olde Town," Audrey added. "I don't even know what all is there now. I hear they've expanded by leaps and bounds. Lots of touristy shopping."

A knock sounded and Audrey started toward the door, but surprisingly it opened before she got there. Six feet of tanned cowboy in jeans, black T-shirt and a Stetson filled the opening. She took a surprised step back.

"Mornin', Missus M. I brought back the genera—oh, sorry. Didn't know you had company. Didn't see a car." The deep masculine voice was familiar enough to send an alert up her spine, and her brain immediately identified it.

"My car's in the garage, and I'm not company." Audrey set down the expired cake mix she held.

He swept off his hat, revealing a shock of cropped black hair and a white forehead. In his other hand, he held a stainless-steel travel mug. His piercing blue gaze locked with hers. Seeing those intense blue eyes rimmed by black lashes, a hundred fond memories assailed her.

Her initial reaction was surprise followed by the warm rush of familiarity. He was taller and broader than the lanky boy she remembered, his shoulders and chest appearing solid muscle under that T-shirt. Creases at the corners of his eyes and mouth only added character to his familiar handsome face. *Now* it felt as though she'd come home.

# CHAPTER THREE

"Jericho Tanner," she managed. She took a few hesitant steps closer to where he stood, instinctively wanting to hug him.

He didn't move forward or even smile, though he seemed unable to take his gaze from hers for several minutes. How long had it been? She'd spent only hasty weekends in Spencer for the past several years, never staying long enough to catch up or see old friends. She'd probably only glimpsed him a time or two.

He and her brother Wyatt had been best friends. They'd done everything together, so every time she'd begged Jericho to play his guitar while she sang on a hay bale stage in the barn, Wyatt had been right there too. In elementary school she and Jericho raised sibling lambs together and shared a blue ribbon.

In junior high and high school when Wyatt joined the swim team and ran track. She and Jericho had attended all his meets, but their passions had been 4H and music.

She was two years older, but in high school he'd been willing to play backup for her at every state fair and local event. Those had been bright days, filled with adventure and the promise of their futures.

After Wyatt's death at fourteen when he'd died of an aneurism on the track field, her mother had shut out Audrey and her father, as though seeing them, being with them added to her pain. Charlie had been Audrey's solace, the loss strengthening their already solid bond. She'd been able to talk to Jericho, and he with her. They'd grieved together. Sharing their loss had helped them heal. Gradually, she'd moved on with her plans.

Jericho's gaze dropped to her white shirt, jeans and bare feet, and made a leisurely perusal on the way back up to her face. People stared at her every day, but his attention was different—personal enough to bring a flush to her skin. Seeing her teenage friend as a full-grown man made her feel as though they were strangers.

He looked good. Better than good. She'd always appreciated that he was tall. She was five nine now; he was still taller. And he'd filled out. This wasn't the young man she remembered. Everything about him, from the grim set of his jaw to the scuffed toes of his boots screamed man. Surprisingly different and yet so achingly familiar that a knot swelled in her chest. It wasn't the resilient independent part of herself that wanted to fold herself into those strong arms and recapture something good and familiar. Rather the youthful hurting girl inside yearned for the comfort she remembered.

She almost flung her hesitation aside and ran forward, but thankfully before she got her bare feet to move, he turned his gaze on Hayden. She would have made a fool of herself. Something she couldn't read flickered in the blue depths. "This is your daughter?"

"Yes. This is Hayden. Hayden, this is Jericho Tanner. He was your Uncle Wyatt's best friend. He plays the guitar."

"Hi," Hayden said. "Bass or acoustic?"

The corner of Jericho's mouth raised in an appreciative grin. "Pleased to meet you. Acoustic." He glanced at Audrey. "She's your daughter for sure."

"I still get the *Spencer Herald*," she said. "I read you're a deputy. Are you still at the *Double T* as well?"

"Yep. Built my own cabin on the ranch."

"Still playing?"

"I play some."

"Come in for coffee," Dorris offered. "We have bacon left and it won't take but a minute to pour some batter on the iron."

Audrey looked away. Dorris had cooked for Hayden. Audrey had simply been there and helped herself. Now her mom was offering to make a special batch for the neighbor. Must be nice to rate special attention.

"I just dropped off that back-up generator I fixed. I don't want to be any trouble."

Dorris pointed to a chair. "No trouble. Sit yourself down."

He hung his hat on a peg near the back door, crossed the kitchen and washed his mug and lid with the soapy sponge as though he'd done it often, dried it on a towel and proceeded to the coffee pot. He poured a full cup from the pot and sweetened it before securely screwing on the lid. It appeared he felt more at home here than she did, and she wrestled with the feelings this evidence of familiarity created. Audrey tried not to notice the way his jeans fit his long legs and slim hips, but the man drew her attention like a magnet. He turned back and caught her staring. "You look good, Audrey. How long are you staying?"

"Thanks. I'm not sure. I'm taking a break to spend time with Hayden."

His gaze flickered back to her daughter at the table. "I read about the stage accident. You doing all right?"

Hayden shrugged. "I got stitches and had a big bruise on my arm and leg, but I'm okay now. My nanny is all right too."

He gave her a nod. "Glad to hear it."

"I don't have anything scheduled until the West Coast in the Spring," Audrey told him. "We're here to hang out with Gramma."

"And for the fair, of course," he said. "I'm working security."

"Besides his deputy position, Jericho works the *Double T* with his father and Judah."

"Little did your grandpa know it would be the *Triple T* one day," Audrey mused.

"Wouldn't sound like the same place," he replied.

Dorris added, "Jericho checks in on me and helps around here too."

"What about Buddy Lowman?" Audrey asked. "Doesn't he still live here on *Big Pine* land?"

Buddy Lowman had been her Daddy's foreman for thirty years. After her father's death, they hadn't continued to ranch, but had leased the land to other ranchers as a sure income. Buddy had continued to live in his place nearby and helped Dorris.

"Buddy had foot and leg problems," her mother explained. "He retired a couple of years ago. Had a knee and a hip replaced and is in Pine Valley."

"Where is Pine Valley?"

"Pine Valley Crescent Senior Center is a retirement village on the east side of town," Jericho offered.

"Why, it's been there at least eight years now." Dorris' voice held that accusatory edge that said, *'If you'd been here more, you would know these things.'* Audrey was convinced her mother deliberately withheld information like this to make herself seem a victim. "They have a community center and a chapel."

Audrey thought over that development. It was difficult to picture the foreman who'd been at *Big Pine Ridge Ranch* for so long anywhere else. Time had marched on while she'd been away. She took her phone from the table and made a note in her appointment app to visit Buddy. He'd been part of this ranch and her life as long as she could remember. He'd gotten her out of more than a couple of scrapes that she could recall.

Another thought struck her. "What about the horses then? Who takes care of them?"

"Lane Shay and Dana Harkness have fixed up Buddy's place and live there in exchange for taking care of the horses," Jericho responded. "They're a couple of college students. Responsible. Reliable."

There wasn't much Audrey could say. Jericho seemed to know more about *Big Pine* than she did, but she hadn't been here for a long time. She nodded in acknowledgement.

Jericho had finished his second waffle, so he got up to refill his cup, fitting the lid on snugly. "Need anything else, Missus M?"

"No thank you, dear. I have more help than I need today."

Audrey hadn't seen her mother smile so appreciatively in years. The woman crossed to Jericho and stood before him, beaming. She touched his wrist affectionately, her pale hand a contrast to his healthy sun-browned skin. "I don't know what I'd do without your help. Tell your father hello for me. I hope he doesn't mind you running over here to set all my problems to right."

"You know he doesn't mind," Jericho answered. "Glad to help."

"Well then I'll see you at the volunteer breakfast Saturday morning." Dorris glanced sideways. "I suppose Audrey and Hayden will join us."

Audrey blinked in annoyance. That had been a back-handed invitation if she'd ever heard one.

"Looking forward to it." Jericho settled his hat back on his head and nodded to her. "Enjoy your visit."

Audrey smiled. "I'm sure we'll see each other around."

"Saturday morning if not before. Nice to meet you, Hayden." He touched the brim of his hat with a nod and exited, pulling the multi-paned door shut behind him.

Audrey made a feeble attempt at nonchalance, then darted toward the door and watched him descend the steps two at a time. She spotted a black pickup, distorted by the vintage glass. A black and white dog with touches of brown had been sniffing the ground near the porch, but ran after Jericho. Jericho opened the door and the dog jumped up into the cab. Jericho got in, closed the door, and the truck moved out of her line of vision. "That looks like the dog the Tanners had years ago, but it can't be."

"Sully is an offspring of those beagle-collies Atwood was always fond of," Dorris answered.

Audrey resumed checking expiration dates on packaging. "He seems to know his way around the kitchen."

"He comes by a few times a week. Such a kind, helpful young man."

Audrey digested that information.

"He never married," Dorris offered.

"I figured he'd have settled down a long time ago." Audrey slipped her phone back into her pocket. "He was always kind, hardworking, easy going."

Her mom flattened her lips into a line. "He'd make someone a good husband. Some people let opportunities like that slip between their fingers."

Audrey didn't miss the not-so-subtle message. "What opportunities do you think I missed?"

"You said he'd have been a good catch."

"We were just friends."

Her mom raised a dismissive brow in that way she had of implying wrongdoing without saying a word. Audrey was used to her disapproval, but it stung anyway. She'd never been the favored child. That was okay. She hadn't begrudged Wyatt their mother's favor, but an ounce of approval or appreciation would sure go a long way.

Audrey finished her list and glanced at Hayden. "Shall the three of us have lunch in town when we go get groceries?"

"You'll cause a stir," Dorris warned.

Audrey had resolved to not allow her mother's digs to ruin her mood or plans for a nice day. "This is where I grew up. I might have been gone a long time, but people still know me. We'll chat a little, take a few photos, and they'll get used to me being here."

"I doubt that, but if you're sure you want to make a scene…" Her mother dried her hands on a dish towel.

"I'm sure I want to go into town. Let's get changed, Hayden."

"Will you curl my hair?" her sweet girl asked.

Audrey extended her arm. "You bet I will."

She was determined to get this part over with, let people see she was still Charlie Monroe's daughter and blend herself and her child into this community. Hayden deserved to have friends her age and enjoy the same experiences other children were having.

It was plain she had a lot to catch up on, but Audrey had set her mind to this. She'd never let her mother's negativity hold her back, and she wasn't about to start now. Spencer was her hometown. They were both going to fit in.

He drove back to the *Double T* with the passenger window down so Sully could sniff the air, and within minutes Jericho parked near the barn. His own home was farther east on *Double T* land. His brother, Judah had his own place too and Bethel still lived in the big house. "Come on, Sully. We've got work to do."

Everything had changed, but nothing had changed. Audrey was no longer his friend's big sister, the girl next door, the friend he'd played with, sang with, grew up along-side. She was an international celebrity, a star recognized by her voice, her face, someone who earned more money in a year then he would in his lifetime. Along with the rest of the Spencer locals, he'd seen the new edition of *People* with a multi-page spread of glossy photos of her Nashville home. Pearl's Café had been buzzing with talk of the magazine feature for the last week, everyone hoping to get a glimpse of their hometown girl who made it big.

Well, he'd gotten more than a glimpse. A gut-punching eyeful actually. He'd guessed her glamorous photos made her look better than reality, but right there in her mama's kitchen, unretouched, wearing slim jeans and a white shirt, her feet bare, she'd robbed him of breath. Seeing her hadn't been as painful as he'd imagined. No, there'd been a dose of exalted pleasure that had accompanied the pain. He'd been right to be fearful of an encounter.

Joe Cavanaugh had been insightful to tiptoe around him —he *was* an eighteen-year-old with a broken heart. Years of self-talk and meticulously constructing defenses should have dissolved feelings of abandonment and inadequacy, but here they were, raw and exposed. True to form, he shut down the feelings before they got a foothold.

The thing was, he wouldn't have done anything differ-ently. He wouldn't have asked her to abandon her dream and stay. Nor would he have accompanied her to Nashville—or followed. She'd always wanted a music career. He'd liked to play guitar and sing, but he loved the land, the mountains, and would have been miserable away from home. Their paths had been destined to separate. He'd made the foolish mistake of falling in love with a rising star.

Spencer's main business and shopping district hadn't changed much since Audrey's last visit, though boutiques south of the courthouse had replaced other retail stores. South on Brook Park Road, it appeared The Wild Card Saloon was undergoing construction between the old and new buildings that had, during a previous renovation, been joined by an outdoor area.

To the east of Brook Park, the garden in front of the brick courthouse, featuring traditional federalist architecture and colonial columns, was seeing the last hardy throes of fall with straggling red and white petunias and sparse beds of blue and white pansies. One good freeze and they'd be gone too.

Audrey stopped her shiny black Escalade on the brick-paved street in front. She opened Hayden's door and walked around to open her mom's door. The double-tiered fountain on the courthouse lawn gurgled and splashed impressively. They reached it and Hayden dashed forward to extend a hand into the cascading water. There wasn't a child in Spencer who hadn't soaked their sleeves—and occasionally their shoes—in this fountain. Copper glistened at the bottom of the pool.

Hayden wore an incredulous expression. "Look at all the pennies!"

Audrey extended her palm, filled with coins. "Make a wish."

Hayden took them, closed her eyes without hesitation or inhibition, stood motionless a few moments, and then tossed them one at a time into the fountain. The falling water couldn't mute the satisfactory plunking sounds of the pennies breaking the surface.

"Did you throw pennies in here when you were a girl?"

"I sure did. My daddy and I used to come to Pearl's for breakfast every Saturday morning. We parked right here, and he always brought a handful of coins."

"Did you get your wishes?"

"A lot of them." Audrey glanced at her mother, but Dorris kept her attention on Hayden's face.

"Do you suppose your pennies are still in there?" Hayden asked.

"No. Some lucky county employee gets to pull on waders and rake them out once or twice a year."

"What do they do with all the money?"

"I don't really know," Audrey answered. "We'll have to ask someone."

"Where's Pearl's?"

Audrey pointed to the row of century-old storefronts along Silverville Road on the north side of the park. Besides the café, the other buildings housed an art studio, potting shed, the sheriff's office, the *Spencer Herald* and the VFW.

A young man, probably in his twenties, wearing ripped jeans, a black polo and a black ball cap got out of a car and jogged toward the courthouse. He glanced over and stopped dead in his tracks. "You look just like Audrey Knox. Oh. Oh! You're her, right?"

Audrey offered him a gracious smile. "Yes. And you are?"

"Um. I'm--wait. Tim. I'm Tim Benson."

"Nice to meet you, Tim. How's the Wi-Fi here?"

"Excellent. Can I—? I mean would you mind?" He fumbled with his phone. "Oh, wait. We're not supposed to disturb celebrities. I forgot for a minute."

Hayden stepped forward. "Here. Let me take a picture of you two together."

"Are you sure? Oh, wow, thanks."

In her knee-high boots with heels, Audrey was a few inches taller than the young man. She casually rested her arm across his shoulders and leaned in for a practiced smiling shot.

"I can't believe this," Tim said in a breathless voice, and it was obvious he was flustered. "I know you're from Spencer, I mean—your name and new album cover are on the billboard outside town and your photos are on the wall at Pearl's, but I never expected I'd meet you. Like right here. I have all of your songs in my playlists."

Hearing that people loved her music never got old. She affably thanked him, and together the three females continued toward the café. Fully expecting a remark from her mother, none came, and she took a relieved breath.

Before heading for Pearl's, they strolled farther along Second Avenue, spotting a florists' and a quilt shop.

"Look, Mom!" Hayden called out. "A nail salon. Can we get mani-pedis?"

Hayden loved having her nails painted with bright colors and fun designs. The sign she'd indicated read Glam Girl Nail Spa. "Sure, Hayden. That sounds like fun. Maybe Gramma would like to spend the afternoon being pampered too."

Dorris flicked a hand dismissively. "The day I can't file my own nails is the day they throw dirt on me."

"No one said you couldn't do your own, Mom. It's a treat to have them done, and the new products make your nail color last for weeks."

Dorris poo-pooed away her suggestion. "Waste of good money if you ask me."

Audrey glanced from her mother to Hayden. "We'll see if they can fit us in."

They headed back toward Silverville Road and rounded the corner where Willa's art studio was located. Pearl's was at the other end of the block. "I'll be disappointed if anything has changed."

By the time they got there, heads were already turning. The bell over the door rang as they entered, but inside the restaurant, expectant silence hung for a few seconds. Someone's phone pinged an alert. Another one across the room.

Several heads averted as people looked at their messages. "Tim Benson posted a photo with Audrey Knox," someone said.

"There she is. It's Audrey."

# CHAPTER FOUR

*A*ctivity resumed, several greetings were called, and
with only that one brief moment of recognition, all
went back to normal. Audrey spotted a few people she
remembered and waved. She took Hayden's hand. "You okay,
baby?"

"I'm okay, Mom."

Another owner would surely have citified the place, but
whoever Pearl had been, she had embraced the charm and
small-town feel, and the current owners honored the tradi-
tion. Beside the cash register was a stack of copies of the
local newspaper and a cigar box with a slit cut in the top.
Audrey fished in her purse for quarters, dropped a few into
the box, and took a paper from the stack as her father had
done every Saturday morning.

She and Hayden surveyed the dessert case filled with
golden-crusted pies and towering meringues, while her
mother greeted friends and neighbors.

"Oh, my stars, girl, look at you." Round-faced Edith
Combs and her husband Marty had operated this place since
Audrey had been a girl. Edith had additional smile lines and

her ample waist under her red apron testified of the good food. "You look just as beautiful in person as you do on the TV. But you're so skinny. You let me order you up the chicken-fried steak."

"Hello, Edith. That sounds great. I haven't had one of those in years."

Edith scribbled on her order pad, but continued talking. "Your Christmas special was the best show of the season last year. Better than Kelly Clarkson's. Better than Pentatonix's. I recorded it and watched it a dozen times. I even played it just this past summer because I love how you sang *O Holy Night*. That's my favorite Christmas song. I remember my mama singing it in church on Christmas Eve, and I cry like a baby every time I watch it."

"That is high praise. Thank you, Edith. I remember you telling me how much you love that song. I thought of you many times while we were recording the show."

Edith's jaw dropped. "You did? Well, God bless you, Audrey. You just couldn't be any sweeter. Or any prettier. Your mother must be so proud of you. Are you doing another Christmas show this year?"

"As a matter of fact, we just recorded it last week," Audrey told her. "I think you'll love the guest stars."

"That's so exciting! Is this your little Hayden? She's as willowy and pretty as her mama. Look at her lovely hair."

Dorris had stopped by a table to talk to a couple of women.

"What would you like to eat, honey?" Edith asked Hayden.

Hayden asked for a menu.

Audrey introduced her daughter to a number of neighbors, ranch owners and a couple of tattooed cowboys. Audrey remembered the Hudson brothers from junior high and high school.

"Ronnie and I were betting on who it was pulled up in

front of the courthouse in that new ESV," Kipp told her. "I thought it was you or some of your people, because we knew you were coming for the fair."

She grinned. "Yep, it's me. I ordered it and picked it up when we landed in Denver. My people don't arrive until next week."

Both of them stood near, but seemed hesitant.

"Come on, guys," she said. "Give me hugs."

Kipp wrapped an arm around her and tugged her against his side for a second, then leaned back. "What color are the leather seats?"

"Slate gray." She leaned toward Ronnie for a quick embrace.

"HD surround vision cameras and the street view on the dash display?" he asked.

With a nod, she said, "You guessed it."

Kipp's expression got serious. "Does it have a screen overhead, Bose speakers and Wi-Fi?"

"It does. Hayden watched *Raya and the last Dragon* and *Frozen* all the way from Denver."

"Pay up, Ronnie," Kipp said to his brother.

She laughed with them.

"Remember all those Friday nights at Grenade?" Ronnie asked. "You and Jericho and some of the others had a pretty boss band."

She remembered the teenage hangout well. "I do remember. Those were fun times."

Kipp pointed a thumb to include his brother. "With some of the other chaperones, we could sneak in beer, but your daddy never let us get away with anything."

"No one ever got away with *anything* around my daddy. Back then I thought he was spoiling all my fun." She gave him a contrite grin. "Now that I'm a mom, I know why he was strict."

"Think you'll sing at the Wild Card some night while you're in town?" Ronnie asked. "Jericho still does a set every now and then."

"He does, does he? Well, I might be inclined to drive in for a drink."

"You could sing *Let it Go* for us."

She gave him a pointed look. "I don't think so. You must have little ones?"

Ronnie laughed. "I do."

"Well, congratulations on bein' a daddy." She fished her keys from her purse and tossed them to Kipp. "Go ahead and take it for a spin. Try not to lose my parking spot, though."

Kipp caught the keys. "Seriously? Don't worry, I'll make Ronnie lay in the spot until I get back."

Ronnie punched him in the shoulder.

Kipp tossed money for his lunch on the counter and his brother followed him out.

Together Dorris and Hayden had found a booth and sat side by side on the red vinyl seats. Audrey joined them.

"You're certainly trusting with a brand-new vehicle," Dorris said.

"It's insured." She glanced at Hayden, who gave her a smile. Audrey perused the framed newspaper clippings of historic events, including several magazine covers with her image. In between an impressive array of vintage license plates and photographs of locals holding up glistening fish was a paparazzi photo of her and Tucker Frost at the Golden Globes.

"There's a picture of you and Daddy," Hayden pointed out.

"Yes, there is," she answered with a nod and a smile.

"Daddy was handsome, wasn't he?"

"Very handsome. That's why you're so pretty." She tapped Hayden's nose.

Edith brought them red plastic glasses of iced water and flatware rolled in checkered napkins. She plucked a yellow pencil from behind her ear and slid a tablet from her apron pocket. "You're having the chicken-fried steak," she said to Audrey. "You want the mashed potatoes with that?"

"Of course."

"Mrs. Monroe?"

"I'll have a tuna sandwich on wheat, not toasted."

"And you, little miss...a cheeseburger for you. Am I right?"

Hayden nodded with a grin, "And sweet potato fries, please."

"Comin' right up in two shakes of a lamb's tail." Edith turned and hurried off toward the window that opened to the kitchen.

"It all looks just as I remembered," Audrey said.

"It's been painted," her mother told her. "And Marty had the shutters removed a couple years ago. They were dust collectors."

Audrey observed the expanse of windows. "So he did."

Hayden still studied the photographs. "Are we going to ride horses while we're here?"

"That's one of the best parts of being on the ranch." She rubbed her daughter's forearm. "I'll show you the creek and the old cabins. We'll see deer and all kinds of wildlife. We can have a picnic whenever we want."

Hayden grinned. "We can buy some picnic food at the market."

Her daughter's enthusiasm and cheerfulness warmed her heart. She could put up with her mother's digs as long as Hayden was enjoying herself. "We're going to appreciate every minute of our holiday."

When Edith served their meals, the woman said to Hayden, "I see you make your own bracelets. I have a granddaughter your age, and she makes oodles of those things. You will have to meet my Annabelle while you're in town."

The Hudsons returned with her keys and an invitation to buy her drinks at the Wild Card. Audrey agreed it sounded like fun.

Their meals were delicious, but Audrey could only make it through half of her enormous portion. She paid and they headed for the grocery store.

"See, Mom, that wasn't so bad. The locals will get used to me."

Dorris didn't respond, simply glanced away.

They walked around the park, discovering the murals painted on the backs of buildings that faced Olde Town to the north. "We'll visit there next time," Audrey promised and looked at her phone. "We have nail appointments in ten minutes."

"Yes!" Hayden said with a huge grin. "Gramma, this is going to be fun. You'll see. I'll help you pick out your color."

She took Dorris' hand and pulled her toward the corner where they'd seen the salon. Dorris acquiesced without a complaint, and Audrey grinned to herself.

An hour and a half later, they returned to her vehicle and she backed out. "Where do you shop for groceries, Mom?"

"At Martin's." She looked at her shiny red nails. "There's a fancy super store at the mall, but I prefer the local retailers."

"Audrey Knox!" As soon as they entered the grocery store, a woman recognized her and gestured to the other patrons and cashiers. "Audrey, it's you, right?"

"See, you can't show up and be plain old Audrey again," her mother said from beside her. Dorris commandeered Hayden and the cart and headed down a side aisle while Audrey greeted the shoppers, answered questions, and posed with them for selfies.

"Wait till my sister Penny sees this!"

"We'll be at your concert at the fair!"

"Are the rumors about you and Brent Dillard true?"

Audrey graciously answered their questions, dispelling the rumors the press had created about her and another music star with whom she'd been seen at an awards presentation and dinner. She asked a few questions in return, hoping to make herself less of a peculiarity.

"You're here for groceries? Do you cook?" one of the women asked.

"I cook whenever I get a chance," Audrey replied. "After being on the road for so long, I miss home cooking. And I'd better finish my shopping now or the whole afternoon will slip away."

She found her mother and daughter in the produce section.

"Did you escape your fans?" Dorris asked.

"Okay, I'm an oddity right now, but they'll get used to me. Hiding or trying to escape would only make them more persistent. I know for a fact. I want them to see me as a regular person."

"I'm planning to grill chicken and have salads for supper," her mother said.

"Good idea. And I'd better go for a long walk or a ride to work off that lunch."

"Edith is right. You're so skinny, a stiff wind could blow you over."

"I'm perfectly healthy. My trainer sees to that."

"She eats on the run," Hayden told her grandmother.

Audrey selected a few avocados. "Here we go. Good fats."

Hayden picked up an avocado. "Can we get some chips and salsa to go with 'em, Mom?"

Audrey laughed. "Sure." She looked at her mother. "She won't let me stay skinny for long."

Her mom turned back to the cart.

They arrived back at the ranch house, and Audrey used the remote her mother handed her for the garage door and pulled the Escalade in between her mother's silver Camry and a much larger tarp-covered vehicle. She'd spotted it earlier, but said nothing. Grabbing grocery bags, she finally asked, "Is that the Skylark?"

"It is."

The red 1967 Buick convertible had been her father's pride and joy. He'd washed and waxed it weekly, driven it to car shows and in the Independence Day parade every year. Audrey had joined him more than once, waving from her perch atop the retracted top. Charlie Knox had been gone for years, but his car still sat here in the garage. If she raised the tarp above the back bumper, she'd see the license plate that read BIG PINE.

Bittersweet sadness rested a dull weight on her chest. She'd had a father for a lot longer than Hayden ever had, and she was thankful for that, but she still missed him terribly. Not a holiday or a birthday went by that she didn't yearn for more time with him. She couldn't give her child a father like hers, but she could create memories for her, and she could make certain Hayden got to experience the joy of friends and the stability of the ranch.

She grabbed bags and headed to the house behind her mom and daughter.

"When's Everly coming?" Hayden asked after the groceries were put away. She'd set out her rubber band and charm chase and was weaving a bracelet on the loom at the kitchen table.

"She's visiting her father in Florida," Audrey told her. "She'll be here for the full tech rehearsal."

"What's that?" Dorris asked.

"After the stage is set up with lights and sound, everyone rehearses as though it's performance day. The technicians and musicians work out all the kinks."

"Didn't help at your last concert when Hayden got hurt."

She'd opened herself up for that one. "The techs took everything apart and put it back together and finally concluded that one of the new hires didn't double check his work. He's been replaced, and that will never happen again."

Her mother sat across from Hayden doing a crossword puzzle. "The nanny doesn't need to come, you know. I'm perfectly capable of keeping Hayden company while you attend to rehearsals and the like."

"Yes, without a doubt you are, Mom. And Hayden is enjoying being here. She's used to being with Everly, though, and she misses her." She stood beside her daughter and smoothed her hair.

Hayden looked up and nodded.

"Are you worn out yet, or do you want to go riding?" Audrey asked.

"Really?" Her daughter gave her a bright smile. "I'm not tired at all."

"How about you, Mom? Do you want to go with us?" She and her father had always ridden the ranch together, and she missed those times.

"No, you two go."

"All right then, let's change," Audrey said with a beckoning motion. "Get a jacket, too."

Ten minutes later, they entered the stables. Hayden had received riding instruction at one of the most exclusive stables in the Nashville area, so she was no stranger to horses. She was, however, unaccustomed to saddling her own ride. Audrey took her to the tack room, where they looked through the well-kept saddles, oiled leather reins and halters. Finding a saddle that had been hers as a girl, she instructed her daughter on choosing a thick comfortable pad. "This saddle probably weighs forty-five or fifty pounds, so we want to make sure the horse is comfortable."

The interior of the building looked the same. The open areas were clean, everything in its place. The familiar smells of hay and horses stirred a hundred fond memories, but a feeling of emptiness settled around her spirit. She'd never again see her Daddy in his work shirt, jeans and boots, leading a horse from a stall, never hear his voice as he spoke nonsense to an animal as he brushed it. She touched her fingertips to the ache in her chest.

Maybe using his saddle would make her feel closer to him, maybe make *Tall Pine* seem more like home. After a lengthy search with no luck, she chose another instead. Odd that it was gone when all the other old saddles were still here and in good condition. Perhaps her mother or Buddy had stored it elsewhere.

They'd carried saddles out into the aisle and hung them over a rail when a twenty-something brunette in a ball cap with a Stick Pony logo and puffy green vest over a thermal shirt came from the back of the building.

"Hi," she said. A long braid hung over her shoulder. "I'm Dana Harkness. My boyfriend and I take care of the stables."

"Nice to meet you, Dana," Audrey said with a smile. "I'm Audrey and this is Hayden."

"My pleasure. I was wondering when I'd see you. Mrs. Monroe told us you'd be here. After Lane and I knew we were living on your ranch, we downloaded all of your music. Saw the piece about your Nashville house, too. It looks incredible."

"That's so nice of you to get my songs," Audrey said. "Yes,

it's a beautiful home, but honestly, we don't get to spend much time there. We're here to enjoy some down time together."

"Well, I won't interrupt you," Dana said and turned to go. "It was great to meet you."

"Maybe you can help us if you have a minute?' Audrey asked.

Dana tuned back. "Sure. If I can."

"I've ridden a couple of those horses in the pasture, but it's been a long time. And two are unfamiliar." She took two leads from a hook. "Which one shall we ride?"

"Yeah, happy to help." Dana scooped a partial bucket of oats from a bin with a tin bucket. "Let's go get their attention."

Approaching the fence that surrounded the near pasture, Dana shook the bucket of oats.

"My daddy trained all his animals to respond to a whistle." Audrey whistled through her teeth.

All four horses responded by galloping toward them.

"Seems as though it's still common training," she said with a grin.

The horses seemed docile, sniffing at their hands and clothing over the fence. Dana held oats in her hand and a mare ate them from her palm.

"The bay is a gentle girl," Dana told Hayden. "I've exercised Ginny many times, and she's friendly. Never skittish."

Hayden stood on a fence rail so she could reach over.

"Talk to her," Audrey said. "Let her hear your voice and get used to you."

Hayden rubbed the horse's forehead and chattered about the ride she'd be enjoying. Seeing her girl like this was a soothing balm for Audrey's heart, an encouragement. It wasn't too late. She and her daughter still had a lot of time to bond and find things they could enjoy doing together. She could make up for lost time.

"I think she likes me," Hayden said.

Audrey grabbed a few oats and let a shiny mahogany mare munch them. She rubbed the horse's forehead and patted her jaw. "Is this Sybil? I think I rode her when I was here four or five years ago."

"Yep, that's her. I usually see her and Ginny together, so they're a good pair for a ride." She handed Audrey a lead, and they slipped the nylon halters over the horses' heads, then Audrey moved to open the gate. Hayden took Ginny's lead and led her inside the building, Audrey following with Sybil.

"Need help with saddles?"

"We can handle it from here, I think. Thanks so much," Audrey told the young woman.

Dana headed outdoors and called back, "I'll be nearby if you need anything."

With Hayden watching every move, Audrey saddled Sybil, then helped Hayden get her saddle from the railing. "Now we put up the girth and the cinch, so when we lift the saddle over her back, the straps don't fling on her." Audrey demonstrated by lifting the saddle and settling it over the pad on the horse's back, then walking to the other side and letting down the cinches. The image of her father's hands as he taught her how to do this carved an ache in her belly. "Now we come back to this side, reach under for the front cinch strap. We always do the front strap first, just in case the horse should move or bolt so the saddle won't slide off and dangle."

She showed Hayden how to bring the cinch through the metal loop and repeatedly wind it through until there was no leather remaining, then pull it tighter. "Not too tight, though. We don't want to hurt her." She fastened the back cinch and then demonstrated how she could place her hand under the front of the saddle and the pad. "Plenty of room for her withers. She's comfortable and the saddle is secure."

"Who taught you to do this, Mom?"

"Your Grandpa Charlie." She paused and gave her child a fond look. "I wish you could have known him. He loved this land and the horses. He never wasted a minute of life. He enjoyed everything and everyone, and people admired him." She'd often thought how odd it was her parents had married, as different as they were. She supposed it was true that opposites attract. She moved a mounting block to Ginny's side. "Can you get up yourself?"

Hayden stood on the block, and putting her foot in the stirrup, took hold of the pommel and pulled herself onto the saddle.

"That's my girl." Beaming, Audrey released both animals from the straps that kept them tethered to the stalls and mounted. She took her phone from her hip and snapped a photo of her daughter's smug grin.

With easy nudges, they led the horses out into the sunshine.

Hayden fished in her pocket for her phone and opened the camera app. "Can you take one for me to send Everly?"

Audrey learned to take Hayden's phone and obliged.

"Why don't I take a pic of the both of you?" Dana leaned a rake against the front of the barn and strode to them. "With your phone, not mine. I'm not a paparazzi."

Audrey laughed. "I wasn't concerned about that."

Dana took the phone and moved back so she could get both horses and riders in a few shots. "There you go." She handed Audrey's phone up to her. "You girls enjoy your ride."

Dana grabbed her rake and made her way into the outbuilding. Hayden and Audrey glanced at each other.

"She's nice," Hayden said.

"And we have a photo of us together." Audrey opened the

gallery on her phone and showed her daughter the photos. After sharing a pleased smile, they rode away from the stable.

Hayfields they passed had been harvested, rows of large round bales now stored for winter.

"Is all this *Tall Pine Ridge* land?" Hayden asked.

"It is. A couple of the fields are for our hay. The others are leased out to other ranchers for grazing and crops. There's a farrier on the front corner of land on the highway."

Audrey led them off the road, through gates into grass pastures where horses grazed. A rancher mending a fence waved them over.

"You must be Audrey," the fellow said. "Vince Rogers, ma'am."

"I know the name," Audrey said with a smile. "You and my daddy were friends."

"For many years. My son joined me and brought in new stock. We lease this section of your land for grazing now."

"They're beautiful animals."

"And this little one is your daughter?"

"This is Hayden," Audrey said proudly. "We've been looking forward to riding. Nice to see you."

"Give your mother my regards."

They turned their horses back and rode on. At the top of a rise, they reigned in and surveyed the countryside. Audrey pointed to a fence line. "That's *Double T* land."

"The tall man who came to Gramma's for coffee?"

Audrey nodded. "My great-grandfather started *Big Pine Ridge* a long, long time ago. Jericho's grandfather bought the *Double T* land beside *Big Pine*. Jericho's dad and my dad worked beside each other and helped each other out. As kids we grew up working on each other's wells and barns, pooling labor to put up hay. Sometimes it seemed like we were all part of the same family. Jericho's mama is the kindest soul I

ever met. She always treated me like one of her own.
Growing up I ate a lot of meals at their place."

"Does she cook better than Gramma?"

Audrey grinned. "I remember her being a very good
cook."

There had been times when Christina had been more like
a mother to Audrey than her own mother had been. Dorris
had always withheld affection, and Audrey had never understood why. It was almost as though she was jealous of the
attention Charlie paid to his daughter, but that made no
sense. Dorris spent no effort endearing herself to anyone.

She'd had Wyatt to spoil and lavish with attention. It
hadn't gone to Wyatt's head though, and often he'd seemed
apologetic about the favoritism. But he'd been special to
Audrey as well, and she'd been close to him and her father.

When the men in both families worked or traveled
together, she'd felt on the outside of their circle. She'd longed
to be a part of something so inclusive and mysterious and
important. Wyatt, Jericho, and their fathers had gone on
roundups as well as buying trips, while Audrey spent a lot of
time with her music and her animals, raising prize-winning
sheep and calves. Christina had often invited Dorris and
Audrey for lunch, and after looking back, Christina had her
own daughter, yet had given Audrey special treatment.
Bethel had always been equally kind and sweet.

"That's him, isn't it?" Hayden asked.

"Him?" Audrey tracked her daughter's gaze.

Sure enough, mounted upon the back of a magnificent
gray and black mottled gelding with a black mane and tail,
the rider galloping toward them came into focus. He reigned
his horse to a stop and touched the brim of his hat. "Ladies."

His voice was familiar, but deeper, coaxing long-buried
memories that teased her consciousness.

The animal beneath him pranced a few steps.

Hard to remember this was the skinny kid with whom she'd caught tadpoles and flushed out gophers, the boy who'd indulged her in her search of four-leaf clovers as though possessing them would lock in a bright future. On humid summer nights they'd imprisoned fireflies in jelly jars and Wyatt had set them free. It had always been the three of them until Wyatt's death at seventeen.

Audrey had been accustomed to her mother holding her at arm's length, but with Wyatt gone Dorris had withdrawn even more. Jericho had quickly become Audrey's companion and sounding board. This cowboy didn't even resemble the lanky teenager who'd played guitar for her at fairs during her high school days.

Scared but determined, and with her dad's blessing, she'd followed through with her dream and left for Nashville after two years of business college. By then Jericho had graduated high school and was studying criminal justice. She'd been gone for nearly a year, invested in her career when she'd gotten news of her father's death. Devastated didn't describe her state of mind or the grief that had consumed her.

Now tenderness toward Jericho, gratitude for his concern and steady presence brought tears to her eyes. This person had been her consolation, her anchor in a sea of loss and confusion. He'd comforted her when she'd felt alone and adrift, held her while facing life without her beloved father had been agony.

He'd always been the rock she needed. But her career was igniting and she was no comfort to her mother, so she'd returned to Nashville and picked up where she'd left off.

Audrey had chosen to embrace her career and shut out the memories. She shut out *him*, because he reminded her of the pain. And maybe somewhere deep inside she felt guilty for not staying when she suspected he wanted her to. But he'd been Wyatt's age with dreams for his own future. Days ago, their encounter in her mom's kitchen had shown her he was a full-grown man, and she didn't know what to do with that realization.

Jericho calmed Khan in low tones and studied the pair who'd galloped across the meadow. Audrey's hair glimmered in the waning sunlight. Noting those pale waves created an ache in his chest. He clenched his fists to gain control of his thoughts and emotions.

"Looks like you haven't forgotten everything you know." He meant it to sound teasing, but maybe it hadn't come out that way, because nowhere was the blinding smile he ignored regularly on those magazine covers in the checkout lanes. He glanced at her daughter. "Hayden seems to be a pretty capable rider."

Audrey looked at Hayden with pride. "She's a great rider."

Khan sidestepped and moved his back end, turning his side to the two females.

"Whoa," Jericho cautioned the animal, and Khan obediently stood still. Jericho leaned to pat his neck. "What do you think of all this open space?" he asked Hayden.

"Grandpa Charlie's ranch is huge."

She was a pretty little thing, which was no surprise. He liked her enthusiastic manner and charming expressions. Something about the way she spoke reminded him of Audrey when they'd been kids, long ago when things had been easy between them. Back then she'd been like a sister...and then she'd blossomed into a woman, and his feelings toward her had changed. Hers had stayed the same. She'd always looked at him like a friend—a brother. And he'd seen her as the woman with his beating heart in the palm of her hand.

He smiled at Audrey's young daughter.

"Is your ranch this big too?" she asked.

"It almost is now. Your great-grandad was one of the first to buy up land that had previously been owned by the government until after the second world war. The War Office had training facilities here. My grandad bought a share eventually and the Tanners and Monroes became neighboring ranchers. You have a proud family heritage."

He glanced at Audrey. As kids they'd learned the origins of the ranch land and nearby forested areas. "The park was originally part of the Louisiana Purchase," he told Hayden. "Belonged to the government until 1915 when Woodrow Wilson signed the Rocky Mountain National Park Act."

"I think I'd like to read about that," Hayden said.

He gave her a nod and a smile and returned his attention to Audrey. Meeting her eyes made his stomach dip. Her pride was obvious. She adored that girl, and he recognized her gratitude for his attention. And then he remembered Audrey's husband had been killed several years ago. These two had experienced loss.

Audrey offered him a small smile, and then her attention moved over his jacket to his hands holding the reins and down to his saddle. Surprise showed in her expression and she brought her gaze back, this time boring into his. For a long moment he felt himself breathing in time with her. She was so pretty, it hurt. Not Grammy Awards pretty, like the pictures at Pearl's, but barely-discernable-freckles, wind-mussed-hair and fresh-air pretty. She'd always tied him in knots. But she was a woman now. He was a man smart enough to know better. He wasn't going to open himself up to being vulnerable again.

"How did you come by my daddy's saddle?"

# CHAPTER FIVE

*H*er tone hadn't been friendly.

Jericho touched the pommel. "Your mom gave it to me."

"Oh, I see." The smile she mustered was just short of being stiff. Definitely not *Country Music Magazine* material. Hadn't she known what her mom had done? The saddle meant a lot to him, but if she didn't approve, he didn't want it to cause hard feelings.

"Mom mentioned you've taken over a lot of the work she and Buddy did." Audrey's gaze slid over the tooled leather.

"Not that much really. Lane and Dana do the day-to-day chores, but I'm overseeing and keeping the accounts. We get more help for hay season."

"Still a big job to look after another ranch. We need to get together and talk. I'm noticing things that could use fixing or replacing. I'd like to hire a full-time manager or at least an accountant."

He'd brought up the idea to Dorris, but she'd been dead set on taking care of the ranch without hiring more help. He'd suggested training one of the present hands to take on more responsibility, but she'd vetoed that as well. She was a stubborn woman, and he hadn't asked for the job of filling in as manager, but he'd done it and had been gently winning over Dorris to consider his ideas.

"I doubt your mom would go for that." He knew for a fact she wouldn't. Audrey was going to makes waves and leave, and then her mom would be calling him again.

But after speaking to other ranchers and staying current on the market, he'd confirmed his suspicions that *Big Pine Ridge* wasn't charging the ranchers enough for their land leases, and he wanted to bring that up to Audrey. "But I do think we should talk."

She glanced at Hayden, who was contentedly stroking her mount's neck, but close enough to hear. "I'm on the deed," she told him softly. "Daddy left it to us fifty-five forty-five in my favor. I haven't been here and I'm thankful you've been handling things that needed attention. I do need your help. You and I can look at accounts receivable and payable, and I'll decide what needs to be done."

"I do what Dorris asks me to do because we've always been like family," he said with a shrug. "But it's not my ranch. I don't want to rock the boat, but I have some concerns."

Her expression softened, and she glanced across the land before looking back at him. "I appreciate how much you've helped her. I really do. Is there a time that will work for you to come by and look over the books together?"

"Tomorrow evening?" he asked.

Audrey nodded. "Come for supper. I haven't forgotten how to be neighborly."

"All right." He tapped the brim of his hat.

She turned her horse and urged Hayden to join her in the direction of the house. She still sat a horse as though she'd been raised in a saddle, which she had. Her hair rose and fell against her shoulders as they rode away. He'd known she was the major owner of the land. In his wisdom, her father had undoubtedly known it would be Audrey who would assume responsibility for the ranch in the long run.

Seeing her raised a million questions and proved again that he'd been lying to himself for years. Out of sight wasn't out of mind. Audrey Monroe had spoiled him for any other woman, not that he hadn't spent several years trying to prove just the opposite. But he'd come to terms with how things were, and he liked this life he'd forged. It had always been his plan to run the *Double T*, train horses and spend his days on this land where he'd been born. Where his father and grandfather had been raised. He liked his job as deputy and wanted to move into the sheriff's position like his father had. Atwood had managed both, and he could too. All it took was hard work.

Audrey wasn't born for this life though. She'd always been a star, had always been destined to shine bright and make a name for herself in the music world. He'd never lied to himself about that. He'd stepped aside and watched her shine. Truth was Audrey had wanted more than he could offer.

The lie he'd told himself had been that he would forget about her in time.

He still felt guilty about the night they'd spent together. She'd been grieving her father, and he should have been smarter, should have had more self-control. But she'd been there in his arms, the realization of his dreams needing him, and he'd been weak.

"I'm sorry," she'd said afterward, obviously confused. Embarrassed. "I shouldn't have done this—it—it was a mistake." She'd gone back to Nashville and married her new manager.

He hadn't forgotten. It hadn't been a mistake for him.

Audrey entered Spencer over Prospect Bridge and drove
along Chickering Road, which ran along the northwest side
of the Gold River. She arrived at Pine Valley Crescent and
parked in the lot in front of the one-level care center. The
morning was cold, so she bundled her full-length coat
around her and carried a small gift bag toward the doors.

She'd been here years ago when her grandmother had
been a resident, and was pleased to see the interior had been
remodeled and decorated with blues and cheerful yellows.
An enormous glass enclosure held finches that hopped from
tree limb to tree limb and peeped with each bounce.

A young woman behind a counter greeted her. "Miss
Knox, I heard you were in town. What a nice surprise to see
you here."

Audrey glanced at the smiling young woman's name tag.
"Hi, Missy. I'm here to visit Buddy Lowman."

"Sure." Missy stood and came out around a short wall. "I'll
take you to Mr. Lowman."

"That's nice of you. Thanks."

"No, it's my pleasure. He's down here in the music room
with the other residents. They're enjoying a singalong this
morning." She led the way down a long hall. "I have tickets to
your performance, and my mom and I are looking forward
to it."

"Thank you. That's very kind of you to say."

Piano music and a few thready voices reached them.

"Here you go, Miss Knox." She gestured for Audrey to
enter the room ahead of her.

Audrey stepped into the room where two dozen elderly
residents occupied chairs or wheelchairs arranged in a half

circle. No one noticed her presence until the woman playing the old upright piano glanced their way, and her fingers fumbled on the keyboard.

"Oh, my goodness," she said, stopping her rendition of *Buttons and Bows*, which Audrey recognized as a popular forties' song.

"Oh, please don't let me interrupt you," Audrey said. "I just came to see my friend, Mr. Lowman."

Missy gestured for Audrey to join her and led her to one of the gentlemen in a wheelchair. Buddy was dressed in baggy trousers and a plaid shirt, his thin gray hair neatly combed. He glanced up in surprise and studied her.

"Let me take your coat, Miss Knox," Missy said. "I'll hang it with mine."

"I'd appreciate that." She shrugged out of the garment and knelt in front of Buddy. He was unmistakably her father's ranch foreman of countless years, but much older and grayer, his face lined and thin. He recognized her, and his eyes lit up. He reached for her hand. "Little Audrey," he said. "What are you doing in Colorado?"

"Visiting my mom. Seeing old friends."

"Have you ridden a horse yet?"

She grinned. "You know I have."

He patted her hand and held it. She glanced at his knobby knuckles. His hands were free of calluses. "I always said you should've been a trainer, didn't I?" he said. "You got horses in your blood, just like your daddy."

She gave him a smile. "I still have a lot of time."

He chuckled and gave a shrug. "Don't take time for granted."

She released his hand and reached for the bag she'd set on the floor. "I remember you have a sweet tooth. My daughter and I made fudge."

"Oh, well, I can't eat nuts anymore."

"There are no nuts."

"We get popcorn during movies. I like John Wayne."

"What's not to like about the Duke?" Audrey glanced around and realized the others were watching them. She stood and turned to see the smiling woman at the keyboard. "I apologize for the interruption. Please continue."

The woman gave an embarrassed wave. "Oh, no. I'm not going to sing while Audrey Knox is here with us."

Audrey glanced at Buddy and then from one face to another. Most of them probably didn't even know who she was. They simply seemed entertained with the interruption. "What songs does everyone like?" Audrey asked and walked to the front of the room. "I can try to help you out."

"I'm Peggy," the sixtyish person told her with a nervous smile. She gathered a pile of sheet music and extended the papers.

Audrey looked through them. "Okay. I can manage a few of these. What do you say we try *Tennessee Waltz?*"

Peggy was surprisingly good on the old upright, and played the intro with a flourish. She nodded for Audrey to come in.

Audrey turned toward the residents, who were waiting with smiles. *"I was dancin' with my darlin' to the Tennessee Waltz, when an old friend I happened to see. I introduced her to my loved one and while the-ey were dancin', my friend stole my sweetheart from me.'"*

Several of them joined her and sang along with feeble voices. Others clapped, their faces glowing with the joy of what she knew must be good memories. Emotion rose and filled her throat and eyes, causing her to stumble over a few words until she caught herself and resumed the lyrics. She wasn't simply singing hits for a crowd who enjoyed her music. There were no cameras; no one had paid for a ticket. She was sharing something personal with these people whose best memories were in the past. Buddy didn't sing, but his expression told her this was a good day. This wasn't the visit she'd expected, but she was so glad she'd come. Next time she'd bring Hayden.

After half a dozen songs, she excused herself, and a couple of aids came to assist the residents to lunch.

One of the caregivers pushed a silver-haired woman in a wheelchair toward Audrey. "Excuse us. Mrs. Beardsley insists she meet you."

"I enjoyed the songs so much," the woman told her. "They take me right back to when I went to dances." Her hair was neatly styled in a French roll held back by pearl combs, and she wore powder and pink lipstick.

"I'm so pleased you enjoyed the music, Mrs. Beardsley," Audrey told her and held her slender hand for a moment.

"It's Thelma, dear. I'm so pleased to meet you. I can't wait to tell my granddaughter, Francie. She's from Spencer, too, but living in Chicago. She's a well-known photographer."

"Shall we take a photo for her?" Audrey asked.

Thelma's face lit and her broad smile pleated her cheeks.

"Thelma doesn't use her phone, but I'll take one and have a print made for her," the caregiver said.

Audrey knelt to pose with the elderly woman, then wished her a good day.

Buddy had been waiting for Audrey to turn her attention back. "This is my friend, Ben," Buddy told her. And to Ben, he said, "This is Dorris."

The gentleman he introduced was standing. "Ben Rumford, miss."

"I'm Audrey," she explained without bringing attention to Buddy's mistake. "And it's a pleasure. Your name is familiar."

"I knew your father," he answered. "And I know your neighbors, the Tanners. I lived most of my life out on Twin

Owl Lake, but renovated and rent out the place now. Sold part of the land to Joe Cavanaugh."

"The sheriff?"

"Yep. He built a fancy new cabin and got married."

"I'm sure glad Buddy has a friend here," she said.

"He cheats at Rummy."

"What? Buddy, you don't." She laid a hand on her old friend's shoulder.

Buddy shrugged and gave her a sheepish grin.

A young aid came to push Buddy's wheelchair. "This was a treat for everyone."

"I enjoyed it too."

Audrey told Buddy she'd be back soon and went for her coat.

Once in her vehicle, she sat for a while, composing her thoughts and emotions. Life changes were always hard. Seeing Buddy so frail reminded her of her father's last days. He'd been gone too quickly. It pointed out that the years moved swiftly, and one had to make the best of here and now. She was certain that coming here was among the best choices she'd made. Hayden was going to build memories with her grandmother, and Audrey was going to have the opportunity to strengthen both relationships.

Nashville felt a million miles away right now.

A light rain was falling and his sister was riding toward the stables when Jericho drove his truck away from his cabin and spotted her. He stopped on the drive and rolled down his window.

"You don't usually go to the Wild Card on a week night,"

Bethel said. "You're leaving before supper?" Her cheeks were pink from the wind, and locks of blond hair fell across the collar of her puffy white coat.

"I'm going over to the Monroe's to look over books with Audrey, so I'm having supper there."

Her gray-green eyes widened with a sparkle. "Audrey invited you to supper?"

"Yes, as a convenience."

"Sounds *very* convenient to me." She gave him a teasing grin.

"She's here for the fair, and she'll be leaving after that. She's trying to make sense of the ranch affairs, and because I've been helping since Charlie's been gone, it makes sense I'd look over the accounts with her."

"Tell her I said hey. I'll save some dessert for you."

He nodded and rolled up the window. Raised working on the *Double T*, his sister might appear deceptively like a petite angel when wearing a dress, but in a pair of Wranglers, she matched her brothers' stamina and expertly accomplished a hard day's work alongside them. Besides overseeing care of the horses and stables, she was the full-time director at Aspen Gold's child care facility for guests, and Bethel managed the staff daycare as well. He knew the dedication and resilience involved in managing full-time responsibilities as well as holding up her end of the work on the ranch, and he admired her. Their father had never cut her any slack because she was a female, and she'd never expected any.

Sometimes he thought his sister should be devoting part of that energy to other things she enjoyed, perhaps friends and relationships, but he was no one to judge. He'd thrown himself into his law enforcement career and his aspirations of advancement. Jericho's job performance and ranch work afforded him the self-worth he needed and relied on. His family and his job were his security and fulfillment, now and in the future. The life he'd created wasn't perfect, for one big reason, but he was content. He told himself it was enough.

As he turned onto the road leading to the Monroe house, fat raindrops splattered on his windshield and immediately became a torrent. He turned the wipers on high and clicked on his high beams. The road was still in great shape heading into winter, so wouldn't need grading until after the Spring thaw in the new year. Light glowed from the lower windows of the house, and the porch light guided him along the side drive to the back door. After shutting off the truck, he jumped out and dashed up half a dozen stairs in two leaps, removed his hat and shook it off.

On the other side of the panes of glass in the painted wood door, Audrey was visible, adding bowls to the dishwasher, an ordinary task the public never saw. Being here seemed personal, and the rush of excitement in his gut troubled him. He was accustomed to walking right in like he did at home, but Audrey's previous reaction had him rap his knuckles on the wood and wait a couple seconds before entering.

She turned at the sound. "Hey, Jericho. Come on in."

He wiped his barely-wet boots on the rug inside the door. "Sure smells good in here. It's a real frog strangler out there. The ground's so hard, the rain's sitting on top of it."

He glanced at the kitchen table, where only a small tray with napkins and salt and pepper sat in the center.

"We're eating in the dining room tonight," she said. She wore a loose sweater with jeans and knee-high caramel-colored boots. "Mom thought it would be nice to make supper kind of special. Go on in and have a seat."

"Okay." He crossed through the kitchen, stopping to wash his hands at the sink. In the other room, Hayden was seated at the table, a tablet lying beside her plate. She glanced up. "Hey, Mr. Tanner."

"You can call me Jericho," he said.

He was glad he'd worn a good shirt and his nice belt. A white linen cloth covered the long table, a vase of flowers in the center, but the four place settings were all at one end. Spotting a basket of rolls and tossed salad in a large wooden bowl made his stomach growl.

"Oh, you're here," Dorris said, appearing with four silver-plate napkin rings. He only knew what they were for sure once she slipped them over cloth napkins and laid one beside each place setting. "It sounds like we're in for quite a storm."

"Everything in here sure looks nice," he said.

The older woman beamed and laced her fingers in front of her. She was wearing color on her cheeks and lips and had fixed her silver-blond hair in curls. "I'll go help Audrey carry in the meal."

Thunder rumbled in the distance. Hayden shut off her tablet and looked at him. "My mom said you used to play the guitar and you said acoustic."

He nodded. "Still do."

"Are you any good?"

He shrugged. "I'm no Erik Bentley, but I can rustle up a tune you'd recognize."

"For real?"

"For real."

"Do you sing too?"

"Some."

"Where do you sing?"

"At the Wild Card. It's a saloon in town where the locals hang out, like a bar and grill with good food. There's live music on the weekends."

She folded her hands over the tablet on her plate and leaned forward, her intent gaze boring into his. Up close her eyes were blue, not the same color as Audrey's, but the same shape. The intent way she studied him was a hundred percent like Audrey. The uncanny resemblance reminded him of all the confusing feelings he'd had back then. "Would you rather hear the same song for the rest of your life or never hear the same song twice?"

Her question grounded him in the present. "That's a difficult question."

"Would You Rather *is* difficult. It makes you think."

"It sure does." He tapped his fingers on the tablecloth and pursed his lips while he considered her surprising question.

Dorris and Audrey came from the kitchen then, both carrying dishes. Audrey set down a platter holding a meatloaf and Dorris presented a bowl of mounded mashed potatoes and another of steamed vegetables. After scurrying back for the gravy bowl, Audrey sat across from him next to Hayden, and Dorris seated herself at the table's head.

"Can I pray, Gramma?" Hayden asked. At the woman's nod, she said a brief blessing and then skewered Jericho with a stare. "So, which would you rather?"

"You're already quizzing our dinner guest?" Audrey asked. She served herself a slice of meatloaf and passed it across the table to him with an apologetic raise of an eyebrow.

"He doesn't mind, do you?" Hayden's expression told him the girl was invested in his answer.

"No, I don't mind." Delighted with the hearty menu, he filled his plate. "Would I rather hear only one song for the rest of my life or never hear the same song twice?"

Audrey groaned.

Dorris passed him the rolls and butter.

"Thank you, ma'am. Well, Hayden, after serious consideration, I've made a decision. Hearing only the same song for the rest of my life would be torture, the degree depending on the song and the singer, of course. So, I would prefer to never hear the same song twice. Of course, I'd have to be able to imagine there were that many songs in the world so as not to run out. But I have a pretty good memory, and if there were some I especially liked, I could sing them over again to myself. When no one else was around. There's no rule against that is there?"

Hayden held her fork aloft while her thoughtful expression revealed she was turning over what he'd said. Slowly, she looked at her mother.

Audrey raised a shoulder and couldn't hide a grin. "He's got a point. The choice was about hearing, not singing. I think he posed a great solution. And he did decide which he'd rather. He'd rather never hear the same song twice."

"Good decision," Hayden said with a nod of agreement.

It was odd how accomplished it felt to have an eight-year-old's approval, and he grinned to himself. She'd asked questions about his musical ability and then this amusing dilemma she'd posed. She seemed to think about music as much as her mother had at this age.

"This is a delicious meal," the sweet-faced girl said. "Thank you, Mom and Gramma."

Audrey and her mother exchanged a pleased look.

"Nothin' fancy, but you can't beat a good meatloaf," Dorris said.

"It's the perfect meal for this country boy," Jericho told them.

"You must burn a lot of calories at your job," Audrey said.

"Some days it seems I do nothing but drive and give tickets to kids on ATVs, but other days I find myself in some interesting--and challenging situations."

"What interesting things happened this week?" Hayden asked.

He buttered his roll. "I got a call to investigate squatters on private land. Owners had heard shots, so I called for another deputy to meet me, and we checked it out. We discovered tents and coolers and ammunition. Appeared more than one person had been living there, shooting game for food, littering cans and bottles."

"Like living out in the woods?" Hayden's eyebrows rose. "Homeless people? Did you see them?"

"No. They had either cleared out or saw us coming and left."

"What did you do?"

"Took photos, confiscated belongings and bagged up all the trash. The landowner put up no trespassing signs. Most times that takes care of the problem and the vagrants move on."

"What else did you do this week?" Hayden asked.

"Well...this one was tricky. I rescued a family of ducklings out of a storm drain."

"Seriously?" Audrey asked.

"Oh yes. My job is fraught with adventure and peril."

Audrey and Hayden laughed, while Dorris ate her meal without amusement. He exchanged a glance with Audrey, who raised one eyebrow as though she couldn't figure out her mother either.

Conversation continued as they finished their supper.

"This reminds me of dinners our families shared over the years," Dorris said finally. "Do you still eat meals with your family?"

"Almost every Sunday," he answered. "Sometimes on a week night. Judah and I have our own places, you know, and Bethel works long hours, but she still lives in the big house."

Dorris drank a sip of water and set down her glass. "You kids always took off after Sunday dinner, and we didn't see you until sundown."

"What did you do all that time?" Hayden asked.

"In the summer we swam in the creek," Jericho answered.

"Winters we sledded until our feet and faces were numb

with the cold," Audrey added. "Once we had a downhill collision, and your Uncle Wyatt had to have stitches in his forehead."

Dorris shook her head. "I remember that."

"Mom told me stories about her little brother." Hayden glanced at Jericho. "You were friends?"

"Best friends," he replied with a nod.

"They were together so much that people mistook them for brothers. They did look a lot alike." Audrey tilted her head in a familiar way that caught him off guard. She'd worn her hair down and the light caught small silver earrings when she moved. She was so pretty, it hurt to look at her.

Hayden's expression lit up. "I want to see pictures of them."

"Wyatt had my father's eyes," Dorris declared. "The two boys looked nothing alike, except they were the same age and both had dark hair, like half the students in their class."

"You and Uncle Wyatt were in school together?" Hayden asked.

"Same age, so same classes," he replied.

"Were you friends with all the kids in your class? How many were there?"

"There were probably twenty or so, and I knew them all, but I didn't hang out with all of them."

"That must be so cool. What about Mom?"

"Your mother is nearly two years older than Wyatt and Jericho," Dorris told her. "Let's you and I clear the dishes."

"Okay." Hayden folded her napkin.

"Would you like another cup of coffee?" Audrey asked him.

"No, thanks. I'm bursting at the seams now. Bethel said to tell you hey."

"I hope I have a chance to see her while I'm here."

"I'm sure you will."

Audrey laid her napkin beside her plate. "We might as well go into Daddy's office and get started."

He followed her down a hall and into what had been Charlie's domain. She took ledgers and several file folders from a drawer and pulled up two software programs on the desktop pc. "You're familiar with this software?"

"I am," he answered. "It's what I use. The last few years I've put together all the *Big Pine* paperwork and sent it to the same accountant who does the *Double T* taxes. You can trust that it's all done well and everything is legal and accounted for."

She gestured for him to take the big leather chair and pulled a smaller one close. She smelled good, the scent of her hair drifting to him. He'd been strong enough to block the old feelings when she'd been the unreachable girl on the radio or on all those glossy covers, but having her right here beside him—their arms brushing—this was a different tune. This was Audrey, the girl next door, the girl with the hundred-watt smile and eyes that sparkled when she laughed. He'd buried a million unspoken words long ago, along with the emotions that went along with them. Seeing her again, being close was like testing the ground for metal and finding proof it was under there. He wasn't digging though. He'd been through it all before. But the feelings and words were down there deep, *whispering*.

# CHAPTER SIX

With supreme effort, Jericho collected himself and focused on the task. It took well over an hour to study the ranch finances. "Everything is in the black, and there are stocks and money in the bank," he said. "But the leases could be earning more."

"Pull up those files, will you please?" she asked. She thumbed through a stack and found the folder with the contracts. "What's the going rate per acre?"

He told her, and she looked over each contract. "A couple of these come up for renewal the first of next year, and the rest within the next two to five years." Audrey tucked her hair behind her ear and glanced over at him. "The original contracts allow for adjustments according to land value. Have there been any?"

"Not that I can see. It's a market-based formula, so we can check to see where the average is right now. Pretty positive some of these amounts are too low."

She put the folders back on the stack and opened another.

"If the leases were bringing in market value," he added, "*Big Pine* could easily afford upgrades and repairs."

She nodded. "Which I've been thinking about. We need a new off-road vehicle, and the harvesting machines could be upgraded. We're not growing a lot of crops, but repairs on the old machinery needed to grow and store what's required for the horses is eating into the budget."

"I agree. New machinery saves on help, repairs, time and money in the long run. Of course, you can't make it up all at once. You'll have to write a gradual increase into the next leases."

She stopped with her finger on a line in a bank statement. "What is Vista AgriServices?"

"Never heard of them."

"There are several payments to them. Twelve hundred twice that I see." She picked up a highlighter and drew a yellow line through the amounts. "Twenty-one hundred here. Is it a supplier or a service of some sort? What's been outsourced?"

"The fields are minimal, so when we have ours dry spread with fungicide and herbicides, I schedule *Big Pine* at the same time. It's RM Charters. You'll see it in the paid out at the end of October last year."

She gave a thoughtful nod.

He took the paper from her. "This is a red flag. Google Vista AgriServices."

Audrey opened her laptop and typed into the browser bar. "Pulls up a lot of similar stuff, but not specifically Vista AgriServices."

They looked at each other. Her confusion was obvious. She logged into the bank account and searched in payees, finding nothing. Concern drew her eyebrows together. "If these weren't sent as bill pay, then physical checks had to have been written."

She pulled open the top desk drawer and pulled out the binder for manual checks.

"I've never even seen that checkbook before," he said.

"There have only been a few written since Daddy died," she said, thumbing through. "These stubs were the checks made out to Vista AgriServices. This is my mom's handwriting."

"What the…?" He stifled his reaction so as not to add to her distress. He'd already had opportunity to pick up on the tension that remained between mother and daughter. Audrey didn't want to step on her mom's toes, but this was business—a business two of them shared. Their relationship had always been strained, and he'd heard Dorris' criticisms firsthand. Audrey had told him once that she was okay with Wyatt being their mother's favorite, because her father's love was enough. Still, the favoritism had to have hurt, and now her dad was gone, which left her without a buffer.

"Do you want to ask her?" he asked. "I mean, she has her own money that she can do whatever she wants with. The only purpose for this account is for the ranch. I'm only an outsider, but I'm thinking you want to know where these payments are going."

"I need to know. Daddy left ownership to both of us." She took a deep breath. Her gaze didn't appear focused on anything. She put her hands on her knees and pushed off the chair. "I'll go get her."

She left the room and returned a few minutes later with cups of coffee. "She's coming."

When Dorris entered, Audrey gestured to the chair beside Jericho. "Have a seat, Mom. We're trying to figure out a couple of things that aren't accounted for and I'm not familiar with."

Dorris gave Jericho a hesitant smile and seated herself. "I'll help if I can."

Standing, Audrey leaned forward to point out the

payments in question. "It's these payments to Vista AgriSer-vices we can't figure out. There are no invoices for services."

"Oh, there are," Dorris said, and opened the drawer at her knee. After flipping through the tabs on the hanging folders, she pulled out three invoices and handed them to Jericho.

"Dorris, you never mentioned this to me," he said. "I've been doing the accounts and I've never even seen this check-book before."

"I didn't think you needed to be bothered with it," she replied.

"I don't look at the bank statements every month," he said. "So, I didn't see these deductions Audrey found. I've never heard of this company before."

Audrey was thankful for his presence, which seemed to keep her mother's temperament even. Audrey moved behind him and read aloud over his shoulder. She had no idea what she was looking at. "Lime, organic matter, nitrogen nitrate, phosphorus, potassium, calcium, all with amounts. What is this?"

"Soil testing results," Jericho answered.

Dorris got up from the chair and moved to stand at the end of the desk and face them. "Yes. See there, all accounted for."

Her mom seemed to think this explained the payments, but Audrey was still baffled. "How did you find these people to do the testing?" she asked.

"Soil testing is a perfectly normal expense," her mom said.

"Did they contact you? Did you get an email about them? Or a letter? A recommendation?"

"Oh, no, nothing like that. It was easy to handle. Nothing to be concerned with. I've taken care of it." Dorris turned to go. "There are brownies in the kitchen."

Her mom left the room.

"She's just walking away." Sick to her stomach now,

Audrey sat back down in the chair her mom had vacated. "Why would someone be doing this kind of testing? What would prompt it?"

"It's not done unless you have reason to believe there's contamination of some sort or nutrition is depleted."

She looked at him with a raised brow.

"Neither is the case here," he explained. "It doesn't make sense. *Big Pine* isn't farming and there's nothing questionable about the soil."

"I don't remember seeing anything like this before." She ran a hand through her hair and looked at him. "She obviously doesn't want to explain it or talk about it, and I'm not going to chase her into the other room and confront her in front of Hayden."

He didn't appear to understand Dorris' behavior either. "Soil tests are free through the state, and even to pay for a more thorough analysis, a university would charge maybe ten or twenty dollars a sample." When he looked at her; his gaze traveled over her hair and face and skittered away from her lips. He looked at the computer screen. "I'm completely at a loss here."

He had a five o'clock shadow that made his tanned skin look darker and emphasized the dips and planes of his jaw. She wondered if his skin would feel warm and raspy to the touch. "Well," she said, distracting herself. "I guess we have to find out who and what this company is."

"Let's do that before we stir up anything more," he agreed.

They hadn't kept in touch for a lot of years, but it seemed perfectly natural to be having this conversation and trying to figure out something that affected *Big Pine Ridge*. He'd been in the thick of ranching this whole time and had a lot more current knowledge than she did. "I want you to know how much I appreciate you being here and helping me like this."

He glanced at her, his dark eyes not revealing his

thoughts. "We're old friends," he said with a dismissive nod. "The sheriff has a lot of resources at his fingertips. More than I do for this kind of investigation. If it's okay with you, I'll ask Joe to look into this corporation and see what he can come up with. This could be one of those scams that preys on people because they're not computer savvy or they're elderly. Not that your mom is incapable by any means, but I do have to wonder if this was a deliberate con."

*Old friends*, she thought uncomfortably, still stuck on those words. "I know what you're saying, and I agree. Yes, please do ask Sheriff Cavanaugh if he can get us information."

"First thing in the morning," he assured her.

A lot of time had passed since they'd been comfortable with each other. She'd been young and determined when she'd left Spencer headed for Nashville. Jericho had believed in her back then. Leaving had been the most difficult decision of her life, but she'd had to try. Certainly, she wondered sometimes how her life might have turned out if she'd stayed. "This wasn't what I wanted to find out, but I'm thankful for your help."

"Any time."

"Would you like a brownie?"

"I'm going to pass. My shift starts early tomorrow, and Bethel said she'd save me dessert."

"Say hey to both of them for me. I want to get over soon and catch up."

Her mom and Hayden were in the family room with a talent show on the television in the background, Mom doing a crossword and Hayden on her tablet. Jericho wished them a goodnight and Audrey walked him to the kitchen door.

"Evenin'." He settled his hat on his head, slipped on his leather jacket and dashed out through the rain to his truck.

The headlights came on; he backed up, turned around and headed along the long drive toward the road.

Audrey watched his taillights disappear into the night, feeling oddly adrift. Her days and nights had slowed down, giving her time to think. Until now even brief vacations had been strategically planned, so the weeks ahead felt liberating. Two consecutive Saturday concerts were the only things on her schedule and other than those, she was free to do as she chose. She made herself a glass of iced tea and carried it to the other room.

"How long does she get to be on that thing, anyway?" Dorris asked Audrey after she'd taken a seat.

"I'm playing Minecraft with my friends," Hayden said.

Dorris gestured with her pencil to the television. "I watched a show where grown men are on those computers, befriending young girls." She leaned toward Audrey and whispered, "Perverts."

Hayden looked at her mom.

"She knows all the rules, Mom. There are parental controls on her games. She uses a fake name and ID and never gives out personal information."

"Well, strangers aren't friends," Dorris said.

"I don't know about you, Hayden, but I'm beat." Audrey picked up her glass. "We could get changed and read in bed together for a while."

Hayden's expression brightened. "We haven't done that for a long time."

Audrey rose from the chair. "'Night, Mom."

"Good night, girls."

Hayden had been sleeping in Audrey's old room, which looked much as it had when Audrey had still been living here and attending college. The walls were a pastel peach with framed photographs of horses. The white-painted antique cast iron bed had a black and white toile skirt and spread and white throw pillows emblazoned with black music notes. The room seemed quite uninspired until one turned around and encountered the posters of The Band Perry, Jewell, Sugarland, Danny Gokey and Keith Urban along with two acoustic guitars, all adorning the entire wall.

She followed her daughter and leaned against the doorframe while Hayden brushed her teeth.

"This clock in here is the coolest, Mom."

A three-foot tall laser-cut birchwood clock shaped like a guitar hung beside the mirror. "I'll put new batteries in it for you. You can have it for your own if you want."

"Really? Awesome."

"We're going to be here for a while," Audrey said, thinking. "Is there anything you'd like to have? Legos or slime ingredients or anything?"

Hayden swiped a moisturizer stick over her lips and put the cap back on. "If it wasn't almost winter, I'd like a trampoline."

"A trampoline. Really?" Audrey rolled that thought around a minute. "Well, wherever we are in the Spring, we'll get you a trampoline. I was thinking more along the line of things to do during the winter. I guess you've outgrown your dollhouses."

"I want to go sledding like you and Jericho did."

"Grab your book and slippers." Audrey turned out the light and they went into the guest room Audrey was using, which held a larger bed than Audrey's old room. "I'll order some snowsuits and winter boots then. And a sled or a saucer."

"A saucer would be fun. Get two so we can go down the hill together. Whose room was this?"

"It was always a guest room, and my grandparents slept in here when they visited. My daddy said he built the house with room for company. I helped Gramma redecorate it when you were little and we came to visit."

"I don't remember."

"You were only three. You slept in a portable crib right over there."

"Did Daddy come too?"

Audrey admired her daughter's delicate features, the curve of her cheek and her long eyelashes. "That was right after he died. We came here to get away. The next time we came to stay a while you were five."

"Do you still miss Daddy?"

Audrey thought carefully before she answered. "I miss how full of life he was. When he got excited about something, he just drew everyone into his passion. I'd never known anyone like that before."

Tucker Frost had been dynamic, which served him well in business, but the business consumed his time and energies. His animated personality and enthusiasm had been hard to resist. From the first time they'd met, he'd been convinced she would be a star, and he set out to make that happen as quickly as possible. He'd seemed to fall for her and had asked her to marry him only months after they'd met. Only after his death, had she recognized there'd never been a moment to relax in his presence.

Memories of singing with the seniors at the Pine Valley Center were unshakeable. She loved to sing. She loved her career. But she couldn't remember the last time before coming here that she'd sung for pure pleasure. No adoring fans, no back-up singers, no sought-after musicians. Only old songs she read from yellowed sheet music, a hand-me-down Kimball upright played by the church organist, and a room full of silver-haired men and women for whom the songs brought back the days of their youth.

No one had gotten out their phone.

She picked up her book from the nightstand and found her place. It felt familiar and good to hold a real print book in her hands and turn the pages. She enjoyed reading on her tablet, but this added tactile pleasure. "There's a charming bookstore in Spencer. We'll go book shopping next week, okay?"

"Okay."

Thunder rolled overhead, and the sound of rain was a steady beat on the roof above, a homey, relaxing sound.

"This is nice, isn't it?" Hayden asked from beside her.

Audrey stuffed down her concerns about her mom's behavior. It wasn't like that money was going to break the ranch, but she didn't like not knowing what was going on, and she really didn't like Dorris avoiding talking about it. She was going to wait until the sheriff came back with some information before thinking about it anymore. "It's really nice being here together. I'm glad we came."

Dorris called Audrey to the landline phone the next morning.

Audrey took the receiver. "Hello?"

"Audrey, I don't know if you remember me, but this is Glenn Randall. From high school. We took Mr. Dickies' shop class together."

"Of course, I remember you. We had a library study hall together, and you always made me laugh. I got detention for that once."

"Wow, you do have a good memory. Not holding a grudge, I hope."

She laughed. "Hardly. Those were the best days ever. What's up?"

"I'm calling to ask a favor for the Spencer Fire Department."

"I hope it's easy. I didn't bring my turnout gear with me."

It was his turn to laugh. "It's easy, I promise. Rumor has it you and your mom and daughter are coming to the fundraiser breakfast at the VFW tomorrow."

"Yes, we'll be there."

"Can I talk you into taking a turn at the griddle and flipping pancakes for an hour or so? It's short notice, and an imposition, but we're thinking you'd be a hit and maybe raise a few more dollars for us. If you don't want to, just say no. It's okay."

"I'd love to do it. I'll ask my daughter Hayden to help. What time would you like us to show up?"

"If you can be there at nine, it would be great. Otherwise, we'll put you to work whenever you get here."

"I'll be there at nine."

"I can't wait for Ashley to meet you. She's my wife. We have a baby, too. Her name is Joy."

"I can't wait to meet them."

Thanks, Audrey."

She hung up and glanced at her mom. "I'm going to flip pancakes at the volunteer breakfast tomorrow."

Thankfully, her mom said nothing and put clean dishtowels in a drawer.

Later that day, her cell rang and she glanced at it. When she and Jericho had exchanged numbers the other night, she'd added him to her contacts. She didn't answer calls unless she recognized the caller.

"Hey, Jericho."

"Audrey. Joe's been looking into Vista AgriServices. The secretary of state searched and found it's registered as a domestic corporation. But get this, the majority stockholder is another corporation. Apparently, it's pretty common practice, but getting to the source requires a deeper dig. The guy suggested we might think about an attorney just in case."

"So, the sheriff's suspicious too?"

"Yes. The secretary of state didn't come right out and say he thought something was fishy, but it was implied. As soon as I learn anything else, I'll let you know."

"She had to have mailed those checks to someone—or handed them over. I want her to give me a name, but I'm not going to cause friction until I have all the facts. Hayden is having a good time here."

"I know it's dicey between the two of you."

"Yeah. Thank you. Really, Jericho, I appreciate the help."

"Any time. Talk to you later."

Audrey tapped off the call. What had her mother gotten them involved in?

# CHAPTER SEVEN

*A*udrey drove them into Spencer the next morning. Parked vehicles already lined the street, so she drove across Chickering Road East, where there was a large lot for Old Towne and The Old Stone Church, and they walked across to the VFW. Audrey bought tickets from a couple of high school girls at the entrance, and they found spots at one of the long tables and hung their coats on the backs of folding chairs.

"Hey, Mrs. Monroe, Audrey. Hi Hayden." Dana wore her Stick Pony cap and a thick cable-knit sweater.

"Hello, dear," Dorris said.

Dana turned to Audrey and Hayden. "You two haven't met Lane yet. This is Lane Shay. Lane, Audrey and Hayden."

"I feel like I already know you both," Lane said with a broad smile. He was tall and slender, with dark hair held back in a ponytail. "I've seen pics, of course, but Mrs. Monroe talks about you."

"Well, thanks." Audrey didn't show her surprise, but instead asked about the logo on Dana's cap. "I noticed it the other day."

"Stick Pony's a rehabilitation center across the highway from *Big Pine*. It's horse-assisted therapy. They're having a grand opening next month. They're staffed and running on a limited basis right now."

"Seems I did read something about a new facility," Audrey said. "Jackson Spencer's project, isn't it?"

"Along with Ryder Barlow," Lane answered.

"We want you to know how great it is we can work for you and have a nice house to live in," Lane said to her. "What with college expenses, I don't know how we'd have swung a decent place."

Audrey glanced at her mom and back. "We're pretty fortunate too. The barns are clean and orderly, and the horses are well cared for. I can tell you're doing an excellent job."

She'd been thinking they needed to include wages for the work these kids did, but had yet to mention it to her mom. There was enough going on without further stirring the pot.

"Audrey!"

She turned to see who had addressed her, and recognized a smiling Glenn Randall. He was a couple inches shorter than she was, with closely-trimmed hair and glasses. "I'd like to talk soon," Audrey said to Lane. "Excuse me, won't you?"

She joined Glenn.

"Audrey. Thanks so much for doing this at the last minute."

"My pleasure. This is Hayden."

He gave Hayden a smile and a nod. "Come meet my wife and baby." He gestured for them to follow him between tables to where a gathering of locals were seated. "This is Ashley."

The petite young woman with short dark hair and glasses stood and greeted them.

Glenn took the baby she held and turned her so they could see her round little sleeping face. "This is Joy."

"She's just beautiful. She has your shiny hair, Ashley."

Ashley's wide smile showed her pleasure and pride.

"These are Ashley's folks," Glenn added.

A smiling older couple beamed and she greeted them.

Glenn handed the infant back to his wife. "Come on, I'll show you around the griddle and introduce you to anyone you don't know."

A long open window with a counter between the meeting room and the kitchen made a serving window where residents were waiting for their breakfasts. Heads turned as she and Hayden followed him through a doorway into the warm room smelling of bacon, syrup and coffee.

A few of the volunteers were familiar, and she was introduced to others. A rotund older man named Giorgio who wore a pristine white apron showed her how to slather butter on the grill. "I'll be making the batter in this big mixer. When you need more, just grab one of these pitchers. You ladies know when to flip?"

"After the bubbles break," Hayden replied. "Mom taught me."

Audrey experienced a moment of delight for having taught her daughter a useful tip and that Hayden had remembered. She gave her a proud smile.

Giorgio grinned. "Right, little lady. You will be able to fit about eighteen cakes at a time. Add three to a plate when you serve 'em up. The fellas will keep the clean plates coming."

After glancing around for a handwashing station, Audrey gestured to Hayden.

Once they got started, the two kept plenty busy. Hayden produced a couple of oddly-shaped pancakes, before Giorgio figured out the glass pitcher full of batter was too heavy and got a plastic measuring pitcher for her to pour from.

Audrey hadn't anticipated the stifling heat from the griddle. At least half the people getting their breakfast told her they had tickets to the concert the following weekend. No one had asked to take photos, however, and she was thankful. Not that she minded; she always stopped to greet fans and pose for pictures, but Spencer was her hometown and being here should be different. She wanted it to be different. Granted, etiquette in this tourist town mandated locals not make a big deal out of the appearance of celebrities in stores and restaurants, but Audrey hoped part of the reason was that she and Hayden belonged here.

She could live with the initial oddity, but she was counting on them getting used to her. Before their shift ended however, Glenn took her aside and asked if it would be okay to get a group photo with her, Hayden, and the volunteer firefighters. "I think it would be a nice addition to an article in the *Herald*," he said. "And maybe the fellas here at the VFW would like copies too."

She barely paused. Her presence at their fundraiser was news, and this was good publicity for them. "Sure, Glenn. I'd love photo too."

Audrey excused herself to the restroom, where she cooled her face and neck with wet paper towels, touched up her makeup, and brushed her hair.

In a matter of minutes, Glenn had rounded up as many volunteers as were in attendance and ushered them outdoors to gather across the front of the building. Among them were two females Ronnie Hudson introduced as Isla Dagleish and Breezy Richards. She knew Tyler and Dusty Cavanaugh from school, as well as Matt Chandler and Tony Burnham. She met Konnor MacDhuibh, the young man who ran the forge on land he rented from *Big Pines*. Glenn introduced Lincoln Simmons who owned Old Time Photos across the way in Olde Town. Lincoln excused himself to unpack a camera and go stand in the street and change out his lenses.

Hayden hugged Audrey around the waist. "We're sure making a lot of friends, aren't we?"

Audrey glanced at the line-up of men and recalled Edith over at Pearl's saying she had a granddaughter Hayden's age. "Yes, we are. Let's go buy a pie to take home before we leave Spencer this morning."

"Okay. How many pancakes do you think we flipped?"

"Wow, well…eighteen at a time, about a billion times, that's got to be—"

"Eighteen billion!" Hayden supplied with her cheerful laugh.

Forty-five minutes later, she and Edith had arranged a playdate for Hayden and Edith's granddaughter, Annabelle the next day. Edith promised to drive her out to the ranch and pick her up a few hours later.

They left the café and headed back to get Dorris at the VFW. They had crossed the street when Jericho emerged from the front door of the sheriff's office. Dressed in his uniform, wearing his deputy hat and a utility belt holding a weapon, she almost didn't recognize him. His handsome professional demeanor caught her by surprise. "You look so…different. All official and everything."

"Look like this every day," he replied. "Hey, Hayden. You did something new to your hair."

"Braids," she replied. "Mama and I made pancakes at the firemen's fundraiser."

"I'm heading over there myself right now. Sorry I'll have missed your pancakes though." He held up a to-go cup with a lid. "But I'm taking my own coffee. Sheriff Cavanaugh bought us a cappuccino machine a while back."

"You can come over to Gramma's one day, and we can make you pancakes," Hayden offered in her cheerful voice.

Audrey locked eyes with Jericho, and he grinned.

"Any time," Audrey agreed.

"Well, okay, that sounds great. I'm glad I ran into you, because I want to ask you something."

"Me?" Hayden looked surprised, but excited to hear his question.

He nodded, his expression serious. "Would you rather have one really big hand or one really small hand?"

Hayden grinned at him, but then her expression turned thoughtful. "Small like a Barbie doll or small like a three-year-old?"

He was obviously amused, but hid it with a serious reply. "Like a three-year-old."

"Hmm." She screwed her lips to the side while she considered. "If I had a really big hand, I could reach things up high and catch balls really well, but if I had a little hand, I could get things out of small places. And I could wear kids' gloves, but with a big hand I'd never find a glove to fit it."

"I can't believe how much thought you two give these questions. Both of the choices are bad," Audrey said.

"That's the point," Hayden replied matter-of-factly. "You have to choose the least bad option." She turned her attention back to Jericho. "I'll take the small hand. I could get a puffy glove."

He nodded at her logic as they reached the VFW.

From across the street a female voice called, "Deputy Tanner!"

He glanced over and gave a wave.

Three girls who looked to be college age checked traffic before running toward him. "This is the deputy who saved me from the bear," the blonde said before introducing him to her friends.

"We heard the whole story from Melinda," one of them gushed.

"And you're a good singer too, we hear," the other commented.

Not one of them glanced at Audrey, which was unusual and welcome at the same time. *Saved her from a bear?*

"Passable anyway," he said with a grin.

"What's going on in there?" the one Audrey assumed was Melinda asked.

"Pancake feed. You should stop in," Jericho replied.

"Want to?" she asked the others.

They nodded.

"Okay, thanks. We'll be back in a few minutes," the girl said and the three continued on their way.

"Saved her from a bear?" Audrey asked.

"Scared it off is all," he said. "She's a hiker."

"Well, you're clearly a hero." Audrey gestured to the VFW. "We're stopping back for my mom before we head out," Audrey told him.

He opened the door and stood aside. She passed in front of him with an awkward exchange of glances.

"I don't think I mentioned it," he said, "but I'll be working your security at the fair. So, I'll see you there. I wanted to let you know."

Hayden had run off to find her grandmother, and once inside Audrey paused to face him. "That's great. You'll likely meet with DeShawn and Bowman. They're my bodyguards for concerts and public appearances."

His gaze moved over her hair to her eyes and made her stomach flutter. "Is all this what you imagined back when we were playing fairs and 4-H events?"

Thinking about his question, she glanced aside, then back. "I don't know. Not exactly, I don't think. I wanted to sing, share my music, make records. I don't know that I ever really considered the business or logistics of actually making a name for myself. I never realized that everyone would think they know me—and most of them do know all about me. They read articles and Wikipedia and have my song lists. But it makes me feel like I'm catching up all the time—like I'm behind in most conversations. They think we have a relationship, and that's just…weird."

She studied his rich brown eyes, his contemplative expression, appreciating that he was listening because he really cared how she felt. She'd forgotten he wasn't a person who talked simply because no one else was. He waited. He listened. He thought before he spoke. He gave a person time to assemble their thoughts, and that was rare in her world now.

"I love the fans, I do." She paused another moment. "They're the ones buying my albums, making it all happen, and yet sometimes it's overwhelming. Being a public figure isn't why I got into music, but it's a repercussion." She caught herself overthinking her reply. "I did choose this life." She turned to see Hayden and her mom talking to Glenn and Ashley. Hayden was cradling the feet of the baby Glenn held and smiling. "But my daughter didn't choose it, and that's the part that troubles me most."

"I get that." He glanced at Hayden and back. "But she's a great kid."

"Thanks. I'm trying to do right by her."

"From what I've seen, you're doing a good job."

Unexpected tears pricked at Audrey's eyes and she blinked them away. "Thank you. I'll see you later."

She turned away before he could see how his simple words had affected her. The incident in Atlanta had poked holes in any confidence she ever had about her parenting abilities. It hurt when the person you loved most turned to someone else for comfort. Maybe doing her best while working and traveling wasn't good enough. She didn't want to choose between being a good mother and her career.

The following morning, Edith dropped off Annabelle at the house. She was a pretty freckle-faced brunette with an infectious smile, and she'd packed a bag with bracelet supplies, hair ties and hairbrush, and several teen dolls that looked like ghouls in make-up. After a few tentative questions over cookies and milk, she and Hayden hit it off and disappeared into Audrey's old room, from which music and laughter pealed for the next few hours.

Audrey called them down for lunch, and they showed up with their hair slicked into glittered pigtails and shiny heart stickers on their cheeks. They each wore a dozen colorful bead bracelets.

"You make really good taco salad bowls, Miss Knox," Annabelle told her.

"Thanks, Annabelle. I asked your grandma, and she said you weren't a picky eater."

"No, the onliest thing I don't like is liver. And chicken livers." She wrinkled up her nose.

"I'm with you there," Audrey told her.

"I've never had liver," Hayden said. "It's gross, huh?"

"Disgusting," Annabelle replied. "My grandpa cooks it on Wednesdays at the café. Grandma takes that morning off to go get her hair done."

Audrey and Dorris looked at each other, and Dorris actually chuckled.

Annabelle's vivacious personality charmed them. Audrey was delighted that she and Hayden seemed to get along so well.

"Maybe Grandma will let us have a sleepover at her house," Annabelle suggested. "She has a room for me, with a

Nintendo and everything. Her dog, Binky sleeps with me so I'm not scared at night."

"What kind of dog is it?" Audrey asked.

"Brown."

"Oh." She glanced at her mom again, and her mom's eyes twinkled. "Is Binky a little dog?"

"No, he's a medium dog."

Audrey nodded as though she could pick Binky from a crowd now.

Annabelle obviously spent a lot of time with Edith and Marty, her extended family. Audrey had fond memories of her own grandparents, and she often lamented her father not being here for Hayden. Tucker's parents had been divorced since he was a child and the family wasn't close. Audrey had only ever met her in-laws once. Hayden was missing out on family connections.

When Edith came for her granddaughter, Audrey asked her in for coffee, and the three women visited for half an hour until the woman gathered Annabelle and they left.

Hayden couldn't stop talking about how much fun she'd had with her new friend. Audrey was delighted her daughter had been able to do something so ordinary, something that other girls did all the time. This was why she'd come to Spencer.

On Monday part of the crew arrived. Gianna called and scheduled a time the next day to go through wardrobe. Clothing was arriving and she was setting up in the trailer for dress, hair and makeup. Musicians and their gear would be arriving the following day and stage and techs on Wednesday. The full tech rehearsal would be Saturday morning.

"Who did you arrive with?" Audrey asked.

"Willow and Tam. We flew in this morning and got a car in Denver. The others are on the bus."

"Great, that gives you time to come ride this afternoon," Audrey told her. "I want you to see the ranch."

"We're at the Grand Vista Hotel. What time shall we come and what shall we wear?"

"Come any time soon and wear comfy clothes like jeans, but bring a coat. It can be chilly out in the open." When she tapped off the call, she found Dana's number and called to ask if she or Lane were available to saddle horses for five riders. Dana told her Lane would be at the stable within the hour.

Whenever possible, Audrey and her team found ways to enjoy the locales they visited together. Sometimes they were fortunate enough to get private admissions so they could enjoy themselves without the constant interruptions of fans. Other times Audrey wore a ballcap and sunglasses and spoke with an accent so she wouldn't be noticed. Sometimes it worked.

Today they had acres and acres to ride at their heart's content, and after they'd ridden, Audrey broke out the wine and had food delivered to the house. Dorris didn't seem to know what to make of the noisy and jovial women or their outbursts of laughter, but she was hospitable.

The next day Everly called to say she'd arrived and checked into the hotel, so Audrey drove her mom and Hayden to the RV lot at the fairgrounds, which held the enormous hotel, the Centennial Event Center, conference center, 4-H barns, livestock pavilions and outdoor arenas. The RV areas were on the far east side of the complex, with gates nearby.

Audrey's bus had been parked, awnings outstretched, outdoor furniture arranged, and the crew was present, grilling steaks. Hayden flung open the rear door of the Escalade and ran to Everly.

Vallie and Monica, Audrey's singers, along with Zane and

the other musicians, were next to greet Hayden and welcomed Audrey and her mom. Dorris eyeballed Gianna's spikey blue hair and row of earrings, but Gianna got Dorris a cup of coffee and settled her on a cushioned chair where the sun would warm her.

Audrey greeted and gave hugs to her crew and friends. "Have you seen Sidney or Cadence?" she asked Zane.

"Sidney is at the hotel." He pointed in a westerly direction. "He said Cadence will arrive Friday. Everyone else is here. Tech is setting up."

"Okay, tech rehearsal Saturday then," she said with a nod.

Hayden appeared at Audrey's side and waited until she'd finished speaking with the guitarist. "Mom, can I stay here with Everly tonight?"

Her daughter hadn't been apart from the nanny for long, but she'd greeted Everly as though it had been months. The young woman was her constant companion, so it was exciting to be reunited. Audrey felt the pleasure of being reunited with her people as well. They'd been together—with the exception of a couple members joining or leaving—for years. Ashamed, she tucked down jealousy and inadequacy. "No, darlin'. But if she'd like to, Everly can come stay with us at Gramma's."

"Thanks, Mom!" Her daughter dashed back to talk to her nanny.

Everly looked at Audrey with questioning eyebrows, so Audrey smiled and nodded. Hayden gave them both a thumbs up.

They stayed for steaks and salads, then drove to the hotel so Everly could grab her bags. The nanny rode back to *Big Pine* with them. Dorris didn't say much, but she watched Hayden and her nanny with furtive glances.

"Can we sign in to Disney channel from Gramma's tv?" Hayden asked.

"Yep, download the app, and Disney will look just like it always does," Audrey replied. "What are we watching?"

"*Raya and the Last Dragon,*" she answered.

"Again?"

"Everly hasn't seen it yet."

"Well...great then." She avoided her mother's gaze.

Everly shared Hayden's room, and the two of them talked and laughed until late. Only a couple of nights ago it had been she and Hayden, and it wasn't as though Everly took anything from Audrey's relationship with her daughter. She had no idea how other mothers felt when their kids made adult friends. Feeling threatened didn't seem right or natural. She doubted if her mom had cared who she spent time with, but she wondered if a measure of jealousy was normal for everyone.

No reason for confusing feelings. Everly had been with them for years and was like family. She'd been present for them every time they needed her. Audrey loved and trusted the nanny or she wouldn't leave her child in her care. She was grateful Hayden was content with her childcare provider.

Audrey had enough things to occupy her thoughts with the concert and the question about the unaccounted-for payments, so she wasn't going to stress over this. She had a big weekend ahead.

Friday morning Audrey drove them to the fairgrounds, where security met her vehicle and led them to the event center. The fairgrounds opened to attendees at noon, but hundreds of behind-the-scenes workers were on the grounds

for the rodeo, 4-H presentations, livestock shows, conces-
sions and carnival rides, so her arrival was no secret. Sidney
Oliver had worked with local law enforcement and event
security to coordinate safety for not only Audrey, but for all
the staff and the public as well. A deputy and a couple of
brawny men in black event T-shirts met the Escalade and
opened all four doors.

"Hey, guys," Audrey said with a broad smile.

"Mizz Audrey." The nearest one flashed her a white-
toothed smile. "You enjoyin' your visit home?"

"I really am. We've been riding and taking it easy. Hayden
and I made pancakes at a fundraiser." Once they were all
outside the vehicle, she turned and gestured to Dorris.
"Mom, this is DeShawn. That scrawny fella over there is
Bowman. Gentlemen, this is my mother, Dorris Monroe."

"Mizz Monroe," the fellas echoed and moved to walk on
either side of their charges.

Dorris seemed unable to hold back a chuckle. "Goodness,
what did your mothers feed you?"

"Shrimp and grits," DeShawn said with a laugh. "She
made 'em for me twice last week when I was home."

"My mom didn't cook at all," Bowman told her. "She a
state's attorney now, but she was a public defender when I
was a kid. My sister and I learned how to call for pizza."

Dorris grinned. "Bowman. Is that your last name or your
first name?"

"It's my whole name, ma'am. Like Pink."

DeShawn chuckled. "He and Pink have so much in
common."

Her mom's expression showed puzzlement, and Audrey
considered rescuing her, but Bowman held out his elbow to
escort Dorris, and she took it while smiling up at him. Her
head barely came to his shoulder, but she was obviously
taken with the big guy. Hayden rescued her grandmother by

changing the subject however. "DeShawn, when are we racing again?"

"Girl, you have to let me win once in a while."

Dorris gave Audrey a curious sideways glance.

Oh boy, here came the criticism. "Mario Kart, Mom. They play a video game together."

"Audrey!"

"Whoo hoo!"

Three young women and a guy all wearing jeans and cowboy hats called to them from the direction of the livestock pavilion.

"Can't wait until tonight!"

Bowman stepped back so Audrey could see the fans calling out from a distance.

Audrey smiled and waved. "Hey, guys!" she called. "I'm excited too."

Inside the event center, they stepped into the usual chaos of testing all the equipment, techs calling to one another in person and on walkie talkies, and the band finalizing set-up. Since the incident in Atlantic City, their set-up crew had been retrained and an expanded checklist put in place, with a supervisory team to retest everything on event day.

In a dressing room with her name on the door, Audrey met Gianna, and they went over the costumes that had been hung in order of wearing. She'd tried them all on the day before so Gianna could check for repairs, so now they went over the order with coordinating jewelry and footwear.

At a rap on the door, Audrey opened it and Sidney joined them. His assistant Cody White carried in a guitar case. "Hi, Miss Knox. Here's the guitar from the bus you asked for."

"Thanks, Cody. Will you stay with me and keep that with you while we do the sound checks?"

"Happy to." He carried the case to a nearby stool and sat with it on his lap.

A few minutes later, a runner came to tell her they were ready whenever she was.

Audrey led Cody and Sidney along the corridor to back of the stage. Half a dozen greetings met her as she took her place. She conversed with band members, catching up. Back-up singers Vallie and Monica joined her and gave her hugs.

"Olde Town is fabulous," Vallie told her. "Wait until you see the photos we had taken at the old-time photographer. We dressed like saloon girls."

"Did you find good food?"

"Honestly," Monica said. "The best place is that burger joint. Everything is called something old time, so it's a name like Olde Time Soda Shop. The food was awesome. Especially the chocolate shakes."

"With real whipped cream and a cherry on top," Vallie agreed. "I had sweet potato fries, and they serve a special dipping sauce with them." She rolled her eyes and grinned.

"On my list," Audrey said.

The audio tech brought a cordless mic and counted into it before handing it to her. "Let's do this," she said, her voice coming over the sound system. "Ordinarily we wouldn't do so many songs all the way through, but it's been a while since we were together, so I'll feel more comfortable—I think we all will—if we blow out the cobwebs."

The drummer called out a whoop and spanked a cymbal, followed by Zane playing his Hendrix flourish on the bass.

"Do ya'll know the difference between God and a guitar player?" Audrey asked into the mic.

Everyone laughed. They were familiar with the old joke that God didn't think He was a guitar player, but guitar players think they're God. The excitement in the air was contagious. She had a team of musicians and singers who loved what they did, and she was thankful for them every day. On tech rehearsal and performance days the energy in the air was electrifying. There was nothing comparable.

The familiar first chords of *Baby We've Got This* incited a shiver of excitement along her skin. Audrey's broad smile was for this amazing group of performers and bandmates as well as for the joyful excitement of singing again. *"Days and chances have slipped through our fingers..."*

Someone in the auditorium cheered at hearing the song. Audrey continued. It was an early hit, one of the first she'd written. A song about love lost and love found. *"...while doubt stole the years and foolishness lingered."*

She sang the song all the way through, plus the whole first set. "This second set, let's do intros and a few lines only," she said to the band and singers. Once finished, she asked Cody to bring her guitar. Another stage hand brought a stool and a stand for the mic.

Jericho had entered with the crew that would be working the show that evening. He'd stopped along with the others to listen to Audrey's soundcheck. Her singing, enhanced by the sound system made her voice so full, so...*intimate*. He'd been listening to her sing since she was a girl, and with maturity her tone had grown richer. He absorbed her voice through his skin, into his bones like sustenance. Her talent had always been breathtaking. He'd played with her because she asked, and maybe she'd needed him to gain her footing, but he'd never been in her league.

Finishing that last intro, she asked for her guitar, and he sank onto the nearest seat. A crew member took an acoustic Gibson from a case and handed it to her. Jericho wasn't close, but he knew exactly what she took from her jeans pocket when she slipped a finger pic over her index finger and one over the thumb of her right hand. His heart skipped a beat. He'd seen her practice this technique a hundred times.

Her guitar had a capo on the neck, and she picked a C

note with her thumb and strummed upward with her index finder playing the chord sound, creating both the base and the rhythm. Alone. No band behind her filling the auditorium. Only the sound of her guitar. With her right hand, she brought in the melody. The tune he recognized held him transfixed. This was her idol Maybelle Carter's song, *Wildwood Flower*, and she picked it in the distinct Carter scratch she'd aspired to all those years ago.

Of course, her voice was richer than the old recordings of the mother of folk and country music, fuller, unique only to Audrey. Jericho's stomach fluttered—or was it his heart? Pride and longing and a million memories overwhelmed him in that moment, and tears prickled behind his eyes. She was so brave and so beautiful he could barely breathe.

"She plays one song like this at every concert," Vida Lucas said quietly from behind him. He hadn't realized the female deputy had dropped onto a seat as well. "All by herself on her guitar, no band or singers. For the pure love of the music."

Jericho leaned forward, elbows on knees, fingers clasped in a fist against his lips.

"Incredible, isn't she?" Vida continued in awe. "I listened to these old songs with my great-grandma. I was hoping to get to catch a little tonight, but this? A front row seat to a Maybelle song?"

Audrey sang the last words of the song. The strum of her guitar faded away. A pin drop could have been heard, and then people seemed to collect themselves.

She glanced off stage at the same time crew and band members applauded.

"Thanks, guys," she said. "You were amazing. Let's do it again tonight."

Jericho and half a dozen other deputies went back to their inspection of the auditorium. He returned for a security briefing.

"Miss Knox?" the head of event center security called up to her. "Would you kindly give the security team a few minutes of your time?"

"I'd be happy to." Audrey made her way over to the stairs and came down to where they stood. DeShawn and Bowman, whom Jericho had met previously, joined her.

"I like to make introductions whenever possible so you know you're well-protected and the security team gets to meet the person they're here for," the security leader said. "These are our deputy sheriffs who will be here this evening, along with our on-staff team."

"Deputies," she said. "Thank you for working the concert. I appreciate your time and experience." She turned. "DeShawn, do we have tickets left for next Saturday's performance?" She pointed her thumb at him. "He's always with me, so he's the one who knows this stuff."

"Sure, I'll have a couple tickets for each of you at the ticket window." DeShawn got out his phone and noted the names on their tags.

Audrey shook each deputy's hand. As she took his, she leaned forward and brushed her cheek against Jericho's. "Do you remember that last song?"

Her softly spoken question near his ear sent a tingle across his shoulder. She moved back and looked at him.

"That Carter scratch was pretty amazing," he answered.

She grinned, took the sterling finger pics from her jeans pocket and held them in her palm. "Remember these?"

He'd given them to her for her graduation. Her initials were engraved inside. He couldn't speak around the acute ache, so he nodded.

"You've been with me all along." She tucked them back into her pocket.

*What had that meant?*

She spoke to Vida for a few minutes. The deputy blushed

as though she'd received honors from the queen, and then Audrey excused herself.

The situation was getting more complicated because of his involvement in helping with *Big Pine Ridge*, then the business with the unexplained checks Dorris had written, and now seeing Audrey in her environment. He collected himself.

She'd chosen her life's path, and it hadn't included him. He couldn't afford to let her get into his head.

# CHAPTER EIGHT

*A*udrey's performance was the subject of nearly every conversation he overheard in town the following week. There was already a new photo on the wall at Pearl's Café. He caught sight of it as he glanced around from his stool at the counter. The place wasn't busy that morning, so he got up and walked over to inspect the glossy image more closely.

She wore a body-hugging, above the knee, black sleeveless dress with cutouts that showed her cleavage, and canary yellow pointed high heels with an enormous black-and-white butterfly on each heel. Leaning in, he noted her black-and-white butterfly necklace.

"Eye candy, eh, deputy?"

At the female voice, he turned to see Brooke Cavanaugh, the life-flight nurse who worked at the hospital. "She's pretty, all right," he replied. "Did you go to her concert?"

"Sure did. Worth every penny. She loves her fans and gives an incredible performance."

"Not working this morning?" he asked.

"I got called in for an overnight shift, so I'm grabbing breakfast before I go home to sleep."

"What will you guys have?" Edith asked from behind the counter.

They'd just given their orders, when Joe's voice came over Jericho's walkie. *"Elderly male reported missing from Pine Valley Crescent Center. All available personnel report to south side of Brook Park for assignments. Respond in route."*

"Toss me a bagel, will you, Edith? I'm out of here."

Brooke's phone rang. She glanced at him. "Hello? Okay, standing by." She touched off her phone. "Wonder who it is?"

Jericho shook his head and took the bag and takeout cup Edith handed him. "Thanks. Catch you later."

"On the house, sweetie," she called after him.

His Tahoe was parked on the north side of the park, so he walked to where the emergency people were gathering on the opposite side and found Joe Cavanaugh with a map spread out on the hood of his sheriff's SUV.

"Tanner," he said. "You're team leader for D section. That's everything on the west side of the river from Willow Street to the Prospect Bridge. Cover Chickering Road from bridge to bridge first. No one but you goes near that section of river. Then work your way back up to the senior center."

"Who are we looking for?"

"People!" Joe called, and immediately drew a gathering. "We're looking for a white male, eighty years old, last seen wearing a blue plaid flannel shirt, khaki trousers and a camouflage ball cap."

He'd just described most of the men at the senior center.

"It's Buddy Lowman," he clarified. "Five seven, a hundred and sixty pounds. Gray hair. Speed is of the utmost importance," Joe said. "If the gentleman is confused or disoriented, he may be wandering or he could have a destination in mind. If we suspect he went over to the river, that's a whole different scenario. Police are investigating the nearest entry path to the water now. Fish and Game are bringing their K-9 unit."

"Do we know how long he's been gone?" Hunter Lawe asked. The police officer had shown up in uniform, as had many officers.

"He was accounted for at six-thirty am, but didn't show up for breakfast. After searching their facility, the center reported him missing just before eight am, so we can guess he's been on his own for maybe an hour to an hour and a half."

Within fifteen minutes, vehicles representing all critical services were pulling in along Brook Park Road. Jericho took the metal D sign from the open back of Joe's vehicle and walked ten feet east toward Chickering Road and set it down so it stood against his shin. A couple of his fellow deputies joined him, followed by volunteers in their orange T-shirts with SPENCER VOLUNTEER emblazed across their backs in white, among them his brother Judah and Matt Chandler, the widowed outfitter. All wore boots and had prepped back-packs. He waited until several more arrived and then gave them each their sections and directions within the grid.

"There's a photo of Mr. Lowman on the RCSD website and on our social media. Grab it for reference. You'll search in twos. Anyone not have my phone number?" He gave his number to a couple of new people. "Judah and I will search the river bank from Willow Drive Bridge to Prospect Bridge. You two search Willow Drive west, yards and businesses all the way to Grand Avenue."

He turned and pointed to Matt and his partner. "You two search Burnham Drive, the Super 8, Eagle View Motel, houses all the way to Grand Avenue."

He addressed the last pair. "You're covering everything south of Burnham Drive all the way down to The Winery and west to Timberline Trail. Knock on every door. If no one is home, leave a flyer. Officer Lucas has a box of them in her vehicle—gloves too. Check trash containers.

"Now listen up," he called to everyone. "It's important no one except assigned officers go near the Gold River. We have to be able to distinguish footprints, and if thirty people tramp through there, all evidence will be destroyed.

"Judah and I will take a team along the riverbank. We'll cross over and search River Road and the bank along the east side of the river. Hopefully, before we get that far, someone will have found Buddy. Report in every fifteen minutes."

Jericho paused a moment, watching to be certain the pairs understood their assignments and then grabbed flyers.

Joe joined him. "If more volunteers show up, I'll send them over the same areas and then widen our search. You two know Buddy pretty well. Can you think of anywhere he might want to go?"

Judah glanced at Jericho and then across the park, as though thinking. "I don't know. He doesn't have family that I know of. He lived most of his life on *Big Pine*. He knows horses."

Across the street an easily recognizable black Escalade parked and the driver got out. Audrey's distinctive hair glistened in the sunlight. She checked for traffic and ran across the street, spotting them.

"I just heard," she said. "What can I do?"

Genuine concern etched her forehead. She wasn't wearing makeup and was dressed in distressed jeans and a long sweater with her worn boots.

"You and your mom probably know Buddy better than anyone," Joe said. "Can you think of anywhere he might head?"

"I can't. I thought about it all the way here. He wasn't himself when I visited him last. He kept calling me Dorris."

"My men have already spoken with the staff at the care center, but there's a chance you might learn something if you go speak with the residents. Is that something you'd be willing to do?"

"Absolutely," she answered. "I'll start with Ben Rumford. They're friends and play checkers together."

Joe took a card from his pocket and handed it to her. "Give me a call if you learn anything."

He headed back to where he'd set up a temporary command center for the search. Missing persons were a high-risk situation in the mountains. Spencer's boundaries were rivers, streams and treacherous trails abounding with wild animals and prone to unpredictable weather.

"I grabbed us each a backpack from the house," Judah told him. "You driving?"

"I'll drive. Grab my vehicle in front of the café, will you?" He handed Judah the keys.

"Be right back." His brother headed across the park.

"This is frightening," Audrey admitted. "Buddy seemed pretty frail compared to the man I remember."

"We'll find him," he assured her, trying to sound confident. Last year an elderly man had left his home and been found dead only hours later in someone's front yard. "Our volunteers are experienced and tireless."

She nodded uncertainly. "People can just walk out of that place?" she asked. "I know it's not jail, but that doesn't seem safe."

"It happens," he said. "Sometimes they slip out around service workers or behind a visitor. Usually, the resident only wants to go for a walk and it's harmless. If it looks like the person is a risk, he's moved to a more secure part of the building."

Judah pulled the black RCSD Tahoe up along the curb. He gave Audrey a casual wave.

"Go find him," she said with a flap of her hand.

"Will do. And you learn what you can from those seniors."

She headed for her car, and Jericho did the same.

By sundown no one had reported finding Buddy or speaking to a citizen who had seen him. Returning critical service workers and volunteers gathered in the park, where Edith and a dozen others offered the searchers drinks and sandwiches.

Audrey sat on the ground with a sandwich on her lap, too concerned to eat. A pretty blonde with a ponytail sat beside her and handed her a takeout cup of coffee. "I'm Piper. I work at Pearl's."

Audrey managed a weak smile. "Thank you."

"I heard you grew up on *Big Pine Ridge* and Mr. Lowman was your daddy's foreman."

"That's right. He got me out of a lot of jams in my teen years. I feel just sick."

"I get it. My grandad is getting up there too, and the last thing I want is for him to go sit at one of those places. I know the staff takes good care of them, but it has to be hard being there."

"He seemed healthy when I saw him," Audrey said. "But a little confused."

"Yeah, that's hard," Piper said.

"We're calling the search for the night," the sheriff declared. "It's too dark for safety now. We can still canvas neighborhoods and make calls, but until morning, we can't do more. In the morning we'll widen the search and explore the river."

Audrey's heart sank. "That's it for tonight?"

Piper placed a comforting hand on her arm.

"At first light," Joe said. "Air search will begin. At this point we don't have reason to believe he went in or near the water, but he could be along a bank or in the woods."

"What about hypothermia?" she asked.

"The nights have been unseasonably warm," Joe assured her. "He might be cold, but he won't freeze. Everyone eat, hydrate, get a good night's sleep, and we'll start again early tomorrow."

"Oh, my goodness, no," Audrey said and covered her face with her hands. "He's somewhere out there in the dark. In the cold, no water, no food."

"Is she okay?" The male voice spoke from above them.

"She's afraid for Mr. Lowman's condition overnight," Piper replied.

Someone sat beside her, and she looked up through tears to recognize Kipp Hudson, his shoulder-length hair pushed away from his face. "Hey, Audrey."

She gave him a weak smile. "Hey."

"You've never seen volunteers work as hard as this group does," he told her. "They get tired, but they keep going. They'll be back first thing in the morning, and no one gives up. I've seen some of them search for days and then the teams carry injured hikers on litters down rocky trails and over streams. Every single person here cares, I promise you."

She gave him a nod, and he wrapped an arm around her shoulder.

Audrey leaned against him.

"Lost my bandana somewhere today. You can wipe your nose on my hoodie."

She chuckled.

"No, go ahead," he said. "I can frame it. With an arrow pointing to Audrey Knox's snot."

She laughed and wiped her eyes on the back of her sleeve. "Only you, Kipp."

He squeezed her shoulders. "What are friends for?"

She nodded.

"Nobody is giving up," he assured her. "Wherever Mr. Lowman is, he'll be okay for one night. It won't be freezing. We'll find him tomorrow."

"Okay."

"Try to eat," Piper said from beside her.

She sat and picked up half of the sandwich. "Sorry. I'm more emotional than usual lately. I'm normally pretty cool and collected."

"There's nothing wrong with caring," Piper told her.

She caught a look between the young woman and Kipp. "You two know each other?"

"I know everyone who comes into Pearl's," Piper said. "Kipp likes BLTs with onion, and he drinks his coffee with cream and sugar."

"If we are what we eat, then you do know everyone," he replied with a grin, then turned to Audrey. "Tomorrow bring a backpack with bottled water, protein bars or a peanut butter sandwich, a pocket first aid kit, socks, sunscreen, sunglasses, a compass oh and a headlamp if you have one. The Trading Post sells everything hikers need. Not that you'll be hiking, but when Buddy is located, he may need food and water until he can get medical care."

Audrey saw a different side of her old friend in his serious demeanor and critical knowledge. "You sure know a lot about this."

"Some of us have been volunteers for years," he said. "I've done this...well for a really long time."

"Ronnie too?"

"Sometimes, yeah. And my sister-in-law."

Audrey looked at Piper. "Marty and Edith provide food and drinks?"

"We make and pack sandwiches and drinks," she answered. "But a lot of times the search center is out along a highway near a hiking trail, so a couple of the guys from the VFW deliver to the locations. There are donation cans set up to pay for it. What we collect is always more than enough, so Marty keeps a benevolence fund."

"The longer I'm here, the more I appreciate the people. I guess I'd forgotten what community was like," Audrey said. "I'd better go home and get some sleep. I'll have to let Mom know Buddy hasn't been found yet."

"Is your daughter with your mom? She must be waiting for you."

"She is, but her nanny stayed on after the concerts, so Hayden has both of them. I think they were going to bake cookies."

"Tell your mom what I told you," Kipp said. "We'll find Buddy tomorrow."

He reached for her hand and she got to her feet.

"Thanks, guys," she said. "I'll see you tomorrow."

"Have to be honest," Kipp said. "I never thought we'd see Audrey Knox joining our volunteer brigade."

"I told my mom the locals were going to have to get used to me," she said. "I'm not a stranger and I don't want to be treated like one."

He grinned and then turned to Piper. "Suppose you could hook me up with one of those BLTs?"

"Sure can. We got some real pretty tomatoes in yesterday."

"Do you have a ride?" Kipp asked Audrey.

"My car's right across the street," she replied.

He gave her a nod, and he and Piper walked toward the café.

Audrey hadn't been exaggerating. The more time she spent around the locals and the more familiarly everyone treated her, the more she loved this place. Taking Hayden away from her grandmother and new friends and going back to Nashville would not be easy.

Jericho had been in Joe's office with Hunter Lawe and Levi since before sunrise. Pine Valley Senior Center's nurse advisor had told them she suspected Buddy Lowman had experienced sundown syndrome, become agitated and confused, and simply wandered off.

"If this is the case, she said he may be more oriented this morning, recognize where he is and seek help," Hunter told them. "The news channels are showing his photo, and law enforcement social media has spread the word to watch for him."

"We need to cover the same areas as yesterday," Joe advised. "If he hid because he was scared or confused, he may be trying to find his way back this morning."

"Levi and I will be piloting our drones and two officers will observe the screens," Hunter said. "We'll be working the grid at daylight. I'll search downriver."

Joe turned to Jericho. "You'll be organizing the teams and volunteers again. In the storage room are a couple boxes of orange T-shirts the VFW donated. Have someone pass those out to new volunteers. Give them the safety talk. Pair them with an experienced partner. You know the drill."

"I do, sir."

"Command center remains in the park. You have Richards working the phones?" Joe asked the police chief.

"Yes, Chauncey and Glenn Randall."

"Gage is sending Emily Davis over to answer phones with Pam today," Joe told them. "So, we're staffed and it's a go."

The sun rose at six twenty-four while Jericho was pairing search teams. The search began with renewed energy and high expectations. Audrey was assigned with Matt Chandler, the owner of Timberline Outfitters, Crosby Cavanaugh and his sister-in-law, Colette.

"Our search location is east in case he went across Willow Drive Bridge," Matt told them. "We'll be searching Olde Towne and the wetlands. Where shall we start?"

"Let's start with the wetlands while we're fresh," Crosby suggested.

"That's right along the north side of the river," Colette said. "Is the riverbank ours too?"

"Only if the drones don't have success by this afternoon," he answered.

"Oh, I hate this," she said. She was slender with blond hair stuffed under a straw hat. "I keep thinking this could be my granddad. He's the same age."

"We'll find Buddy today," Audrey told her.

They climbed into Matt's Ford Ranger and he drove away from the park toward Willow Drive Bridge.

Colette touched her arm. "Buddy was your ranch foreman, wasn't he?"

"For as long as I can remember. I visited him a couple weeks ago."

"I was ahead of you in high school," Colette told her. "I heard you sing at fairs though. I always thought you were good enough to make it big."

"Thanks. Those days seem like a lifetime ago."

Matt pulled off the road onto the grass, and they got out. The sun was warm and bright. Audrey surveyed the acres of weeds and wildflowers growing at lower elevation than the road. "It's almost like a creek full of vegetation."

"That's exactly what it is," Crosby said. He opened his backpack and produced a can of insect repellant. "Anyone forget theirs?"

"I didn't think of it," Audrey said. "But I have the recommended peanut butter sandwich. I didn't know this would be my first visit to Olde Town since I've been back. I could go for one of those burgers I've heard so much about."

She accepted the aerosol can Matt handed her and liberally sprayed her arms and legs and clothing. Handing it back, she took a red bandana that had been her father's from her pocket and tied it around her hair.

Crosby got out his phone. "Selfie for my mom."

Audrey groaned. "You waited until I had a bandana on my head?"

"It's more authentic. She'll love it."

They posed for his photo and then headed into the weeds.

Audrey stayed beside Matt, who wore a walkie tuned into the search channel at his waist, so she heard all the reports. Sector by sector, the reports came back negative. The four of them plodded through murky ankle-deep water and thick foliage. At a low hum and whir, their group paused with insects buzzing around them and the gentle lap of the water nearby to watch a drone flying along the bank of the Gold River.

Audrey's throat tightened and she got a sinking feeling in her chest. "They hoped to find him this morning. It's nearly noon. If he fell into the river, he could have been swept anywhere downstream."

"This is still a rescue search," Crosby told her. "And it will remain one until there is no hope. We aren't there yet, and everyone is still searching."

She pulled herself together and nodded. "Yes."

Two hours later, sweaty and covered with burs, they stood outside Olde Time Soda Shop.

Audrey adjusted her hair under the bandana and pulled her sunglasses over her eyes. "I'm going in. It's air-conditioned and the smells are making my stomach growl."

"Okay." Crosby opened the door and they entered. They ate and used the restrooms with a minimum of sideways glances. Locals knew what they were doing, and tourists didn't much care. No one had recognized Audrey.

This wasn't the way she'd intended to explore Olde Town, but she saw the interior and exterior of every shop, bakery, café, museum, the visitor's center, and each establishment's employees. No one had seen Buddy in or around their businesses. Audrey and Matt questioned the college students who transported visitors in golf-cart like vehicles from the parking lots to the stores. They searched behind buildings and around trash containers. None had been dumped, so Matt searched inside those as well.

"Like I didn't smell bad enough before," he said as they joined Crosby and Colette at their agreed upon meeting place. He removed his gloves and wiped his face and neck with a wet wipe. It was after seven pm.

The ride back to Brook Park was silent, Audrey lost in her own thoughts and fighting discouragement. "What happens next?" she asked, tugging off the bandana and bending forward to run her fingers through her hair. She poured water on the kerchief to dab her cheeks and neck.

"They'll continue the search until it seems unlikely he's alive," Matt told her kindly. "And then the game wardens will strategically search the river."

At the thought, Audrey's heart sank.

Static came across Matt's walkie, followed by Jericho's voice. "Teams, return to Brook Park as soon as possible.

Repeat. The search is called off. We have reason to believe Mr. Lowman is not in our search parameter."

"What does that mean?" Colette asked.

They had stopped and now ran across the street to where the sheriff and Jericho were watching something on a laptop and listening to the crackling reports on their walkies. Jericho glanced up.

Either he read the distress on her face or she looked like someone who'd waded through the wetlands in the blazing sun. She glanced at Colette whose face was flushed, nose sunburned, and had strands of hair stuck to her cheeks and neck. Okay, they all looked like that.

Jericho walked their way, his gaze fixed on her.

She pulled her hair into a ponytail. "I'm okay."

"Are you sure?"

"Yes. What do you know?"

"We just got word from someone who we believe gave Buddy a ride and dropped him off up by Drake."

"Drake? That's northeast," Matt said.

Audrey didn't know how to react. "Is this good news?"

"Absolutely," Jericho answered. "We won't be searching the river. We have a solid lead."

"Yes," she said, and then again with more confidence, "Yes!"

"Sheriff Cavanaugh is in contact with Larimer County now. One of the shelters they contacted has someone who might be Buddy."

"Oh, thank goodness." She put her hands to her cheeks. "Oh my. Now what?"

"We're waiting for confirmation."

"Okay."

She and Colette shared a relieved smile. Colette stretched an arm around her shoulders and hugged her.

"There's water and food in the shade over there." Jericho pointed and went back to join his senior officer.

Audrey had guzzled a bottle of water by the time Jericho called her name.

She ran to where he and the sheriff were studying something on his laptop. He smiled. "Here's the photo they sent."

She leaned in front of him to peer at the screen.

# CHAPTER NINE

$\mathscr{I}$n the photograph, her old friend looked tired and confused, and he was wearing green scrubs, but it was definitely Buddy. "It's him!" she cried, then turned and called to the others. "It's him! They found him!"

One by one the search teams returned, all tired, but everyone relieved and thankful. Audrey called her mom and gave her the good news. "I'll be home shortly."

She turned to Joe. "Will someone go get him?"

"Officer Ephram has already been dispatched and Brooke Cavanaugh is accompanying him. She's a trauma nurse. They're on the way."

"Where will they take him?"

"He'll spend a night or two in the hospital and be evaluated."

"Thank you, Sheriff."

He grinned. "This was a good ending."

"I can't believe all the people who show up and pull something like this together."

"Our departments couldn't do what we do without the

volunteers. Not with the trails and rivers and the terrain. They're a big part of our success stories."

Matt and Colette said their goodbyes, and Audrey unzipped a small pocket on her backpack to retrieve her car remote while walking toward her vehicle.

Jericho caught up with her as she reached it, and she turned to face him. He looked tired, too, a day's growth of whiskers darkening his cheeks.

"Are you okay?" he asked. "It was a long day."

"For everyone," she agreed. "I'm just thankful Buddy is all right. I barely slept last night."

He nodded. "Go home and rest. I'll call you when I know he's arrived at the hospital."

"Okay, thanks. A shower and some sleep sound really good." She glanced at others walking toward their cars. "The scare aside, it felt really good to be alongside the volunteers, not being singled out, but as part of a team doing something important. I think I get why you like your job so much."

"I do like my job," he agreed. "But what you do is important too. First, you're raising a really smart and personable daughter."

She met his eyes and blinked. Her own eyes watered, likely from the emotional two days she'd just experienced.

"On top of that you bring pleasure to a lot of people. Music isn't frivolous. It's a part of our culture, the fiber of our memories and life stories. Music has a time and a place."

"I saw that the day I sang with the residents at the senior center," she said. "It was as though the songs took them back to good times and maybe to people they remembered. To their loved ones."

He nodded. "We respond to music. We identify with it. It brings out emotions and validates our experiences—highs and lows, sort of authenticates our hurts. Our loves. Our losses."

His words meant more to her than the gold-plated gramophones sitting on the mantle in her Nashville home. Surprisingly, his appreciation meant everything. Her subconscious alluded that she'd disappointed him in the past. Sleeping memories almost woke.

She was hot and tired and probably smelled like a trash container, but she closed the space between them and pressed herself against him. Raised her face to rest her damp cheek against his rough one and held him fast. His strong lean body and the arms he wrapped around her were shelter, security, familiarity. Peace.

"Thank you, Jericho."

"I only stated the truth." She felt his words against her breast, in his breath against her ear.

"For everything." After another moment's indulgence, she inched away. "You must have things to do. I'd better go."

She still held her car remote, so she unlocked the Escalade and opened the door, pausing to glance at him.

"I'll call," he said.

Jericho had a shift the following day, and then three days off. On Friday he woke at dawn, stocked a backpack and went for a hike on one of the less-traveled trails, the difficulty guaranteeing he wouldn't run into beginners.

Along the needle-like creek trickling down the mountain, he spotted blue grouse, marmots and fox squirrels. His steps flushed a band of pigeons from the underbrush. At the top, an outcropping of rock provided a flat space to sit, eat his protein bar and drink water. He hadn't stopped thinking about Audrey's hug the other night. He'd decided it had been spontaneous after the emotional day she'd had followed by her relief. However, it hadn't seemed impulsive. She'd been looking right at him, and he'd have given anything to know her thoughts. Her gaze had gotten soft-like and misty, and she'd deliberately reached for him, holding him as though he was her lifeline.

It hadn't been the most glamorous hug; they were both hot and tired, and they'd both smelled like bug repellant. But it had been the most satisfying hug he could ever remember.

He'd stopped aching for her a long time ago. It was foolish to waste energy thinking on something he'd never have, and he was sensible. Practical. Realistic. Audrey was bigger than this small town. She'd always been destined to be someone spectacular and to shine. She was the sun and the breeze.

He was like this rock he sat upon. Warmed by her heat, cooled by the night air, but a part of the mountain and the land.

He wasn't kidding himself. But they'd meant something to each other once. She wasn't going to stay, but maybe…if she was interested…they could mean something to each other until she left again. This time she wouldn't take his heart.

Jericho was playing with Chickering Road at The Wild Card that night, so after a ride and chores, he showered, ate supper with his folks and headed into town.

When he arrived, a good-sized crowd already occupied tables and barstools. Chickering Road had been together in many forms for about fifteen years. They'd recently reorganized after the original creator left, and members came and went as their interests changed and careers permitted. Jericho wasn't an official member, but played and sang with them as often as his schedule allowed, honoring special occasions when friends asked him to sing.

Bethel was there with a few friends, which he'd guessed when she hadn't been at home for supper. She waved him over to their table and bought him a beer. Her friend Stella asked him about their search that week, and they caught up. "I was relieved to hear Mr. Lowman was all right. He always chats with me when I go to the care center to give the residents their flu shots."

Stella Novak was closer to his age than Bethel's and had been a nurse at Edna Burnham Memorial Hospital for a few of years. He'd invited her to dinner a couple of times, and she was a lovely young woman Jericho really liked, but there'd been no romantic sparks, so they were friends.

The band's longtime drummer, Tammy Zimmerman, wearing a Paul McCartney T-shirt caught Jericho's attention. "We're down a singer, so would you mind putting together a quick set without Vince?"

"Excuse me," he said to the ladies, and joined Tammy to come up with a song list. He and the band were comfortable playing together and had learned each other's strengths and weaknesses. They had an approved set within a few minutes and planned to take requests to fill in.

"Let's go," Tammy said, took her seat at her drum set, and counted off the rhythm.

The first song was her choice, and it made him smile while she enthusiastically played.

"'*Well, she was just seventeen,*'" he sang.

The girls at Bethel's table were the first on the dance floor.

Jericho laughed when he reached the chorus and the dancers all joined in on the 'whoos.' Tammy loved her Beatles songs.

They were finishing up a set before their first break when a buzz of excited voices drew his attention to the small group entering the Wild Card from the back door.

Ronnie Hudson and his wife, Delaney entered first, Ronnie waving to Ace at the bar, and behind them were Kipp and Audrey. He'd noticed Kipp and Piper with her the other day and hadn't thought much of it, but this surprised him.

He set his guitar in the stand and visited the restroom before ordering a beer at the bar. Someone had started the juke box, and a familiar voice filled the saloon. He'd barely had a swallow when Audrey came up beside him. "Hey."

"Hey," he responded. "Is it weird to hear your song playing?"

"I've heard it so many times, listening to the demos with the engineers and the producer, making adjustments and editing. It's almost like it's not me. But hearing it when I'm in a store and now here is kind of weird. I love that so many people enjoy my music, though."

She wore an off-the-shoulder cream-colored sweater, jeans and red boots. She was so pretty, looking at her made his chest ache. "How are you doing?" he asked.

"Good. I visited Buddy at the hospital today. Of course, no one would tell me anything, but he seemed just fine."

"Good to hear." His attention wavered to her bare shoulder, and he forced his glance to the room. "Are you and Kipp…?"

"What?" She looked in the direction he'd indicated, seeing the brothers laughing at something another friend had said. "Oh goodness, no. I mean, there's nothing wrong with him. He's a great guy and I like him a lot, always have, but no. Nothing like that."

She looked back at Jericho, and an awkward moment passed between them. Maybe he shouldn't have asked. Maybe she wondered why he had. Her gaze took in his hair, caressed his lips for a moment and then she deliberately focused on his shirt.

"Here, take this stool, Audrey." The nearby cowboy got up and gave her a broad smile.

"That's kind. Thanks." She sat on the stool beside Jericho.

He was still in disbelief that she was in Spencer and now sitting right beside him.

Ace interrupted his silent musing with, "What can I get you, Missy?"

Audrey glanced at Jericho.

"Want a drink?" he asked. "It's on me."

She told Ace, "Thanks. I'll have a glass of white wine please."

The man returned a minute later and hadn't skimped on the portion. "It's on *me*," he said with a wink.

Audrey still didn't know what to make of the undercurrent between her and Jericho. Everything about him was familiar except the tension.

"Hayden's with your mom tonight?" he asked.

"She's at a slumber party with Annabelle and a couple other girls at Edith's. They're planning Halloween costumes. I can't imagine what they'll come up with." She took a sip. "I'm so happy for her to make friends her own age and do kid things."

It felt good to be here, enjoying casual conversation, seeing old friends, making new ones. She'd been telling herself since day one that they'd come here for Hayden, but being honest, this time in Spencer was as much for herself as for her daughter. She'd needed new perspective and immersing herself in real life was giving her a lot to think about and making some things clearer. Tonight, she was as happy as an eleven-year-old at her first slumber party.

She'd only drank half of her wine when someone called out, "Are you gonna sing for us, Audrey?"

The question was followed by a chorus of agreement.

"I'll sing if Jericho sings with me," she called and looked at him.

He finished his beer and took her hand. "Like old times, huh?"

She drew him past tables to toss Kipp her car remote. "Would you mind getting my guitar out of the back for me, please?"

While he was doing that, she familiarized herself with the band members she hadn't met and greeted those she knew.

"I can't believe I'm playing with Audrey Knox," Tammy said, her face flushed. "I'm gonna need pictures of this or no one will believe it."

They discussed songs and everyone knew several of hers. "Let's do *One More Kiss*," she suggested. "I wrote most of this song back when I still lived here, but I didn't finish it for years."

Kipp showed up with her guitar. She thanked him, took the Gibson from its case and showed them the chords. "Jericho, you can grab a bass line like this."

He found the chords on his guitar. "Got it."

Excited friends and patrons clapped and smiled in anticipation.

One of the band members brought another mic stand and adjusted it for her.

"It ain't the Centennial Event Center," Ronnie Hudson called out.

"It's better," she told him. "It's home."

Tammy counted down the smooth rhythm.

*"'The moon is high over the water. It's late and we should go, yet here we are, still counting stars, still listening to the radio.'"*

Jericho recalled listening to this song on the radio not long ago, the sound of Audrey's voice affecting him as deeply as it always had.

*"In the magic of a summer night there's nowhere I'd rather be, because..."'*

He found the harmony note and joined her: *"Your eyes say one more kiss. What I want is one more kiss. Can we share just one more kiss - before we say goodnight?"'*

She looked at him and smiled. Everything about this was familiar. And comfortable. The two of them, lost in a song. *"'My mama has the porchlight on, she's waitin' by the door. Yet here we are, still in your car, waves lappin' on the shore. Your hair smells like summer nights, and there's no one else I'd rather hold..."'*

Enthralled by her, Jericho almost missed his note on the chorus. *"Your eyes say one more kiss. What I want is one more kiss. Can we share just one more kiss - before we say goodnight?"'*

The band played a creative interlude and she and Jericho sang the chorus once more before ending the song. The Friday night crowd applauded and whistled.

"Audrey, will you play us a Maybelle song?"

Jericho looked for the female requester and spotted Vida Lucas who had come in and was standing to the side of the room. He remembered how much his fellow deputy loved Audrey's folk songs.

Audrey glanced at him and then the rest of the band. She played those songs solo and obviously didn't want to step on toes. Every band member set aside their instrument. Tammy left her drums and stepped off the platform to stand out front.

Jericho grabbed a stool for Audrey and adjusted her mic stand. She slipped on her silver finger and thumb pics. "I guess ya'll know how much I love Maybelle Carter's music. That amazin' lady was the grass roots of folk music, and her songs influenced bluegrass and pop. The country music we know today was derived from those early styles. This one was written by A.P. Carter and Virginia Franks. If you don't know it, you'll recognize it was transformed by Woody

Guthrie into *This Land is Your Land."* Audrey strummed her guitar in the style she had perfected and sang, *When the World's on Fire.*

Vida was the first to join Audrey after she'd packed her guitar and stepped off the platform. "Thanks so much. Those songs remind me of my great-grandmother. She played them over and over on her old Victrola. I was fortunate to inherit it and her entire collection. Jimmy Rodgers, Johnny Cash."

"Seriously?" Audrey asked, wide eyed. "You have original Carter records?"

Vida nodded. "I'd be happy to have you come over and listen to them sometime."

Audrey got tears in her eyes. "Oh, that's so generous of you. I'd *love* that."

The band played a set without Jericho so he could sit with Audrey.

"It was great to play with you," he said as they enjoyed cold drinks. "It's been a minute."

"I never had to twist your arm," she said. "You enjoyed it too, didn't you? Back then, I mean."

He nodded. "I did."

"I've seen you in your uniform so much lately, I almost forgot you have a casual look, too."

"These are my best boots," he said. "I guarantee I don't have as many pair as you do. I haven't seen you wear the same pair twice. Not to mention the butterfly shoes."

She grinned. "You noticed those?"

"Hard to miss 'em, blown up in that photo on the wall at Pearl's."

The server set a fresh glass of wine in front of her and she smiled a thanks.

He'd seen her guitar up close tonight. "That's an L-5 archtop you play," he said.

She nodded.

"I've watched black and white YouTube videos of the Carter family. Yours looks exactly like Maybelle's 1928 Gibson acoustic."

She ran her finger around the rim of her glass and gave him a mischievous smile. "Yep."

He leaned closer. "Is that Maybelle's guitar?"

She glanced around and leaned in. "Yep."

Mind blown, he sat back and put both hands on top of his head for a moment. He was a guitar person, and knowing she owned an astonishing piece of music history stole his words.

"I love to play it, but I don't let on about its history," she said softly. "It's insured, but I keep a close eye on it."

He scooted his chair closer to hers. "I thought it was in the Country Music Hall of Fame. How did you come by it?"

"It was loaned to the museum at one time, but then auctioned by a Carter family member." She took a corn chip from the basket on the table. "You're dying to know, aren't you?"

"I can't even imagine," he replied.

She ate the chip, taking her tauntingly sweet time chewing. "Five hundred and seventy-five thousand. My advisor calls it an investment."

"Holy shit, Audrey."

She laughed.

"My investments would buy me a plot at Gold River Cemetery."

"You can play it if you want."

"I couldn't."

"Don't make me dare you."

"I'm not twelve anymore."

"Obviously."

What was going on? He'd been thinking of nothing but her since that hug at the park. He'd made up his mind, and his heart was definitely out of the equation. He finished his beer as the band started a slow song, something about being heartbroken and lonely.

"Dance with me," she said from beside him.

"I don't know…"

"Come on." She stood and took his hand.

# CHAPTER TEN

*A*udrey relaxed in Jericho's easy hold. She hadn't felt this comfortable anywhere or with anyone in years. She'd picked up on a smidgeon of concern over how she'd arrived with Kipp, but Jericho knew she'd been friends with him since high school. Maybe he was being protective. Maybe it was something else.

Playing her song with him had taken her right back to their days at festivals and county fairs. Jericho said music took people back to times and places, and these were the same exhilarating feelings she'd had when she and Jericho had performed together years ago. Those years were fun and carefree. Wyatt had been right there with them.

Jericho toyed with a strand of her hair on her bare shoulder, his fingertips sending a shiver up her spine. In any other place or time, she'd be paranoid about someone taking a compromising photo and blasting it all over social media, but the Spencer locals had been nothing but friendly and respectful. She couldn't imagine anyone here wanting to embarrass her or Jericho. He was an esteemed figure in

Rockwell County, which was likely helping her ease into their social groups with minimum fanfare.

"Have we ever danced together before?" she asked.

"At Matt Chandler and Nikki Spencer's wedding," he answered easily.

"And you remembered." She looked up, and he cast his gaze over her shoulder. "I can't recall why her name was Spencer. That was her mother's name, wasn't it?"

"She was born while Elysse was in high school," he answered. "Apparently the woman was the black sheep of the family, married several times after that. I think she's living in Spain with her fifth husband now."

"And Matt's a widower," she remembered.

"Yep."

"What's it like, being neighbors and friends with everyone you grew up with?"

"Normal."

Warmed by the affection she was feeling for this man, she leaned close and rested her head on his shoulder. "I've liked feeling normal for a few weeks. Even tonight, singing here was simply playing for friends. It felt good. Does it always feel that good to you?"

"I guess so. I don't have anything to compare it to. But from what I saw at the event center, the crowds, the body-guards, I could never do what you do. You were really impressive."

She raised her head and met his gaze, their faces a mere breath from each other. "Thanks. You are really impressive at your job, too."

"Yeah?"

"Yeah. I definitely wouldn't rob a bank knowing you were on duty."

She felt his chuckle against her breast. "You have no need to rob a bank."

"I might need ransom if someone learns about my L-5 archtop."

"*I* know."

She smiled at him, enjoying this playfulness that seemed so unlike either one of them. "How much will it take to keep you quiet?"

"A kiss would do."

Her heart seemed to pause and then caught up by marching double time. She glanced aside. "Here?"

He seemed to think a minute. "Need some air? There's a big dark park across the street."

She waited to respond until he met her eyes. "I was just thinking it's a little stuffy in here."

He found Vida and asked her to guard Audrey's guitar case; Audrey left her purse with Bethel. He took Audrey's hand and they eased out the front door, hoping their departure was unnoticed.

"It's not that dark," she said after they'd crossed the street and walked where gas lamps lit the pathways. Muted music echoed from the surrounding buildings, absorbed by the trees the farther they walked. She couldn't remember holding hands with anyone besides Hayden, and it felt nice. Intimate. His hand was large and strong and warm.

"Just you wait a minute." He led her toward the bandstand and up the steps into its shadowy interior.

"Why, Jericho Tanner, I might think you'd done this before."

He released her hand and faced her, wrapping his arms loosely around her waist. "Came across high school kids out here a time or two when I was a rookie."

She rested her palms on his upper arms, liking the feeling of being held so tenderly. One side of his face was outlined in the light that filtered in, casting the other side into shadow. His features were comfortingly familiar, his faintly woodsy scent a reassuring reminder of the past, while the sensation of blood pumping through her veins at an accelerated rate indicated this was all new.

"I never did this when I was a teenager," she said. She raised a hand to outline the shape of his cheek in the dim light.

He bracketed her jaw with both hands, and she caught her breath, raised on tiptoe, closed her eyes.

"How can you still be as beautiful as ever?" he asked.

She didn't respond...didn't breathe.

His warm lips closed over hers in a gentle exploration, the intoxicating sensation making her lightheaded. His kiss was the answer to a question she hadn't asked, hadn't known she'd wondered about. Everything about this felt good...and right.

He angled his head slightly, deepening the kiss, stealing will and reason. He plucked a series of delicate kisses across her lips and paused to look at her.

She couldn't help a smile. "If I'd known how much I'd like this, I would've kissed you that morning you walked into my mom's kitchen."

"Your mom and Hayden might've been surprised."

"Not you?"

"Oh, especially me."

She tilted her face upward and he kissed her again, this time more fervently, and she pulled away to catch her breath. "You just want me for my guitar."

"Is it working?"

"Absolutely."

He laughed and hugged her, the familiarity of their intimacy sparking a longing and peeling back layers of denial. For many reasons, she had always denied feelings for Jericho. He'd been her brother's friend, younger than herself, which made little difference now. But they'd wanted different things, and that had always been a factor.

He'd had a plan to enter law enforcement and help run the *Double T*. She'd wanted to test her wings, follow her dream and build a music career. It wasn't that she hadn't wanted a partner to love and who loved her. She wouldn't have married Tucker if he hadn't been as invested in her career as she'd been. Maybe that had been his appeal.

It wasn't that she hadn't wanted children, because she had. She had adored Hayden since the moment she'd been born. Her husband had encouraged her to get back to recording and performing, had been supportive of her life-style on the road. If it was possible, Tucker had been more driven than she. When she got honest with herself, it felt as though he was her manager first, her husband second. They hadn't actually ever been close, and she attributed that to time spent apart. It had worked for both of them.

An arrangement like that would never have worked with someone like Jericho.

His lean body felt good against hers, strong, protective. She'd never needed anyone to take care of her. Honestly, she'd resented anyone who'd treated her as though she was helpless. His words about the importance of what she did still made her feel proud. He admired her, but he wasn't in awe of her. Maybe that's what she liked best. That and the fact that they'd had a connection before she'd become successful.

Audrey realized she'd pressed herself so close she could feel his every breath, the beat of his heart under her cheek. He'd been her comfort more times than she could count, always there, her safety line, her rock. Her pleasure in his arms felt right. Natural. He ran his palm up her side and flat-tened it across her back. A series of shivers cascaded through her limbs. She closed her eyes.

After a minute he said, "Kiss me again before we go back."

She leaned away and wrapped her arms around his neck to meet his lips. He held her tenderly, threading his fingers into her hair. The moment was sweet and poignant.

"I like how you kiss me slow," she said.

"Sounds like a song," he replied.

She laughed. "Are you going to write it?"

His body lost its relaxed posture and he let his hands slip to his sides. "We'd better go."

"Is something the matter?" she asked.

"The others might wonder where we've disappeared to." He took her hand and guided her down the steps onto the path.

"What happened back there?" she asked.

He didn't stop walking. "I might be a little sensitive about songwriting."

"Why?" she asked.

"Never mind."

"No. Tell me."

He paused on the sidewalk across the street from the Wild Card. "It's nothing. I need to get back to the band. We'll talk another time."

Audrey was confused with the abrupt change. They'd gone from playful conversation and honeyed kisses to this swift return to the saloon.

Jericho resumed his place with Chickering Road, and she took a seat with the girls and the Hudsons, and focused on the friendly chatter.

That night she lay awake scouring her memories for a some-thing she'd said, a song she'd written. Did he think *Speaking of Mistakes* with its lyrics of not counting on the guy was about him? Surely not. She'd been the one who'd left Spencer. He'd always been dependable. There was something she was missing.

When she picked up Hayden the next morning, her daughter was bursting with excitement about the ideas she and her new friends had for costumes. "We'll be here for Halloween, right Mom?"

"Yes, we will. I've planned for us to be here through Thanksgiving and the Christmas holidays."

"Annabelle and Brinlee and June all go to school together," she said wistfully. "They've known each other since kindergarten and first grade. They have birthday parties and sleepovers all the time."

Niggling guilt crept over Audrey at Hayden's revelation at seeing how the other girls had a group of friends. "It's nice they've included you and made you feel welcome."

Hayden twisted a blond braid around her finger. "School sounds really cool. They're all planning to do cheerleading when they're older. Did you do that?"

"No, I was busy with 4-H. The horses and my music took all my time."

"But you had friends?"

"Yes. I did."

"Do you think I could try going to school?"

Audrey's heart sank. She didn't want to disappoint Hayden, neither did she want to rob her of her childhood or teen years. Now that she'd seen how these other children socialized and attended classes together, Hayden was obviously finding changes she'd appreciate. What had Audrey expected? She'd wanted these experiences for her daughter. "I don't know how that could work, since you've been home-schooled and tutored. We'd probably have to have you evaluated for a grade level."

Hayden turned to Audrey with a hopeful expression. "They've only been in school since the end of August. I'm sure I could catch up."

"I'm sure you could too." She thought a minute. "I just don't know what would happen when I had to leave."

"Maybe Everly and I could stay here and you could come back when you're not on tour or recording."

Her vulnerable heart wounded, Audrey managed a smile. She'd come here so Hayden could experience things other kids enjoyed. Had she thought to simply give her a taste and then once her daughter loved the life, rip it away? Obviously, she hadn't thought this through, hadn't considered the ramifications. "I'll think about how we could make it work, okay?"

"Okay, Mom." Trusting. Hopeful. "Can I find music on your phone?"

Audrey handed Hayden her phone and a few seconds after her daughter opened the app, music played through the speakers via blue tooth.

That afternoon, Audrey, Everly and Hayden traveled to Olde Town to check out the shops. Burgers from the Olde Time Soda Shop were a priority, so they enjoyed them with chocolate shakes. In the center of the space between the soda shop, a short strip of stores and a museum was a statue of a Pony Express rider atop a horse. They paused in front of a cupcake shop for selfies with tourists who recognized Audrey, and then across the way discovered a rock shop. Hayden was fascinated by the bin of polished agates and selected shapes and colors she liked to fill a velvet pouch. Everly bought postcards to send to her grandfather who collected them. After touring the Pony Express Museum, Hayden skipped ahead along a street with more shops, and they browsed in several.

"I can't remember a time when you didn't have any tours scheduled," Everly commented as they sat on a bench eating popcorn.

Audrey had put on her sunglasses. "I know. Honestly, I've been struggling ever since Atlanta."

"I get it. That was a scare."

"It's more than the scare," Audrey explained. "I'd been thinking it, but I realized that Hayden is getting older, and I'm missing out on these years." She munched a kernel of popcorn. "You've always taken the best care of her, and I trust you implicitly. I wouldn't have achieved what I have without you. You get credit."

"It's been an amazing experience for me," Everly said. "I adore that kid." She looked to where Hayden was peering into a shop window. "Besides that, my position has provided well, and I've traveled. It's been a good life for me."

The knowledge pleased Audrey. "I understand no one can wait indefinitely for me to figure out what I'm doing." She tipped her face to a breeze that smelled like fresh rolls and bread. "I've tried to be fair with you and the team and the band, but I suspect some will take offers and move on."

"I haven't heard anything, but I don't travel with them," Everly replied.

"I need to tell you I'm really considering what comes next," Audrey said.

The young woman nodded her understanding. "Hayden told me she wants to go to school here."

Audrey gathered her thoughts. "And I want that for her. I want her to have a grounded life with friends her age. I'm just not sure how to make it happen. I don't know how I can pause my career without letting people down, without losing everything I worked for. Sidney's been really good about giving me space, but I know he's impatiently biding his time. I have a lot to figure out. Where to go from here, how I can tour…" She placed her hand on Everly's arm. "I won't spring anything on you without talking things over first. I don't want to be unfair to you."

"You never have been," Everly said.

They finished their popcorn and watched Hayden talk to a baby boy in a stroller. The mom smiled, glanced over at Audrey and Everly, and gave a little wave.

"I feel like I've always been part of her life," Everly said. "Since she was small."

"You have. You've been an educator and a caregiver. A friend and even disciplinarian when you needed to be. She loves you."

"I love her too." She drank from her water bottle before meeting Audrey's eyes. "If I'm being honest, I've been a little jealous of you and Dorris. I know that's silly. You're her mom and Dorris is her grandma, and that's how it's supposed to be. I'm not family, but I've felt a little left out."

Empathy rose in Audrey's chest and her breath caught. This young woman had given so much of herself to her and to Hayden. She'd chosen this job and had committed her time and energy to them.

"We *are* family," Audrey disagreed. "You've been like another parent to Hayden."

Tears pooled in Everly's eyes.

"Thanks for being so honest. I've been embarrassed about my feelings," Audrey admitted. "That day…in Atlanta…when Hayden looked for you first, that did a number on my mom ego."

"The accident, you mean?"

Audrey nodded. "I was hurt. But not by anything you've done. Ever. It was my own fear of failing her. My quandary over the choices I make about my career and my daughter."

"Audrey," Everly said wide-eyed. "You're a great mom. You've kept Hayden close even when the easy thing would have been to leave her in Nashville with me."

Everly leaned forward to hug her.

"And that's part of the problem," Audrey said over her

shoulder. "She's missed out on what she's experiencing here now. She wants to go to school and I want her to have that."

They straightened their sitting positions on the bench. "Whatever you decide," Everly said. "I'll support you. I don't have any plans to leave. But I also don't want to butt in on your mom's hospitality."

"No. You're here with us. That's the way it's going to be. If she's disagreeable, you let me know."

"Dorris is perfectly polite to me."

"But cool. I get it."

"Can we get our pictures taken dressed like saloon girls?" Hayden asked, coming to stand in front of them.

The two women exchanged an amused glance. "We might as well take advantage of the whole tourist experience," Audrey said. "Spencer might be my home town, but Olde Town is pretty new to me, so for today I'm a tourist."

"Cool!" Hayden motioned for them to follow her.

Halloween evening was nippy and Audrey and Brinlee's mom, Iris, drove the girls to a few neighborhoods and waited at the end of streets with insulated jugs of hot cider while the group of girls Trick-or-Treated.

The friends had cleverly decided to be tourists. Audrey and Everly had helped coordinate costumes consisting of gaudy Hawaiian shirts, tennis shoes, assorted hats, fanny packs and old cameras hung from straps around their necks.

Hayden and her friends returned with their bags bulging.

"Thanks for helping us, Mrs. Knox," Brinlee said. "You have a really cool mom, Hayden." Like the others, she had a faux sunburn around where sunglasses had been when Audrey applied the effect.

"I appreciate your respectful address," Audrey told her. "Knox is actually my stage name. You can call me Audrey."

"You all look ready to move on to the next event," Iris said, and the kids agreed. They headed for Audrey's vehicle.

"Hayden said she might be starting school with us," Anabelle said. "Are you moving here?"

"We're still figuring that out," Audrey answered with a smile.

"You really made an impression on these girls," Iris told her afterward, as they sat at a table watching the girls and Everly roller skate at the renovated rink that was part of GoKart Ranch. "Me too."

"It was a lot of fun," Audrey told her. "Brinlee and the others have really welcomed Hayden into their group. I can't tell you what that means to us."

"She's a delightful girl," Iris said. "I'll be honest. I guess I was expecting someone, well spoiled, but she's kind and down-to-earth. A treasure."

"Thanks."

"You're not what I expected either. You're nicer and humbler than most of the moms in PTA at the middle school."

Audrey accepted that information with a raised eyebrow.

"Except you can sing like a freaking diva."

Audrey looked at her.

Iris smiled.

They both chuckled.

"Thanks," Audrey said again. She'd had a lengthy meeting with the grade school principal and guidance counselor, and Hayden had taken standardized assessment tests to see where she placed for attending with her peers. She'd promised Hayden she would check into school and she had.

All Audrey had to do now was make a decision.

It was November before Audrey heard from the lawyer. After Joe followed up with the secretary of state, Audrey had asked him to recommend someone to check into Vista AgriServices. She'd been grooming a horse and paused to take his call to make plans for a video chat that evening. Afterward she called to see if Jericho would be available to join her.

"Will you have dinner with me afterward?" he asked.

She was quiet a moment too long.

"It feels like you're avoiding me, so if I'm making this weird, never mind."

"It's not that," she said. She was avoiding him, but not because she didn't want to see him. She simply didn't want to make any decisions based on something that perhaps wasn't or couldn't be there. She hated being indecisive. She'd always known exactly what she wanted and had gone for it. This lack of confidence was making her question herself, and feelings of uncertainty stressed her.

She walked to open a door at the front of the stable and gazed across the pastures toward Tanner land. "I'd like to see you and have dinner…but I don't want to raise eyebrows in town."

He took a second to respond. "No eyebrows except mine at my place. I can cook for you."

"You can cook?"

"Nothing fancy, but sure. And I promise to keep my eyebrows in their proper places."

She wasn't sure how wise this plan was, but her smile told her it felt right. "Sounds good."

"I'll be at your place at six," he said.

*Like a date.*

He showed up at a quarter till, dressed in dark jeans, nice boots and a white shirt, open at the collar. Not wanting to look as though she was trying too hard, she'd put nearly everything she'd tried on back in the closet and was wearing jeans, boots and a royal blue blouse with a denim jacket.

"Hey, you look nice," Hayden said to him when she saw Jericho in the kitchen.

"I clean up once in a while," he teased.

"So, I have a question for you," she said, her impish smile clueing Audrey of her intent.

"Let's hear it," he said

"Okay. Would you rather sneeze nonstop for fifteen minutes once every day…?" Hayden paused for effect, then raised her finger before continuing. "Or sneeze once every three minutes of every day while you're awake?"

"Oh, we're asking the important questions now," he said with a completely serious face. "Well..."

Everly came to the doorway, and Audrey motioned her in. "This is our friend Jericho Tanner. Jericho, this is Everly. She's part of our family and Hayden's nanny."

"It's a pleasure," Jericho said.

Everly smiled.

"Okay," he said. "Sneezing for fifteen minutes could definitely be inconvenient, but then once every three minutes would interrupt the entire day. I'm going to take the sneezing all at once and get it over."

"Good choice," Hayden said and raised a hand for him to give her five.

"We'll be playing RingFit," Everly said and reached for Hayden's hand.

When Jericho gave her a quizzical glance, Audrey explained, "It's a fitness video game Everly is obsessed with."

Dorris was already seated in Audrey's dad's roomy office, and Audrey had a laptop set up. Joe had joined and they were expectant for the lawyer. They waited only a few minutes before he joined.

Audrey made introductions between her mom, the sheriff, Jericho and the attorney.

"I'll get right to the point," the man said. "With the information I got from the secretary of state, I've looked into this corporation. It's not an uncommon practice for ownership to be hidden under another company name, and that's the case here. The person behind this is a businessman in Spencer by the name of Cale Hartwood. The soil tests could have been performed anywhere and for a lot less money, so this is not a reputable practice, but a means of charging an exorbitant fee for profit."

"Cale Hartwood?" Audrey said. "Wasn't he the owner of the *Spencer Herald* until recently?"

"That's him," Jericho said.

She turned to Dorris. "Mom, you know who Cale Hartwood is. You never mentioned him. Why didn't you say something?"

Obviously uncomfortable, Dorris shrugged. "It seemed logical at the time. He said soil tests were always done before a sale or a prospective buyer decided to purchase land."

Audrey pinned her mother with a shocked stare. "Purchase land? *Our* land?"

orris brushed imagined lint from her lap and said nothing.

"What prospective buyer are you talking about, Mom? Someone trying to purchase *Big Pine*?"

Dorris flattened her lips and didn't meet Audrey's eyes. "It's a lot of land, and when Mr. Hartwood said there were investors interested and willing to pay top dollar, I figured why not look into it?"

The blood pumped in Audrey's head, and her heartrate increased. She took several deep breaths. "Mom, you couldn't have sold *Big Pine* without my approval and signature. Surely, you're aware of that. Do you know what trouble you could have gotten us into doing something like this behind my back?"

"You weren't here," Dorris said defensively. "I didn't think you cared. You have your own life and your own money."

Audrey pursed her lips, tempering her anger. "This is Daddy's land and it was his parents' and grandparents' land before him. Sweat and blood and years of work and dreams went into this ranch. Don't suppose for a minute that I don't care. I care! *Big Pine Ridge* is our family's inheritance and future. This is *Hayden's* legacy. She touched her fingertips to her temples, then dropped her hands. "Do you know the legal battle that could have drained us of *everything* if you'd attempted to sell without me?"

"Miss Knox," the lawyer broke in. "Your mother wasn't the only one Hartwood scammed. He approached others with this same con. I don't believe he could have afforded to buy land himself, but he could have taken hefty finders' fees from the investors.

"Since there are multiple cases adding up to quite a sum, this is in the hands of the state's attorney now. They'll be investigating and prosecuting, which lets you off the hook for fees. You'll be contacted soon and asked for the evidential documents. This won't happen quickly, so be prepared for it to take time."

Audrey deliberately attempted to relax her rigid posture. She collected herself. "Thank you. For everything."

The attorney left the call.

"Thanks for all you've done, Sheriff," Audrey said.

"That's my job, but you're welcome," Joe replied. "The good thing is we've caught Hartwood at this, so his scam is over."

The video call ended, and they sat in tense silence for a moment. Audrey worked to subdue her simmering anger.

"I'm sorry I didn't see this," Jericho said from beside her. "Maybe I could have—"

"No," Audrey interrupted him with a jab in the air. "You have no reason to apologize. You've been helping out of generosity, and you had no way of knowing this had gone on behind our backs." She pointed at Dorris. "*She* was hiding her actions. I'll take responsibility, because I should have paid closer attention. I should have hired a ranch manager instead of expecting you to burn a candle at both ends with two ranches. *I'm* sorry."

"I didn't want a stranger in our business," Dorris said.

"Exactly." Audrey got up from her seat and stood behind it to glare at her mother. "You didn't want someone checking, so there was no accountability."

"You weren't here," Dorris said again, as though it was Audrey's fault she'd made this blunder without talking to anyone. "There's no reason I shouldn't think about the future and what I could do with the money from a sale."

"What about Daddy's land? *Our* land—land that he worked his whole life? Did that mean nothing? If you only wanted money, I would have bought out your share. There's a provisional right of first refusal, so I have first choice to buy out your share. You realize that, right?"

"All I know about what you're doing is on the magazines in the grocery store."

Heat infused Audrey's face and limbs. "You're not easy to talk to, Mom. I don't tell you things because I don't want to hear your criticism."

Dorris' mouth pressed into a line. "You've always done whatever you wanted. You don't consult me. I don't consult you."

"Well, we have to talk about it eventually." There was no reasoning with the woman. An apology was the least Audrey expected, but none was forthcoming. Holding her breath in wait would be fatal. "Jericho, if you will please continue on a little longer, until I've made some decisions. If I should decide to leave, I'll hire someone. If I decide to stay in Spencer, I'll still find someone, so I'll start a search now. But we need you in the interim, if you're willing."

"Yes, of course," he said.

"You might stay?" Dorris shot her wide-eyed gaze to Audrey. "In Spencer? On the ranch?"

"Hayden wants to attend a real school, have friends. She's really happy here. Everly will always be with us, whatever I decide. Leaving was easy the first time," she admitted. "I knew what I wanted, and I wanted a career in music. Daddy supported that. I admit I was single-minded." She turned and looked at the enlarged photographs of horses on the wall behind her father's desk. "Now I have Hayden, and what she wants matters most. I love my career. I love performing and recording, and I love my team. But I love Hayden more, and she has to come first."

"I had no idea," Dorris said.

"Because we don't talk, Mom. You've never approved of anything I've done, and I don't expect that to change."

Dorris stood. "Would you like coffee, Jericho?"

Audrey stared at her dismissive mother, then shook her head. Why should anything surprise her?

"No thank you, ma'am. Audrey and I are going to have dinner."

Dorris nodded at him and left the room.

"That's it?" she called after her. "That's all you have to say?" Audrey stared at the empty doorway. After a moment of stunned silence, she turned back. "Can you believe her?"

"I confess I don't know her well enough to be surprised," he said. "But I know Hartwood, and nothing he does surprises me. I just hope he gets what's coming to him. And soon."

"It's the idea that he'd come to her with this scheme, thinking he'd profit off the illegal sale of *our* land that galls me."

He stood and rubbed her arm through her sleeve. "Come on. Let's go feed you. I have wine."

She relaxed her tense posture again. "Yes, please. Let's go. I'll tell the girls I'm leaving now."

"I'll drive," he said a few minutes later, after she bundled in her coat against the chilly evening and they'd left the house. "And bring you home later."

"Do you think you'll have plied me with so much wine I might not be fit to drive after dinner?"

"No, but it's not far, and it's gentlemanly."

"I might need a designated driver." Audrey felt contrite for being so angry in front of Jericho. He had to understood her frustration with Dorris though. She was already struggling with decisions, and then to have to deal with this stress was a lot to handle.

When they arrived at the log home, Sully had been lying on the porch, but bounded to greet them. Audrey knelt to pet him. "He looks like the dogs you had when we were kids."

"He's probably third or fourth generation of those beagle-collie mixes. Dad had his mother bred with a similar breed to produce his litter." He opened the front door and stood aside.

"Does he get to come in?"

"Yep. He's spoiled."

"When you mentioned a cabin before, I had a different image than this." The main floor of the sprawling log home was open, with beamed ceilings and a stairway to upstairs rooms. "How many bedrooms are up there?"

"Three up there and a master down here."

Leather sofas formed a seating area in front of a huge stone fireplace with a live-edge mantle. The area was void of decoration, save a few pelts hanging on one wall and his guitars on another. "It's visually stunning and humble at the same time."

"Like you," he said.

Her cheeks warmed at his surprising words. She removed her coat and he hung it in a coat closet beside the stairs. Behind the stairway was a roomy kitchen with stainless steel appliances and a farmhouse table and two chairs.

"I'll start a fire," he said. "There's wine in the fridge if you want to open a bottle. Will you set the oven to four twenty-five please?"

She complied by figuring out the digital settings, then found a corkscrew. A covered bowl of leafy green salad chilled on a shelf when she found the wine. His glasses were practical with no stems. She poured and carried two to a low table in front of the facing sofas, worked off her boots and seated herself. "Seriously. I like your place a lot."

"Thanks. I'm comfortable here. Are you okay?"

She glanced aside. "Not really. I have so much to think about right now. I came here for Hayden, and now there's this whole ordeal to figure out."

"The lawyer said it's up to the state's attorney now, so you're off the hook. That's a really good thing. And look at it this way. It's also a good thing you did come when you did—before your mom did something really stupid. At least you've caught it."

"She's not a stupid person." Audrey looked up at him. "That's why I can't figure out how she fell for this and went along with it, thinking she might sell the ranch without me."

"Drink your wine."

"You're right." She took a sip. "We're not going to talk about this anymore tonight. I want to enjoy dinner."

"Good plan." Once he had the blaze going in the fireplace, he straightened and gave the Wi-Fi a command to start a playlist. Harry Styles sang *I Adore You.*

"I was kind of amazed to learn how well the Wi-fi works out here." She handed him a glass.

"There are four towers between town and the lodge," he said. "Can't have big shots missing calls."

She held out her glass and he touched his to it. "You remembered I like white."

"I remember a lot of things."

Jericho studied her with her feet tucked up on his leather

sofa, a sight he'd never anticipated. A long time ago they'd spent a night together, a night that had started with him consoling her. He should have used restraint. He'd recognized that afterward, but he'd been crazy about her. Obviously short-sighted. Afterward, she'd run as fast and as far as she could. No way not to take that personally. Rejection hurt.

But he'd had plenty of time since to develop an emotional shield. If he didn't care, didn't love, he couldn't get hurt. He'd filled that void with work, and it had served him well.

"Vida asked if we'd want to visit her mid-week and listen to the Carter records. She has a couple of days off," he said.

"Sounds great. I'd love that."

He set down his glass and went into the kitchen area. "I'll heat the salmon. I baked potatoes that will still be hot."

"Do you cook often?"

"Only occasionally. My mom still makes a family meal every night, so it's easier to eat with them."

"She was always a great cook."

"They've been taking trips since Dad retired though, which they deserve. Judah and Bethel and I handle the ranch while they're gone."

"Neither of them is married?"

"No. Judah was pretty serious once, but that fell apart. He has a house toward the creek."

"This is from *The Spirit Moves* album, isn't it?" she asked about the next song that started.

*Changes* by Langhorne Slim played now. "You know the album?" he asked.

"I saw Langhorne Slim's interview with *Entertainment Weekly* where he said this track is about the beauty and terror of having breakthroughs and transformations in life, only to discover that there are infinite amounts of both." She finished her wine. "I think I'm going through both now."

"Beauty and terror?"

"Yeah."

Jericho reached for one of the guitars hung on the wall. He perched across from her, listening closely. "Think this is G, right?"

"Then F sharp," she said. "To C."

He told the Wi-Fi to stop, played and sang a couple of lines.

She joined him to sing, *"I'm goin' through changes now."*

They had always been attuned to one other, able to sense the other's move musically. Emotionally, probably not as harmonious. He'd always wanted Audrey, but being emotionally vulnerable was frightening so his walls were study and tall.

They sang the song once all the way through and their voices faded away, replaced by the sound of twigs snapping in the fire. The two of them seemed insulated from the world in that moment. The firelight dancing on her hair gave him a quaking feeling in the center of his chest. A warning signal it would be wise not to ignore. He wouldn't make the same mistake again. She was still out of his league.

A timer went off. He laid the guitar on the sofa. "Let's eat."

She followed him into the kitchen.

"My mom's going to call Dorris this week, and she asked me to talk to you. She'd like the three of you—and Everly if she's in town—to come to Thanksgiving dinner."

Audrey hadn't even thought about Thanksgiving yet. She and Hayden were usually either alone or invited to one of the band member's family dinners. Memories of the Monroes and Tanners together for holidays assailed her, and a pang of loss for her brother struck her anew.

"Did you already make plans?"

She shook her head. "No. No, I was remembering the family dinners we had when we were young. I think it would be really good for Hayden. I'll talk to my mom. I don't know what Everly has planned."

"Let her know she's welcome. The food will be great."

"I'll call Christine and see what we can bring," Audrey told him.

They finished the meal and he poured more wine.

She folded her napkin and laid it aside. "That was delicious."

"You've probably eaten a lot fancier dinners."

"In fancy places perhaps, but that was some of the best salmon I've ever had."

He stacked the plates in the sink.

"I can help you with dishes," she offered.

"No chores tonight," he said. "Sing something just for me."

"Really?" She watched as he rinsed and dried his hands.

He returned to hold her chair, indicating she stand. "Really."

"Okay." She padded in her socks over to the wall where the rest of his guitars hung. "May I?"

"They've never belonged to anyone famous, but you're welcome to play whichever you like."

With a grin she chose one, settled on a leather footstool and tucked her hair behind her ear. "Jericho Tanner's guitar is as good as Maybelle's any day."

Those words surprised and pleased him. Made him feel as though he'd drank all the wine. She wasn't a flatterer. He picked up a wooden box from the mantle, removed the lid and extended it so she could see tortoiseshell and smooth bone finger pics. She selected a couple. "What do you want to hear?"

He lowered himself to sit in front her on the ottoman. "Oh, I don't know. Are you working on anything?"

"The pressure's on to come up with a drop single, so I've been kicking around a couple of ideas." She played an intro, and he listened with his eyes closed. *"Seems all I ever did was wait. Seems all I ever did was want."*

He opened his eyes and watched her. She was as lovely as she'd always been. He liked the feminine curves of her cheek and jaw, how intense her gray-blue eyes were when she was thinking. She revised a chord and went on.

*"But when you saw me, you really saw me. When I knew you, I really knew you, and I don't know where the next line goes from here."* She continued to play, but looked up at him.

"It's beautiful. What if you flipped the first two lines?" He went for a guitar, imitated her chords and sang, *"Seems all I ever did was want. Seems all I ever did was wait. But when you saw me, you really saw me; I knew a love I could not anticipate."*

Audrey's expressive eyes showed so many things in that moment: Surprise, hesitancy, delight. Her lips curved into a smile. "Man, you're good."

He grinned. "All the girls say that."

She laughed. "Right. This place looks like a real playboy's lair."

He went back to picking the melody of the song.

"Do you have paper?" she asked. "I want to take notes. Are you good with being my co-writer?"

He fought the tug of hesitancy in his chest. She'd used one of his songs without an acknowledgement before, but the question didn't seem congruent with that instance. He got up and found her a tablet and pencil. "If you want me to be."

"I really do, Jericho. We were always great together." She set the paper aside, circled her fingers around his wrist and held him with a gentle grip, looking up at him with her eyes shining, her lips parted.

He held his guitar so it didn't swing forward, leaned over and kissed her.

She released his wrist and rested her palm along his jaw. He'd wanted to kiss her ever since they'd entered his home, wanted to hold her and lose himself in the joy, however brief, of her full attention. He would not be vulnerable. He still ached for her, but she could be gone any day. He knew the cost.

"Come closer," she urged.

He eased away and straightened to slip the guitar strap over his head and lay the instrument of the floor. She did the same, and he joined her on the sofa, wrapping his arms around her. She melded against him with a sigh, their lips clinging.

"Your kisses are better than the wine," he said aloud.

Her eyes widened, and she grinned, their lips a breath apart. "Similar lyrics are already taken."

"Jimmie Rodgers knew what he was singin' about."

She wrapped her arms around his neck. Through the smooth warm fabric of her blouse, he spanned her back and ribs, her silky hair fanning over the backs of his hands.

"We still have something special." His voice was gruffer than he'd intended, but he couldn't get enough air into his lungs. "I'm here for you."

"Is this unfair?" she asked.

"Only if I let myself think there's more to this than there is," he said. "I know what I'm doing."

Audrey loved his voice, deep and raspy. She threaded her fingers into his hair and leaned away enough to look into his eyes, their blue depths stirring memories. Being held like this was familiar. Seeking comfort in his arms was familiar. Tonight, she'd needed distraction from the situation with her mother, comfort from her confusion and relief from anger and disappointment. *I'm here for you.*

Her stomach felt as though she was on an elevator, dropping floors.

*She'd sought comfort in his arms before.*

Audrey shivered as though she was cold, buried memories breaking the surface of her consciousness and assailing her. He'd kissed her like this, held her... She leaned away and shoved a hand into her hair. "What's wrong with me? Why didn't I...? Why didn't I remember?"

Jericho's puzzled expression showed his confusion. "Remember what?"

"That night after my father's funeral."

She saw the truth in his eyes then.

"Oh my—" She got up, moved away from him and faced the fireplace. "What kind of person am I? What's wrong with me?"

He got up swiftly and moved to rest his hand on her shoulder.

She turned to face him. "How could I have forgotten something like that? We—we were...*intimate.*" Her throat constricted. "What you must have thought."

Putting distance between them, he returned to sit with his elbows on his knees and studied his hands as he pressed his palms together. "I admit I was really confused. And when you came back this time, I was dealing with how you'd left so easily and seemed to have forgotten all about us—whatever it was we had."

"No. No, it wasn't like that."

You were distraught. You'd lost your father. I only wanted to console you, but it turned into more." He looked up. "I thought you were ashamed."

"We'd always been friends." She held her hands palms up, imploring him to understand." You were Wyatt's best friend. You were younger than I was, and I felt like I'd done something wrong. Maybe I was ashamed, but only because I'd been unfair to you." She held her hands over her face. "How is it possible I just blocked that out?"

"Forgetting helped you, and that's what you needed to do. In my line of work, I've seen how people deal with shock.

Everyone's different. Looking back, you were undoubtedly suffering shock along with grief."

She came then to kneel in front of him and took his hands in hers. He must have felt as though he wasn't enough, as though she'd used him, because to him she'd walked away and forgotten so easily. "I'm sorry. Sorry about that time, about how you must have felt. Please forgive me."

"Please forgive *me*. You were vulnerable."

"No." She covered his lips with her fingers. With her other hand, she cupped his rough jaw. "You were always there for me. Always. I'm the one who left you."

He circled her wrist to move her fingers from his lips. "It doesn't matter now. We're both okay."

She moved the guitar aside and they sat without touching. She took in his heart-reaching eyes, the curve of his lips. She was hesitant to trust her feelings. She'd made so many mistakes.

Jericho rested his arm along the back of the sofa behind her, and she turned to fully face him. She loved his dark-lashed blue eyes, the way they softened when he looked at her. Raising her hand, she rested it alongside his jaw and stroked his cheek with her thumb.

He covered her hand with his, turned his head and pressed a kiss into her palm. A tingle shot up her arm and turned her insides to jelly. He made her feel as though she was the only person in the world. She was accustomed to attention and admiration, but with him she felt cherished. The profound sensation was breathtaking.

She leaned in to press her lips unreservedly against his and experience the first real intimacy she'd known in too long. Under her other palm on his chest, his heart beat steadily. The heart of a good man, a man who'd always been here for her. When she threaded her fingers into his hair, he crushed her against his chest and kissed her hard, stealing her breath.

Moments later, his hold loosened and his gaze met hers, trailing to her lips and back up. "You mentioned to your mother that you might be staying in Spencer."

"I'm trying to figure out what comes next," she managed.

"Because Hayden wants to stay?"

"She does. She really likes it here." She drew her finger across the bow of his lips. "I came here hoping to strengthen our relationship before she gets any older."

"What about you?" he asked. "What do you want? You've sacrificed a lot for your career."

"That's the issue," she said. "I'm not willing to sacrifice Hayden's happiness. She deserves to know what it's like to go to a real school and have friends her own age."

"What about your happiness?" he asked. "Can you do both?"

"I ask myself that all the time." She kissed him. "But this is making me pretty happy."

Her ringing phone interrupted the ardent moment.

She leaned down to her handbag on the floor and slid out her phone. "It's my manager. I'd better take this."

"Sure." Jericho got up and refilled their glasses.

"Hello, Sidney."

"Audrey. Jodi Fenton was in an accident and is in the hospital." Sidney Oliver's voice held an urgent edge as he spoke of one of country music's legendary singers who was also on Audrey's label.

"Oh my gosh, that's terrible. Is she all right?"

"She'll be fine, but she can't walk for a couple of weeks. I'm calling because she won't be able to do the Stockholder's Showcase."

"Oh." Audrey rolled that information over in her mind.

"I've adhered to your wishes and haven't booked you anywhere."

"And I'm thankful for the reprieve."

"These are the stockholders, Audrey. The deep pockets the label courts. The board has asked you to step in, and we really can't say no. There's a lot on the line here."

"I get it," she said. "It's when? The twentieth?"

"Yes. One night. A short set. I'll get as many of your band and team as I can pull together last minute."

He was right. This night was needed for the label as well as for herself. "Okay," she said.

"Okay? Oh, thank goodness. I thought I was going to have to fly to Colorado and grovel at your feet."

"No, I get it. I've done it before. I can stay at my place."

"There's one problem, and if you don't already know, I'm sorry I'm the one with the news."

"What is it?"

"Zane is on a six-week tour with Dirk Elliot, so he's out."

"Okay. I didn't expect the entire band to hang around waiting for me."

"I know he's your main guy and male vocal, so I'll do the best I can on short notice. Unless you have any ideas."

"One night," she said thoughtfully. "I do have an idea. Let me know how many of the guys you can pull together. I'll let you know how my idea goes."

Audrey ended the call as Jericho returned and sat himself on the sofa beside her. He smoothed his hair and took a sip of wine. "What's happening on the twentieth?"

# CHAPTER TWELVE

"Jodi Fenton can't do the Stockholder's Showcase, so I have to do it. Zane is on tour."

"So…no lead guitar." She hadn't come right out and asked him if he'd fill in, but he got the implication. Should he be flattered?

"Or male back-up."

He trailed his gaze to hers and tilted his chin in hesitant curiosity. He rolled his glass between both palms, thinking. "Are you asking me?"

She faced him. "The Ryman Auditorium isn't a huge venue like the Centennial Event Center at the fairgrounds here. It's more the size of the outdoor arena. You've played to crowds that size with me before." She turned her palm up and lifted her shoulder. Her grey-blue eyes sparkled. "It's where Johnny Cash met June Carter. For real, wouldn't you love to see that?"

He didn't know if he'd love to see it or not. He was more comfortable confronting bears and criminals than considering what she asked. "You're trying to persuade me to come perform with you. In Nashville."

Her grin was charmingly contrite. "I'm feeling you out. Was it persuasive?"

"I had something else in mind concerning being felt out."

"I'm serious here."

He finished his wine and rested the glass on the table. She was talking about staying in Spencer, but where was her heart really? He didn't want her to leave, but he'd gotten used to the life he'd created, the life he wanted. And he'd gotten used to her being gone. That was his reality. What if she stayed and he wasn't enough for her? *Again.* Maybe he should be flattered. The Ryman Auditorium.

"How many does the place seat?"

She grabbed her phone, typed and scrolled. "Twenty-three hundred. It's where the Grand Ole Opry was filmed, though the stage is new. The acoustics are fabulous. Elvis sang there. Willie Nelson. Paul Simon." She touched his shoulder. "*Keith Urban.*"

"Hell, that scares me more."

She put down her phone. "I'm not twisting your arm. If you don't want to do it, I'll find someone else, and it's okay. I won't be mad."

He'd shut down these feelings of inadequacy a long time ago. But having her close, holding and kissing her tested his resolve. He could say no. Play it safe. "Disappointed?"

"Maybe a little, but it'll be all right. I know it's not your thing."

"But it's yours."

"It is this time. I can't say no. You can. You don't owe me anything."

He rubbed a hand over his jaw. He'd enjoyed every second of this evening, had fallen back into the ease of creating music with her. He maintained his resolve to protect his heart. His self-worth and fulfillment were in his work and the ranch—but there was no reason he couldn't have fun. No reason he couldn't do this for her, no reason to miss a new experience. "You did agree to come to Thanksgiving."

She rolled her eyes. "Hardly a comparable commitment."

"Stop. I'll do it."

"Yes?"

"Yes. But I'm not wearing anything that sparkles and I play my own guitar."

She threw her arms around his neck. "This is going to be so much fun."

Jericho stood uncomfortably while Gianna smoothed the slim-cut black western shirt over his shoulders and checked where it was tucked into his jeans. She took a square of flannel from her sleeve, knelt and polished the toes of his boots.

"They're new," Jericho said. "I've barely walked in them, so they can't be dirty."

She straightened with a smile. "I'm done fussing. You're perfect. Your black hair with that shirt and those jeans will be stunning beside Audrey. The perfect contrast. And I heard your songs at tech rehearsal. Pretty amazing. You two sound as though you've done this your whole lives."

"We pretty much have." He opened his guitar case, took out his Gibson and looped the strap over his head carefully so Willow didn't bust a blood vessel over his hair when she got here.

Gianna grinned. "Remember to smile. You're not going in front of a firing squad."

"Yeah? I learned yesterday that this will be streamed live." Saying it made his legs quiver.

There was a tap on the door. Audrey entered wearing a black and silver sequined gown that hugged her curves and displayed a tantalizing swell of cleavage. Her pale hair hung in shiny waves. This was the Audrey Knox from the magazine covers, and while he loved her at home in jeans and clean-faced, her glamorous image took his breath away.

"Wow," she said appreciatively.

"Wow back at ya," he said with a grin.

"This was brilliant," she told Gianna. "Silver and black."

"Don't be shy when the cameras come out," Gianna told Jericho. "You're going to be on the newsstands alongside the A-list celebrities, so show 'em that sexy cowboy vibe."

He'd seen enough magazine covers for the information to turn his stomach over. He was no Dirk Elliott and didn't pretend to be. Performing on this scale was so far out of his comfort zone, the act created a new zip code.

Audrey stepped forward, taller than usual in her sparkling heels. She covered his hands with hers, forcing him to look into her eyes. Her hands were warm and steady. Her makeup and lashes were professionally faultless, but the eyes were hers...soft, sincere. "Don't think about any of that." Her voice transmitted the soothing effect she'd intended. "Don't think about the audience or the cameras. Think about the music. Have fun. Enjoy this. It's just like the two of us have done a hundred times before. Remember the smell of popcorn and the sounds of the arcade in the background?"

He glanced from the rings on her fingers back up to her lovely face. This was Audrey, the same beautiful, sensitive woman he'd always known, the person he'd played for and sung with since they were kids. He wasn't going to count on her staying in Spencer or committing to a relationship, but what they had right now was good. He wanted to do this for her. "Okay."

"Okay." Her smile told him everything was going to be all right.

She took his hand and accompanied him along the corridor that led to the stage where they'd set up and rehearsed. The building was filled with people now, the atmosphere crackling and the audience applauding as the previous performer finished his set.

Willow handed Audrey her phone. Audrey beckoned for him to come close.

Hayden's smiling face was on the screen. "You guys took look awesome."

"I'll second that." Everly put her face next to Hayden's to agree.

"I want to ask you something." Hayden's expression had turned serious.

"Okay, hon. Anything." Jericho focused on her.

"If you weren't singing with my mom tonight, who would you rather sing with—Gwen Stefani or Kelly Clarkson?"

This clever kid's sense of humor always snuck up on him. He grinned and glanced face-to-face at Audrey, who shared a similar expression of amusement.

He kept his expression serious when he looked back at the phone. "This is something I've pondered myself, and I do have a preference. Your mom will always be my first choice, of course, but—"

"Of course," Hayden said.

"But my decision would have to be…Kelly Clarkson, because, well, she's *Kelly Clarkson*."

Hayden nodded. "Right?"

"We're all set to watch the show," Everly said. "It's going to be awesome."

Jericho and Audrey both said, "Thanks." Audrey tapped off the phone and handed it to Willow.

"You have a great kid. Intuitive and smart." Sometimes she reminded him of Audrey, other times of his sister.

"I think so too." She gave him a proud smile.

The male performer took his leave. Gianna fussed over Audrey's jewelry while Willow fluffed her already-perfect hair. The crew and band members made changes, and that was Jericho's cue to dodge Willow and take his place on stage while the lights were down. Finally, the announcer introduced Audrey, and the audience cheered when she swept onto the stage in sparkling silver magnificence

This wasn't just any crowd. These were the investors, executives and influential people who funded and promoted the label. And she obviously impressed.

"On behalf of everyone at Songbird Records, I'd like to thank each one of you for being here this evening," Audrey said into the mic, her recognizable voice enhanced to perfection. "I've always been proud to be part of the Songbird family. With my very first album, ya'll took a chance on a young girl from the Colorado mountains. You believed in me and in my music and I'm forever thankful. Tonight's Showcase is an opportunity for your artists to express our gratitude and show you we have a lot more comin' to be excited about."

The audience members applauded.

"You might not recognize this fella singin' with me tonight, not because he's not amazing, but because he likes to stay behind the scenes. I didn't have to twist his arm too hard to get him here with me tonight though. He's been playing backup and singing with me since I was a little girl, and we've made some beautiful music together. This new song we're gonna sing for you is one of them, so please welcome Jericho Tanner."

The lights lit him, so Jericho smiled and raised a hand in

greeting, then lowered it back to his guitar as the band came to life behind him.

Audrey offered a smile meant only for him and sang, *"'Seems all I ever did was want. Seems all I ever did was wait, but when you saw me, you really saw me. I knew a love I could not anticipate.'"*

Nerves fluttered, but he joined her, harmonizing on the chorus, and the song they'd written together was revealed to the world for the first time. He understood the thrill of writing and performing a piece that millions would hear and hopefully love, creating a song that spoke to hearts. They'd composed a guitar solo, and he played it flawlessly, lost in the moment and the music.

The crowd loved their performance. Cameras clicked. The lighting changed, and the next songs were Audrey's recent hits and one that had earned her a Grammy.

At the after-party, they drank champagne and visited with executives. Jericho let Audrey and Sidney do all the talking, meanwhile deflecting blatant flirtations.

"Photos please, Audrey?" someone with a camera called.

"Do you want your photo taken with me? Audrey asked him softly. "I can avoid it if you don't. I respect your choice."

Their photos would make covers and celebrity news. He'd be the object of questions and presumption. Did he care? "I'm here," he said. "We did this together, so I'm not hiding."

She took his hand. "If you're certain."

"I am."

They approached an enormous lobby, where a red carpet had been rolled out in front of a huge backdrop proclaiming Songbird Records' label. Willow appeared to fluff Audrey's hair, Gianna adjusted her gown and Tam glossed her lips.

Willow leaned toward Jericho, but he stopped her with squared shoulders and a glare. She backed away.

Audrey giggled and led him to the epicenter of attention.

"Where did they come from? They're like glamour fairies."

"They're doing their jobs." She smiled brightly. "Look at the cameras."

This thing between them was growing frighteningly real, what with the song they'd written together and Audrey considering staying in Spencer. If she imagined he might choose this life, she was wrong. This was her dream, but it wasn't his life. He hadn't gone after her the first time, and he never would. Neither did he imagine she'd step away from the glitz and notoriety to stay long in Colorado.

This involvement was temporary, and he was as reconciled to the fact as ever.

Audrey's home was a gated brick mansion on a couple of acres with rolling lawns and lush trees. He'd viewed the magazine spread, but seeing the place in person was entirely different. A huge flagstone foyer divided into an enormous kitchen one direction and a living room the other. Audrey had changed out of her dress before leaving the venue and wore jeans and boots. He still wore the shirt he'd performed in. Indicating he should join her in the kitchen, she strolled to the refrigerator, took out a bottle of wine and a plastic-wrapped board of cheese and meat. A basket of crackers sat on the island. After handing him a corkscrew and the bottle, she unwrapped the board.

He popped the cork and poured wine. "Who got this spread ready?"

"I told the housekeeper I'd be here and be staying one or

more nights. She got groceries and prepared the charcuterie board."

"The what?"

"The cheese tray."

He tasted a square of aged gouda. "Nice."

She showed him the rest of the house, and he admired photos of Hayden that were displayed on the mantle in her living room. He gestured to the white sofa and chairs. "The furniture is new?"

"No, we just don't use it. We're only here a few months a year. There's a theater room where we watch TV and a music room with comfortable furniture. I'll show you."

The music room was indeed as she'd described. There were soft leather sofas with fuzzy throws, another fireplace, two keyboards and an assortment of guitars. Framed album covers hung on one wall. Another wall held framed records, and shelves with photos and sound equipment, but his attention was drawn to the shiny gold Grammy statues on the mantle. He admired each one, but one in particular caught his attention.

National Academy of Recording Arts & Sciences

Audrey Knox
Artist

BEST SINGLE OF THE YEAR
MAYBE I'M THE ONE

Barely a twinge of disappointment registered. "Your home is incredible," he said. "And your accomplishments are well-deserved."

"It's a trophy house," she said.

He turned and studied her.

She shrugged. "Yes, I was able to buy this house. Has it brought me joy or satisfaction?" She shook her head. "Hayden brings me joy. My friends and my music bring me joy. I've realized I could live anywhere and have those. This is only a container."

She left him thinking while she got the bottle and returned to pour them more wine. "Want to sight-see tomorrow?"

"I'd like that if you don't mind."

She settled on a sofa. "It's not as big of a deal here. Nashville is full of singers and songwriters. It's more the norm to see them in public than in other cities."

He discovered a photo of Audrey and the man he'd seen pictured with her in a few articles years ago. "Did you and your husband buy this place together?"

"For financial reasons Tucker thought we should invest. He discovered this property and apparently it was the perfect asset. And it was supposedly befitting of our status. I didn't care so much about that, but only that my baby needed a real home. He wasn't in town much—or at least not when I was. One of us was always on the road. He had an office here, but he rarely used it."

"That must've been lonely."

"I didn't think so at the time. I was busy recording and touring. I had Hayden and Everly and a housekeeper. Back when I first moved to Nashville, Tucker had become my manager. He believed in me—in my talent. He was invested in my career, and that was great. He was so sure we should be married and that we'd be a good team. After Daddy died, I was floundering. I came home after the funeral and he asked me again, so I said yes. We got married right away. We were a good team career-wise.

"He barely saw Hayden, and that was hurtful. I didn't make a big deal of it. I didn't press him. To tell the truth, life was easier when he was gone. She was three when he died in a small plane crash." Audrey drew a line along a seam on the leather cushion with her thumbnail. "I was sad of course. It sounds terrible to say, but nothing really changed. Except I had to get a new manager."

"Sydney?"

She nodded. "He's been with me ever since."

"After seeing this place in the magazine feature, I was a little nervous about you coming to my cabin."

"I love your home. You designed it, you live in it. It's very much you."

"So, what are you thinking?" he asked.

"I'm thinking I'll finally clear out Tucker's office this weekend, if you'll help me. And call a realtor."

"You're going to sell?"

"I'm going to sell." She patted the sofa cushion beside her.

He joined her, setting his glass on the nearby table and wrapping her in his arms. He'd never imagined having this time together, having her attention all to himself, but he was still cautious. He'd been too open, too trusting before, and he'd been hurt. After the initial trauma, he'd refocused, hadn't let anyone see the wound. Emotional distance remained his safeguard, but in her presence, it was wearing thin, especially now that she'd remembered their night together.

To be fair, he never told her how he felt about her, so he bore a good share of the blame for what had happened in the past. He'd mistakenly thought the song he'd written and sent her was a confession of his feelings, but the admission had been too vague—and obviously too late.

Her scent enflamed his senses, her soft curves and warmth tempting him to caress and explore. She tilted her face upward, inviting his kiss, which he didn't deny. Since he'd watched her transform from merely a childhood friend into an alluring woman, Audrey had always been everything he wanted. Kissing her was more than a prelude to something more. Kissing her lips, tasting her, was a sensory pleasure he never wanted to end. Not that he didn't want more, because every nerve and cell in his body begged for physical release. But this moment was too good to rush.

She eased a few inches away and looked into his eyes. "Thank you for tonight. I know it wasn't easy."

"It wasn't so bad."

She smiled. "You don't give yourself enough credit. You're a really talented guy."

"Or I can fake it well."

"You're not a fake." With a soft fingertip, she traced his lips. "You're the real deal."

"With my sexy cowboy vibe?"

She grinned. "That doesn't hurt either. But you have talent."

"I learned to play for you," he said. "And I'm not sorry, because now I enjoy playing for friends, but I'm not a performer."

"I know. That's why it means a lot that you made this exception."

He was thankful she understood tonight had been a one-time thing. "You're welcome."

She stood and drew him to his feet with her. "You haven't seen the upstairs yet."

"I'm sure it's great."

With an alluring smile, she met his gaze. "When I said we could stay here for the weekend, we never discussed sleeping arrangements."

His heart missed a beat. "Where would you like me to sleep?"

She flattened her palms on his shirtfront and kissed him. "I think you know."

He studied the arch of her brow, her elegant cheek-bones...he wanted this moment to last as well. "I was hoping…"

Her lips tilted at the corners and she spoke, "Here's one for you. Would you rather sleep with—?"

He cut her off. "I'd rather sleep with you."

The following morning Audrey spoke on the phone with Hayden while she made waffles, and Jericho peeled oranges and plucked grapes from their stems. The rich roasted aroma of dark coffee filled the kitchen. Everything about their night together and this morning felt right. Better than right. Perfect. She liked watching him perform the ordinary everyday tasks of preparing fruit and pouring juice. She had no idea where this was going, but they were both unattached consenting adults, and enjoying each other wasn't hurting anyone. Their night together had been tender and meaning-ful, and thinking about it now created butterflies in her belly. Seeing his fingers adeptly peeling an orange brought to mind the way he touched her. Warmth climbed her cheeks, and she ended her call.

As they ate, they shared hesitant, but knowing smiles, their recent lovemaking a complex current of satisfaction and expectation ebbing between them. When Audrey leaned to pick up his plate, he wrapped his arm around her waist and pulled her close to rest his cheek against her midriff. She threaded her fingers into his silky midnight hair.

"I can't get enough of you." The words came out a ragged admission. "The way you smell. Your soft skin."

His endearments were unfamiliar praise, and her heart

quickened. She leaned forward to kiss him, delighted and frightened at the same time. He accepted that she kept the kiss sweet, and she loved that about him. He'd been sensitive to her wishes and took his cues from her, but she understood on a deeper level, there was fire burning underneath. She'd experienced the heat the night before. It would be so easy to spend the day in his arms, but she had limited time now that she'd made her decision.

She gave him one last kiss and cleared the table.

Obviously, Jericho was not used to idle time, because once they'd eaten, he was eager to move furniture and empty file drawers. Tucker's top desk drawer was locked, so she emptied others.

"I don't know how much of this to save." Audrey alternated between shredding papers and filling boxes. "My eyesight is blurry from all this small print. You'd think I'd been drinking. Did you spike the coffee?"

"Maybe you need glasses."

She frowned at him, but then had a thought. "Tucker had readers." Pulling open another drawer and fishing around, her fingers came in contact with a set of keys. "One of these must open that drawer."

After trying a couple of small keys, one turned in the lock. She slid out the drawer and spotted several envelopes among pens and rubber bands. She found the glasses too and slid them on to look at the mail. These weren't bills or official documents, but personal correspondence.

Among the envelopes were a couple of birthday cards from Tucker's mother, a note Audrey had written before Hayden was born, and a larger envelope addressed to Audrey Monroe. Seeing her maiden name caught her by surprise, but the handwriting set off her radar. The packet had been neatly sliced open, so she slid out the papers and unfolded them.

It took several seconds to comprehend what she was

looking at. Sheet music, both treble and bass notes neatly hand-drawn on the staff lines. The song title written in black pen read *Maybe I'm the One*. No songwriter's credit had been included. The key looked familiar, but the time signatures were different. She focused on the neatly-written lyrics, and frowned.

She flipped the envelope back over and read the return address. There was no name, but the address was the same county road and rural route as *Big Pine Ridge Ranch*. The postal stamp was dated nine years ago.

Her ears filled with the static sound of her blood pumping rapidly. Reading the lyrics more closely, the neat lowercase handwriting was familiar. She hadn't seen it in a long time, but this was Jericho's distinctive printing.

"What is this?" she said aloud.

He paused in packing books into a box. "What are you looking at?"

"This is your writing. Your notes composed on these staffs."

"What?" He set down a stack of books and came to see. Taking the sheet paper from her, he studied it briefly and handed it back expressionlessly. "I guess it's been a while since you've seen it."

"I've never seen this before."

He had turned away, but her words stopped him. He studied her. "What's that supposed to mean?"

"It means I've never seen this before." She picked up the envelope. "It's addressed to me—to Audrey Monroe, but I never got it."

"Well, someone got it, because that song was your first single. I've heard it on the radio about four million times."

"You wrote *Maybe I'm the One*."

"Yes."

Realizing his song had been stolen, she felt sick to her

stomach. *Stolen by her.* But not by her, by Tucker. "You never said anything."

His brows lowered. "I wrote it for you. I figured you could do whatever you wanted with it."

She stood but didn't move toward him. "That's wrong."

He didn't reply, but a muscle in his jaw twitched.

"All this time you thought I'd taken your song without acknowledgement?"

"Didn't you?"

"No. Jericho, this is the first time I've ever seen this. When Tucker showed me the song, it was on professionally printed sheet music. He said he bought it in a batch of music from a struggling writer." She laid the sheets on the desk. "Didn't he think you might come after the rights? Did he ever contact you?"

Jericho held his mouth in a flat line. "No, he didn't. Who knows what he thought? The song came out after I read you'd been married."

"So, all long—all these years you thought I stole your song?"

"I don't think I ever thought of it as stealing. It was yours. I guess I thought you used it without acknowledgement."

Her legs crumpled from under her and she grabbed the edge of the desk to sit back on the chair. A discordant clash of anger and guilt and remorse coursed through her shaking limbs. "How could Tucker have done this?" She straightened in the seat and stared unseeingly out the bay of windows. "I didn't really know him."

"You must have loved him."

"I thought I did. I was enthralled with his knowledge and the people he knew, and he was so positive that with the right songs and the right connections I'd be a successful recording artist. I figured we'd be good together, and we were. We were both driven and admittedly too busy to have time to fight...or find fault in each other."

"You'd have been a success with or without him."

She knew the lyrics by heart but she read Jericho's handwriting. *Like a shooting star you shine bright, brighter than all the others. Your love is sweet and your love is big, bigger than other lovers. We all have to play our parts, but if tomorrow you look back -- if you wake up and think your good sense is gone...I'll still be here, because baby, maybe I'm the one.'*

He'd written these words for her. How could she not have known? Understanding the depth of emotion they held, tears welled in her eyes.

He'd moved to stand at the corner of the desk and she met his gaze.

All along he believed she'd ignored or rejected his declaration of his feelings for her. *'I'll still be here,'* he'd written. "I'm sorry I didn't realize how you felt," she told him. "I was focused on coming to Nashville."

"I knew that. It was all you ever wanted."

"You were hurt because I didn't know about this."

"I know now. Can we let it go?"

She got up and pressed herself into him, her face against his shoulder, and he folded his arms around her. "I can't figure out why you're not mad. I am."

He smoothed her hair over her shoulder, but said nothing.

She'd let the conversation go, but she wasn't forgetting. As soon as she could speak to her attorney, she intended to make certain Jericho's name was on the copyright.

# CHAPTER THIRTEEN

*M*onday morning conversation stopped abruptly when Jericho entered Pearl's. In his hat and uniform, he paused inside the door, attuning himself to the atmosphere. He glanced from person to person. Joe Cavanaugh's expression was impassive as he sat at the counter. Piper showed amusement as she paused in pouring old Jonas Finch a cup of coffee. Jonas glanced over his shoulder and grinned. Edith emerged from the kitchen with two laden plates, spotted Jericho and broke into a delighted smile.

They'd seen the show. Or at least the photos. It took all his resolve not to rake his gaze to the wall to learn if an enlarged photo from the showcase had been hung. He didn't need to look. He removed his hat and jacket and headed for the row of hooks on the side wall. "Go ahead. Say whatever it is you're gonna say and get the yammerin' over with. Then we won't ever talk about it again."

"You looked so handsome," Edith piped up. "Why, my old heart fluttered at the sight, and I see you every week right here in our very own place. My, but you are photogenic, and

I felt so proud that someone with so much talent loves my lemon pie. And Audrey? Why that girl was a vision in that silver dress. I could listen to the both of you sing 'til the well runs dry."

He pressed his lips together resolutely and made his way to the counter.

"Thinking about going on the road?" Joe asked, his expression stoic, but his eyes filled with teasing mischief.

"You know damned well I'm not going on the road," Jericho replied. "It was a one-time favor."

"Must've been one amazing time," Piper said. She refilled a small cream pitcher and slid it to Jonas. "We've all heard you at the Wild Card and knew you were talented, but now all of America knows."

"I don't know about all of America," he denied. "Ratings were still pretty good for NCIS that night." He glanced at Joe. "Audrey mentioned it."

"Do those ratings include people recording shows?" Edith asked. "Because I recorded NCIS so I could watch you two."

Dusty Cavanaugh entered the café, pulled off his gloves and stuffed them into his coat pocket. "Sky looks like snow."

He took a seat beside his brother. "Hey, Jericho."

"Before Thanksgiving?" Edith clucked and filled the brewer basket with fresh coffee grounds. "It won't last."

"Deputy Tanner's waiting for you to say something about seeing him on television," Joe said to his younger brother.

Dusty glanced over. "Oh, sorry. I didn't catch it."

Jericho eased into a satisfied grin. "See there? Not all of America saw it."

"Kendra recorded it though," he added. "We're watching it tonight."

His remark was followed by an outburst of laughter.

Dusty shook his head. "What?"

"What will you boys have?" Piper asked.

"The rancher's special," Jericho said. "Over easy, wheat toast and black coffee please."

"That sounds good to me," Dusty told her. "But break my eggs, please."

Piper tucked her pen behind her ear, clipped their orders to the wheel over the kitchen window and plunked stoneware mugs in front of them.

"How are things going with Dorris and Audrey?" Joe asked in a low tone. "Audrey was breathing fire during our chat."

"She's still plenty mad about Dorris considering a sale behind her back. Dorris seemed a little sheepish, but she didn't apologize." Jericho glanced to make sure no one over-head and spoke quietly. "The woman is so hard on her daughter. She gets in these little backhanded digs. Like a thousand little cuts, you know? I don't know how Audrey has tolerated it all these years, but I do understand why she hasn't made an effort to be here more."

Joe gave a nod. "I've only talked to the woman a few times. She stays pretty much to herself. Charlie was a straight-up guy though. Kind of larger than life. Everyone loved him. Not two people I'd match up, but opposites attract or something like that."

Jericho's breakfast arrived and he tucked into the meal. "Hard to figure people sometimes."

"I don't know anything concrete," Joe added. "But I do know the feds are putting together charges against Hart-wood. The process is slow as always. I haven't seen him around town in a while."

"And now with the holidays coming, everything will move even more slowly," Jericho surmised.

"I want us to keep an eye out for him. Drive across the river and cruise Spencer Heights today. Check his place and see if there's any indication he's there or not."

Jericho agreed with, "Copy that."

Audrey had called Christine Tanner as soon as she'd returned to *Big Pine*. Jericho's mom was delighted the families were going to be together for dinner. They coordinated side dishes and hung up. Audrey immediately ordered flowers to be sent the day ahead.

Everly was flying out to spend the holiday with her grandfather and a cousin, so Audrey and Hayden drove her to the Spencer airport where she boarded a small plane to Denver. On the way home they grocery shopped with their baking list.

It was still morning when Hayden got Dorris to join them in the kitchen. They cleared space on the table and counters and set out supplies.

"I'm having a chest freezer delivered tomorrow," Audrey said. "We can make enough breads, cookies and pies to freeze for both Thanksgiving and Christmas, and enough for gifts as well. I thought we could go to the senior center together. I'll call ahead and see if we can either join their party or plan an event. Maybe sing carols and pass out cookies. What do you think?"

Hayden grinned her approval. "That sounds like fun. I want to meet Buddy."

"I told him I would bring you," Audrey told her daughter. "What about you, Mom?"

Dorris paused in rolling out pie dough and gave Audrey a cautious look. "Do you want me to go?"

"Of course, I do. We're a family. We have a lot to catch up on, and we can't do that if we don't do things together. And talk."

Dorris gave her a sidelong look. "Okay. That sounds nice."

"Can I take some pictures of us?" Hayden asked.

"You don't have to ask," Audrey replied. "We need family pictures, don't we?"

Hayden stood on a chair in an attempt to get them all into shots and also include their crusts and the flour-covered table. They laughed at her antics and the resulting photos.

"Look at you girls." Dorris studied the images on her granddaughter's phone. "I was pretty once too."

Her wistful remark caught Audrey by surprise. "You're still a beautiful woman, Mom. Daddy thought you were the prettiest girl in all of Rockwell County. He told me so. He always carried a photo of you in his wallet."

Dorris didn't meet her eyes.

"Maybe we could look at old pictures. I'd like to see the family before I came along." Hayden wore a bright expression. Her cheerfulness and optimism always encouraged Audrey to stay positive.

Audrey answered before her mother could discourage them. "We can do that, sweetie. You can see your tomboy mama with her blue-ribbon goats and sheep."

Hayden grinned.

After they had several dozen cookies cooling and pies in the oven, Audrey set out ingredients for royal frosting and rested her fingertips on the table edge. She took a deep breath. "I'm selling the house in Nashville."

Hayden looked up in surprise. Concern filled her bright blue eyes. "Where are we going to live?"

"I don't have it all thought out yet." Audrey wanted to be truthful with her, not worry her, and make her feel included in what came next. "I'm going to fly back after Thanksgiving and work out the details. I'm also arranging a meeting with Songbird Records. I want Sidney and my publicist, Cadence there. We'll see what we can agree on for keeping tours short and doing only a couple a year. It will take finesse to save the traction I've made as far as public image and sales."

Now Hayden's eyes were wide with anticipation. "Would we live here?"

Audrey met her gaze. "We'll live in Spencer for sure."

The squeal the girl emitted pieced her eardrums. Hayden jumped up and down and ran around the island to crush herself against Audrey and press her face into her midriff. A moment later, Audrey recognized sobs instead of laughter.

She stroked her palms over Hayden's slender convulsing frame. "Honey, are you happy or sad?"

"I-I-I'm h-h-happy," came the muffled reply.

A look exchanged with Dorris showed her mother had become emotional as well.

"Are you happy too, Mom?"

Dorris gave a single nod.

Audrey dropped to her knees and wrapped her arms around her child. This decision had been important, and she'd known it. Thankfully she'd taken the step to come here when she had. Their lives may have not taken this turn if she'd ignored her instincts. "You're the most important person in my life, Hayden. You come before everything and everyone else. I always want you to know that."

Hayden eased away and swiped her face with her palms. "I know. And you're the most important person to me. But Everly and Gramma and Jericho are important too."

"They definitely are."

The girl looked at her grandmother. "We're staying."

Dorris nodded and gave her a smile.

"Will we live here with Gramma?" Hayden asked.

Audrey straightened and wetted a washcloth for Hayden's face. "We have to plan what comes next. Everly likes Spencer. I'm pretty sure she'll stay with us. Gramma might appreciate having her own space again, but we can talk about it. All this *Big Pine* land is ours, baby. We can build ourselves a place if we want to."

"We can?" Hayden's eyes widened. "Can I get a goat?"

The abrupt change of topic arrested Audrey's thoughts. "A goat?"

"You had goats and sheep you said."

She agreed with a nod. "It *is* a ranch."

"What about fainting goats? Have you seen those videos? They wear sweaters!"

Audrey laughed. "You might want goats that stay on their feet."

"Are there fainting sheep?"

"I don't think so."

Dorris washed her hands. "Want a cup of coffee?"

"I'd love one," Audrey replied.

That evening with all their baked goods wrapped and stacked in containers, most in the freezer, Audrey located a shelf of photo albums in a built-in cabinet in the family room. She piled albums on the trunk that served as a coffee table, and the three of them relaxed and looked at pictures. Dorris had removed her shoes and wore a pair of fuzzy slippers. The sight reminded Audrey of early breakfasts when they been a whole family.

The images of Wyatt created a dissonance of emotions for Audrey. Those years had been the happiest she remembered as a child. Wyatt had been smart and funny, a typical little boy who teased and annoyed his sister one minute and then melted her irritation with a colorfully drawn picture of her or one of her pets the next. She studied his beloved face in a school photo, noting the arch of his dark brows, the smooth line of his smiling lips. So achingly familiar. She longed for those carefree days.

While her mother and Hayden chatted about birthday

and Christmas photos, Audrey opened a box of loose photos, many black and white, some in vintage cardboard frames. "These are Grandma and Grandpa Monroe. This is the old farmhouse that used to be over by the grove. I barely remember it."

She thumbed through another stack. "Who is this couple?" she asked and leaned to hand Dorris the picture.

"Those are Atwood's parents." Her mom pointed to the lanky boy on the porch. "That's Atwood."

"Jericho's grandparents," Audrey mused. The resemblance between Atwood as a boy and how she remembered Jericho was significant. Judah looked like his father as well. "Do they have these same pictures?"

"I don't know. Your father was the one who saved photographs."

"Let's take these to show the family when we go for dinner."

Dorris only shrugged.

The next day they prepped their side dishes. Dorris made her cranberry relish Audrey had always loved. On Thanksgiving morning Audrey baked a sweet potato casserole and made fresh rolls.

When they arrived, the Tanner home was filled with savory holiday smells. Jericho had helped his mom add all the leaves in the table and position a folding table at the end. The house had been updated, repainted and had new furniture since Audrey had last seen it, but two vintage chandeliers still hung in the enormous dining room and Christine's collection of Blue Willow dishes remained displayed on recessed open shelves. The table was set with gold-rimmed white plates and red linens. A long evergreen table scape laden with festive glass ornaments adorned the center.

"Thank you for the centerpiece." Christine hugged

Audrey and then held her at arm's length to admire her. "Look at you. You're more stunning than I remembered."

Audrey wore a green plaid sheath dress and knee-high boots. She'd had a similar ensemble made for Hayden, but hers was red.

Christine turned her attention to the eight-year-old. "Oh, my." She took a step closer and touched Hayden's hair in gesture of what seemed like wonder, the moment acutely reminding Audrey of the woman's mothering ways. She'd always treated Audrey and Wyatt as though they were her own. "I haven't seen you since you were a toddler. It's so nice to have you with us today."

"Thank you, ma'am," Hayden replied.

"Will you call me Christine?" She wore her fair hair shoulder-length and was shorter than Audrey remembered. "You look so beautiful in red." Audrey sensed that Christine would have loved to hug Hayden, but was respectful of having just met her. "After having two rowdy boys," she said, "I loved buying dresses for my daughter. Bethel endured them on special days, but she was happier in jeans like her brothers."

"I like leggings," Hayden told her. "Mom got me Hocus Pocus ones for Halloween."

Christine wrinkled her nose. "'I smell children.'"

The two of them laughed, delighting Audrey. She gave Jericho's mom a grateful smile, thankful for the warm welcome.

In the kitchen, Audrey helped fill serving bowls and carry them to the table. As they all took their seats, she noted she'd been seated across from Jericho. He gave her a smile that warmed her all the way to her toes.

"This is like when we were kids," Judah said. "Except you two take up more room," he added elbowing Jericho and Bethel on either side.

Atwood was seated at the head of the table, and Hayden sat between Audrey and her mother where her daddy had always been. Wyatt had always been on her other side. Her throat closed around the keen loss that welled up, so she breathed evenly and closed her eyes for a moment. She had Hayden now.

When she opened her eyes, Jericho met her gaze with understanding compassion…and more. She reacted with a sharp intake of breath. More held a million possibilities.

She hoped her smile showed her appreciation. She glanced at his siblings, then his mother, catching Christine's knowing expression.

Atwood said the blessing. Bowls and platters were passed.

"Hayden, ask one of your questions," Jericho suggested halfway through the meal.

"Really?" she squeaked.

"Sure. We'll put on our thinking caps."

"What kind of questions do you ask?" Atwood asked congenially.

"Would you rather," Hayden replied rather timidly, but then seemed to warm up to the idea. "Okay." She rested her fork on her plate and thought a minute. "Mr. Tanner, would you rather have a dance off with Beyoncé or a sing off with Ariana Grande?"

Christine giggled and whispered to Judah, "I'd pay to see him in a dance off with Beyoncé."

Judah and Bethel shared an amused glance and looked to their father for his reaction.

"Dad, do you know who Ariana Grande is?" Bethel asked.

"The skinny little girl with the ponytail," he replied as though insulted they'd questioned his pop culture knowledge.

Bethel raised her eyebrows in surprise.

Jericho gave Hayden an appreciative nod as though to say, *'atta girl.'*

The smile Hayden returned was bashful, but pleased.

Atwood took a sip of water from his glass, rested his elbows on the table and folded his hands over his plate. His thoughtful yet amused expression was very like Jericho's when he was considering how to answer one of Hayden's questions.

"I have to choose one of those two, right?"

Hayden nodded. "Not optional."

"Okay. Well, I might hurt myself trying to out dance Beyoncé, so I'd try a sing off with Ariana Grande. I saw Jimmy Fallon hold his own."

Laughter burst out among the adults, but Hayden frowned. "Who is Jimmy Fallon?"

"He's on tv after you've gone to bed," Audrey explained.

"I can find the YouTube video of him with Ariana for you," Bethel offered.

"Sure," Hayden said.

Atwood continued eating.

"Okay, ask me one next," Bethel persuaded.

Hayden flattened her lips while she thought, then asked, "Would you rather give up your cell phone for a month or give up showering for a month?"

The quandary was met with chorus of ohs and wows.

Judah grinned. "Well done, Hayden."

"Not that tough of a call," Bethel said to her brother with an indignant side glance. "I work with the horses every day, so I'd choose to shower." She leaned into Judah. "And you would have to thank me."

Judah shrugged, but nodded in agreement. His expressions were intriguingly familiar, probably because he and Jericho had similar features, but together the siblings reminded Audrey of herself and Wyatt.

She glanced at her mother. These interactions must remind Dorris of her losses, but her expression remained impassive.

"The Winter Festival is coming up in another week," Christine said. "We should think about attending together for a day. I love seeing the ice sculptures."

"I've read about the festival in the *Herald*, but have never been," Audrey replied. "I'm sure Hayden would enjoy it. We could join you for a day, right Mom?"

Dorris rubbed her fingertips on the edge of the tablecloth. "I'm not much for crowds."

Obviously paying close attention to this new idea, Hayden glanced from her grandmother to her mom. Audrey tilted her lips and gave her daughter a tiny shrug. Leave it to Dorris to shoot down a fun idea.

"Let's plan it." Jericho got out his phone. "I'll check which days I have off. I'll take a vacation day if I need to."

Hayden beamed, and he winked at her.

Once they'd finished eating, Bethel and Jericho gestured for the others to stay seated while they cleared the dishes. Christine made coffee and carried a carafe to the table, then seated herself and attempted to make conversation with Dorris.

"Let's go help," Audrey said to Hayden, and the two of them joined the siblings loading the dishwasher and putting away leftovers.

When Audrey reached for the roasting pan, Bethel handed her latex gloves. "Don't ruin your manicure."

Bethel and her mother were both fair-skinned with dark blond hair, while Judah and Jericho had black hair like Atwood's had once been. Bethel's hands were slender, her nails short and unpainted. She had a youthful appearance and yet a serious manner of speech that reminded Audrey of Hayden.

Jericho reached around Audrey at the sink to wet a dishrag, resting his other hand at her waist. She looked over shoulder and smiled.

Once he'd moved away to wipe the stove, Audrey lifted her gaze to Bethel who had seen the exchange. Her sly smile spoke volumes, and Audrey blushed.

"Maybe you'll sing for us later," was all she said.

"Maybe," Audrey answered. "We brought some old photos because we thought it would be fun to look through them together."

"I'd love that," Bethel agreed.

The dishes were finished and Christine ushered them into the comfortable family room where Jericho started a fire in the brick fireplace. Light fixtures and furnishings had been replaced, but the room still held the homey ambiance Audrey remembered.

"Look, it's snowing!" Hayden hurried to stand before the three wide windows overlooking a picturesque expanse of pastureland dotted with tall conifers. To the right, stables were enclosed within white fencing. The snow was pretty and the view likely looked like a Christmas card to her eight-year-old daughter.

The Tanners were warm and welcoming. Conversation was easy. Holidays hadn't felt this special for a long time. She and Hayden had either been alone at the Nashville house or in a hotel somewhere.

Hayden rejoined the gathering to tell Christine and Bethel that she would be starting school in Spencer soon. As the older woman looked at Hayden and listened to her talk, Christine's adoring expression caught Audrey by surprise. The woman seemed to soak in everything about Hayden as though she was seeing someone she'd been missing or had longed for. The impression stayed with Audrey.

"Where are the photos?" Bethel asked.

"I carried them in. I'll go get them," Jericho offered and returned with a tote filled with albums and loose photos.

Atwood reached to a shelf and took down a couple of albums to share as well. For an hour or more they poured over the photographs with, 'Who is this?' being the most-heard question. Christine opened a box holding loose school pictures. "I never did get these in separate albums for you kids. Now I'll have to sort them out and remember who is who." She flipped one over. "At least I wrote dates and grades. Look, Audrey, here are a couple of yours and several of Wyatt."

Audrey took the photos and studied them. She'd always thought Hayden looked like her, but was surprised to recognize only a marginal resemblance. She laid out several pics on her lap. Bethel's were easy to identify. And no wonder people had said Jericho and Wyatt looked alike. They could have been brothers, and Judah had similar features.

The longer she studied the photos of Jericho and Judah at ages seven, eight and nine the more an uncanny comparison became mind-numbingly clear.

The conversation around her faded to only the beat of her heart thudding in her chest. *"Oh, my God,"* she whispered. *"Oh, my..."*

A series of images flashed in her mind, images from a night she'd blocked out for sanity's sake...Christine looking at Hayden...

# CHAPTER FOURTEEN

$S$ ince she'd come to Spencer, her life had been a series of shocking discoveries, pointing out she'd been self-delusional her entire life.

Obviously, since she'd blocked out what had happened between her and Jericho and immediately accepted Tucker's marriage proposal, she'd assumed Hayden was Tucker's child.

The truth had been evident all along, and yet she had been blind—or had fooled herself. And Jericho. He'd forgiven a lot already—but this? Missing eight years of being a father?

She corrected her thinking. It was possible he wasn't Hayden's father. Jericho's hair was as dark as midnight. She glanced at the photo of Bethel on her lap. She was fair and blond while her father had ebony hair like Jericho's. So, a black-haired man fathering a blond child was possible.

It was certainly likely Jericho had fathered a blond-haired blue-eyed child.

Hayden had blue eyes like Christine, not dark blue like herself.

She'd have to have a paternity test done so there was no doubt.

Audrey's dinner wasn't sitting well. Her heart chugged like a freight train climbing a hill. Attempting to hold her composure, she stacked the photos, hoping no one noticed the telltale trembling of her hands. She leaned forward to place the stack in the box on the low table and glanced up.

She met Christine's gaze. Jericho's mother only gave her a kind smile. Not judgmental or accusatory.

Christine may have suspected previously, but the moment the Monroes had come into her home and she'd set eyes on Hayden, she'd known. She'd recognized what was glaringly apparent to her and not to Audrey. Would she say something, call her out? No. Not here and not like this. Would she point it out to Jericho? Maybe. Maybe when they were alone, she'd tell him what she believed.

Audrey's heart thudded so loudly she couldn't hear conversations going on around her. She concentrated. Jericho was replying to something Hayden had asked. He left the room and returned with a guitar. Audrey recognized it as one he'd played years ago. He handed it to Hayden. "I'll be right back. Want me to grab a guitar for you, Audrey?"

She shook her head. "You play."

Several minutes later, he could be heard stomping snow from his boots in the foyer. He returned and settled across from Hayden, where he opened an app on this phone and tuned both guitars by turning the pegs. He explained the strings. "These are E, A, D, G, B and e," he said. And these are the frets. He counted them for her, then showed her how to place her fingers on the frets. "Now which one is the second fret of the A string?"

Hayden pointed to it on the guitar she held.

Audrey's throat tightened.

The others were talking among themselves, but Audrey

was completely focused on watching Jericho with Hayden. She thought back over all their analytical discussions regarding musical would-you-rather questions. They thought alike.

She would have to tell him. She wouldn't sneak around trying to get a sample of his DNA. He deserved to know the enormity of this question. Especially after Nashville. She'd been evasive long enough.

She declined dessert, choosing to watch Hayden enjoy the attention of possible family and join in what might become traditions. Her imagination took over, giving her daughter another grandmother, a grandfather, an aunt and an uncle. She couldn't let herself dwell on the father aspect. A disappointment would be too difficult to accept.

She wrapped leftovers with Christine and Bethel, filling a bag to take home. Christine hugged her soundly at the door as they prepared to leave. "I'm so glad you and Hayden are here and planning to stay. I hope we'll be seeing you more often."

Audrey's cheeks burned. She wanted to say something, but she didn't know what.

"It's all going to work out," Christine told her. "When we do things out of love, it works out."

"Thank you," she managed. Christine knew. She'd seen the resemblance the moment she'd met Hayden. Audrey had to be the one to tell Jericho. Coming from someone else would be unforgiveable. If the truth wasn't unforgiveable already.

He carried containers, placed them in the back of her vehicle, then cleared snow from the windshield. "Lane clears your drive," he told her. "Is he at *Big Pine* today?"

"He and Dana were having dinner with friends in town, but they're probably back by now."

"If not, give me a call from the highway. I'll be right over to plow."

"Okay," She met his dark gaze. "I'd like to come over in the morning, if that's okay."

"Better than okay," he said.

She'd started the Escalade from inside, so it was warm when they got in.

The drive to the house had already been cleared. Once inside, she put away food and washed a few dirty dishes they'd left on their way out earlier. She joined Dorris and Hayden who were watching a Christmas movie, but her mind was in a whir. After the show ended, she tucked Hayden into bed, got a book and returned to the family room. She stared at the pages, but couldn't concentrate.

What had she done?

"Will Cale Hartwood have to pay back the money?" Dorris asked.

Audrey refocused her thinking.

*Right now, Mom?* Some people had a knack for knowing when things were tense and bringing up another problem. "Apparently Hartwood hasn't been seen around Spencer in a while," she answered. "And the case against him is in the hands of federal investigators now. It could be a long time until we have a resolution." She smoothed her fingers over the pages of the book she held. "If he has the money, he'll probably have to pay it back. The money doesn't bother me."

"Because you have plenty."

"Even if I didn't have plenty. The problem is that you went behind my back, thinking to sell land that belongs to both of us."

"I understand why you got angry." Dorris muted the television. "The land means more to you. Your father always said you could be whatever you wanted and do whatever you liked, and he assured you the land would be here too. You had a lot of choices."

"I suppose I did. He wanted me to be happy."

Dorris set down the remote and flattened her palms on her knees. "Times were different for me. My father was..."

"What?"

"Disapproving," she said simply.

"Of you?" Audrey asked. "Or of your choices?"

"Basically me, probably because I wasn't a son. As his daughter, I didn't have the options you had. You weren't afraid of displeasing your father. You were the apple of his eye and had nothing to worry about."

"That must have been hard." Her mother's disclosure was the most she'd ever heard her say about her own father. "Did you displease him often?"

"Never dared."

"But you chose a kind, generous husband," Audrey mentioned. "That must have pleased him."

Dorris picked up her crossword puzzle book. "He definitely approved of Charlie Monroe."

Maybe the treatment her mother had experienced had something to do with her disapproval of Audrey. Shouldn't people strive to be better parents than the ones they'd had? Dorris wasn't the most stressful thing on her mind, though. That night Audrey barely slept, praying Christine hadn't said something to Jericho.

She gave herself a clay facial and showered early, dressed in jeans and boots and drove to the *Double T*. The sun was high and warm. The snow would be melting. She hadn't eaten or made coffee because her stomach was clenched with nerves. She had no idea how she was going to tell him what she knew already in her heart. She needed proof, and she needed Jericho to be part of the discovery, whatever it was.

Jericho opened the door as soon as the Escalade pulled up in front of his cabin. Audrey got out wearing sunglasses, the sun highlighting her pale hair, and made her way to the porch.

"Mornin'," he greeted her.

"Hey, Jericho."

Her pensive manner cautioned him. Was she having second thoughts about what had happened in Nashville? Or did yesterday's family gathering have something to do with what he was sensing? He opened the door and ushered her in, taking her coat.

"Would you like a cup of coffee?"

"Do you have tea?" she asked.

"I'll find some." He heated water in a pan on the stove. "Not very fancy. Don't have many tea drinkers visit." He set out a mug. "Is everything all right?"

She rubbed her palms together in an uncharacteristically nervous gesture. "I need to talk to you."

Once the water was hot, he dropped in a teabag, poured himself coffee and carried both mugs to the living room.

She glanced toward the fireplace.

"Are you cold? I can start a fire."

"No." She held up a hand to stop him. "No, don't—don't bother. Do you have to go to work?"

"Not until later. I took a shift tonight so one of the other deputies could travel this weekend. What's going on?"

She sat perched on the edge of the sofa, knees together, her fingers laced in her lap. She tucked her hair behind her ear, her telltale nervous gesture.

He waited. He could be patient, but he didn't like the tension.

"I have to tell you something, and I'm not sure how to say it."

"Just say it."

"There's already been so much misunderstanding between us…" When she locked her gaze on him, her deep blue eyes were filled with concerns he didn't understand.

He kept his expression impassive to encourage her.

"I'm embarrassed that for so long I blocked out something as important as that night we had together."

"Audrey, we already talked that out. I understand. You were grieving and then you felt guilty or embarrassed—or like our friendship had been damaged. At the time hooking up had to have seemed like a mistake. I was pretty messed up for a long time after that, but I'm over it now. You don't have to explain again."

"I'm not explaining this time." Her hands trembled.

She was scaring him. A hollow ache expanded in his gut. "What then?"

She looked away, but then back as though she was forcing herself to meet his eyes. "I think Hayden is yours."

The statement spoken barely over a ragged whisper echoed in his head as though she'd shouted it into a well. "What?" His brain conjured up images of the slender little girl with the big blue eyes and pale hair. Hayden teasing Audrey, asking him one of her questions with a serious expression…shyly talking to his dad yesterday… "What?" he asked again.

"I promise you I didn't realize." Audrey's face was paler than before. "When I got home after Daddy's funeral, I accepted Tucker's proposal. We were married immediately. When I knew I was pregnant I never questioned that the baby was his. Ever. She's blond—like me. She has blue eyes—like Wyatt. Tucker had brown hair and brown eyes, but I never questioned that she didn't look like him, because I had no reason to. I—I thought she took after me."

Her cheeks flushed and she looked at her hands. She glanced back up and leaned toward him. "Jericho, I'm so sorry. And—and I'm still not a hundred percent sure."

Jericho's thoughts were all over the place, and he struggled to pull them together. If her revelation was true, and Hayden was his, he'd missed eight years of her life. He got to his feet. "You think Hayden is mine?"

"I don't know for sure. But I think she is."

He rubbed his neck in frustration.

"I'm positive your mom noticed it right off...the way she looked at Hayden yesterday. The way she looked at me." She paused. "Did you tell her about us? About what happened all those years ago?"

"I didn't tell anyone about us," he answered absently. How much more could he take? He'd protected himself well, and as soon as he'd allowed a tiny crack in his armor, here she was with more. He could shield himself again. Not let her in. Not let anyone in. That felt safer. Alone was safe, but loneliness was a pain in itself.

The bright blue-eyed child was already firmly ensconced in his heart. The possibility that she could be his engaged so many emotions he couldn't keep up with the poignant tidal wave tossing his feelings and his thoughts into confusion.

Eight years. While he'd been filling the void of love, intimacy and belonging with work, Audrey had been raising his child.

"I told you so we could have a paternity test done," she said. "And know for sure."

He paced around the sofa. Yes, of course they'd need a paternity test.

"I understand if you're angry."

He held up a hand. "Give me a minute here. I'm reeling."

"I'm sorry."

"I guess if you could block out the fact that we had sex, you could block out the possibility that the child you were carrying might be mine."

"It wasn't fair to you," she said.

"No, it wasn't."

"I'm sorry," she said again.

He let himself look at her. He knew Audrey better than anyone. She hadn't left because he wasn't good enough for her, hadn't rejected him because he wasn't good enough. She hadn't even known how he felt about her at the time because he was Wyatt's friend—her friend.

She hadn't headed to Nashville because he wasn't talented enough or ambitious enough. She left to pursue her dream because she was focused and always had been.

He didn't harbor bad feelings toward her. He'd always been proud of her, but he'd been wounded all the same.

As he was wounded now.

"Stop being sorry." He held up a palm. "Just stop. We feel what we feel. And we do what we think is best at the time."

"I've hurt you more than once," she said.

"I know you well enough to know you did nothing maliciously."

He felt numb, almost as though this was happening to someone else. He detested the feeling of not being present. That's why he didn't drink much. He needed to feel in control, and this entire situation was cataclysmically out of his control.

He was going to need time to come to grips with this...*possibility*. It wasn't actually a fact yet. For now, he was going to have to shut down his feelings until he could get a handle on them. That was what he did. Disengaging came naturally.

Audrey sensed the change in Jericho's demeanor, and it terrified her. Her life had become a gigantic mess, and she had only herself to blame. Tears threatened. Her throat was tight from holding back regret and fear. Something inside her must be broken for her to have blocked out crucial truths, which now revealed were shaking their lives and futures. She wasn't malicious, she was broken. She would never intentionally hurt this man who held her heart.

Jericho strode into the kitchen and returned to hold out a box of tissues.

She plucked a few from the box, but she didn't cry.

He set down the box and sat across from her. "Of course, we'll do a paternity test. Together."

Matter-of-factly.

She nodded. She wanted him to take her in his arms, but needing his comfort was selfish. Her chest ached.

"If it's positive," he said. "Which you believe the test will be...how will we tell her?"

She looked at her hands and back up. "I don't know. Just tell her, I guess. Tucker is pretty much only a story to her. He was rarely around, never attentive."

"Did he know?"

She shook her head. "No. He couldn't have."

"It will still be shocking news," he said. "For everyone."

Audrey stared upward and took a shaky breath. "Everyone."

"You're a public figure. The facts of your life are out there for the world to see. How is this going to work?"

"I don't know." She wanted to reach for his hand, but an uncomfortable emotional distance yawned between them. "I really don't know."

He picked up his phone and checked online for a few minutes. "Looks like home tests are quick, but legally binding tests should be done in a medical facility. We'll want the test to be legal."

He was thinking clearly. Objectively. Not like how she felt inside. "Do you know a doctor you can trust?"

"Gage Ewing. I'll call his cell so I don't have to go through his receptionist."

After speaking to his friend, he ended the call. "Samples need to be collected by a non-biased authorized third party. He qualifies, and we can go in tomorrow. He said he could make it like a routine exam if you prefer Hayden not be suspicious. I'll go in at a different time. Results will take two, possibly three business days. He'll try to rush it."

"That was thoughtful of him to think of making the test seem routine." Audrey would know when she returned from Nashville. She'd already set her adjusted career plan in motion and was determined to make it work. "Okay. Thank you."

"I can't deny it, Audrey. If she's mine, I'll be wrecked over losing years with her. But I can't deny how much I want this to be real."

Her heart lifted in a moment of hope.

"I already love Hayden."

Bittersweet news. He wasn't hoping for them now. He was hoping because he wanted Hayden to be his. She was thankful Jericho loved her daughter. He would be a great father.

The tension between them frightened her. She wanted nothing as much as she wanted to press herself against him, feel his strong arms around her, and know everything was going to be all right between them. "Are we...are we going to be okay?"

"I need some time," was all he said.

Disappointment sank in her heart. She couldn't expect him overlook what she'd done and accept this without thought or question. He deserved better.

"Of course." She stood. "I'm flying to Nashville day after tomorrow to meet with Sidney and Cadence at Songbird Records. I've hinted to them about my plans, so they'll be prepared for our discussion on cutting tours to a bare minimum. I have contractual obligations with the label to record and promote, so we'll have to negotiate, and Cadence will plan how to spin the changes to the media."

"I know Hayden is happy about settling here," Jericho said.

"She's the reason I'm doing this."

"You'll miss that life."

"I won't miss hotels or the bus or constant traveling. I'll perform enough to keep me fresh and in the public eye, but not so much that I feel as though I don't have a home. Over the years our lives have become really small, and this is what I want now. I want to live in a community where Hayden and I have friends and family."

She didn't meet his eyes as she went for her coat, but it was there between them, the unspoken possibility of who Hayden's family might be.

"I'll text you Gage's number," he said. "Just let him know when you'll be at his office tomorrow."

She nodded.

"I'll go afterward, so he can send tests to the lab right away. They should be available when you get back."

She'd said all she knew to say. This awkwardness was new, and it felt awful. "Until I get back then."

He walked her as far as the wooden stairs. Heart aching, she got into her vehicle, pushed the starter and drove away. If she looked at the rearview mirror, she'd see him alone on the porch. He'd had plenty of practice watching her go.

After two days of going over the situation in his head, Jericho ate supper with his family and later told Bethel to go enjoy her evening. He joined his mother in the kitchen. His family had always been safe. They wouldn't or couldn't leave him. He trusted them and he didn't trust a lot of people. People disappointed.

His mother, always intuitive, glanced over from where she was loading the dishwasher. "Something bothering you?"

He washed out a pan, rinsed it under hot water and picked up a towel. "Yes."

She straightened and dried her hands. "This has to do with Audrey."

He nodded. "Obviously, we've been a thing the past few weeks."

"I picked up on that."

He proceeded to tell his mother what Audrey had told him the previous morning. Head down, he glanced up at her. "Are you shocked?"

"Definitely not now. But I was shocked the minute I saw Hayden come into our house on Thanksgiving. I knew in that instant she was yours. I didn't know you and Audrey had been that close."

"We weren't," he said. "Not then, I mean. After Charlie's funeral she was so sad. That's when it happened. Just the once. And then she took off for Nashville and married her manager."

"You don't have to explain. I'm not judging. Things happen. I'm relieved she recognized it and told you. I didn't want to be the one to say that little girl is your spitting image."

"You could have," he said.

"And I would have, but this is better."

"I feel cheated," he said. "If she's mine, and we're all sure she is, then I've missed all this time with her. I missed being her dad. And how will she react to finding out?"

Christine took her son's hand and led him over to the small table in front of windows that looked out over stables and pastures. She pulled a chair to sit near him and took his hand again. "I understand your pain. I can't imagine what it's like for you to learn this now. What it's like waiting for test results. I can only imagine how you feel about missing Hayden's childhood. But I do know what it's like to love an eight-year-old and a nine- and a ten-year-old, and what it will be like to see her in school plays and chorus and at swim meets or softball games or whatever she chooses to do.

"You have all of those years yet to go. Let yourself look ahead and not behind. I might be putting the horse ahead of the cart here, but if she's your daughter, you will see her graduate and one day walk her down the aisle."

He flattened his lips and nodded. "You're right. I have to change my thinking. Just because we don't have a past doesn't mean we don't have a future."

"Exactly. You can do anything you put your mind to. You always could. I never told you how much fun it was to see you with Audrey on that live Showcase Special." She grinned. "That was something I never thought I'd see."

"I never thought I'd do it. And someone would have to blackmail me to get me to do it again."

Christine laughed. She patted his hand and stood, going

back to the dishes. "Go ride or something. Blow the stink off."

That made him laugh. She had always said that to him and Wyatt and Judah to get them out of the house. He gave her a brief hug and headed for the back door.

Audrey's meetings went as well as could be expected. Songbird didn't give an inch on her minimum promotional efforts, but she had no desire to buy out her contract and had been prepared to agree to three brief tours a year for the next two years. After that her contract would be up for negotiation again. Songbird had option clauses on her next two albums as well, and she assured them the songs and recordings wouldn't be a problem. An idea had been dancing around in her head for several weeks, so she mentioned it to Sidney and Cadence at lunch after the meeting.

"I own hundreds of acres of land in Colorado," she told them. "Hayden and I have talked about building our own home. But there's something else nagging at me."

"What's that?" Sidney asked.

"A recording studio."

Sidney and Cadence looked at each other and back at her. Cadence set down her glass of wine. "That's an ambitious undertaking. How would you staff it?"

"Hire techs and sound editors. The thing is, I wouldn't have to absorb all the expense on my own if I made the studio available to other artists."

"How would that work?" Sidney asked. "It's a long way from Nashville."

"Which is the draw." Audrey leaned forward. "Spencer is a

tourist town with one of the most exclusive hotels in the country. Aspen Gold Lodge caters to celebrities with its tight security, amenities and dining. And the area is filled with summer and winter activities. Skiing, horseback riding, boating, fishing. I can think of half a dozen artists off the top of my head who'd love to bundle a fishing trip with a recording session."

"John Denver did it in the seventies and eighties with his Caribou Ranch Studio," Cadence agreed. "Michael Jackson and Billy Joel recorded there."

"John Lennon," Audrey added.

"You might just have something here," Sidney told her. "Want me look into specs on construction and requirements? Not exactly my forte, but I can check around, ask studios for insider tips. Maybe help find a contractor."

Audrey gave him a grateful smile. "I'd really appreciate it."

"Let's keep it just between us until the plans are firm— maybe until construction is underway," Sidney said.

"A studio will be impressive and we'll let the media know at the right time," Cadence agreed. "Not only did you think of a way to stay home and still record, you're diversifying your income streams." She lifted her glass in appreciation.

They toasted the idea.

"Now let's look at our schedules," Sidney suggested. "And see what we can get booked. I've already been approached for next year's Christmas special."

"I love doing those," Audrey agreed. "As long as I'm not gone over Thanksgiving or Christmas."

"They're filming in October," he assured her.

Audrey stayed the night in the enormous home that already had several offers. Being there reminded her of the night she'd spent with Jericho, and how optimistic she'd felt about the future. She packed personal items in her luggage and arranged to have the rest of her belongings packed and put in storage.

Hours after she arrived at *Big Pine,* Everly's plane landed at Mountain Jay Airport, so she and Hayden drove to pick her up. On the ride back to the ranch, Audrey told Everly that she was accepting an offer on the Nashville house and relayed the plans she'd laid out with Songbird Records.

"Spencer is our new home. If it's what we all think is best, I'll be building a house for us on the property. We'd like for you to stay if that's something you want. You can help us plan a guest bungalow for you. You can have time to think about it."

"I don't need time," Everly said from beside her. "Honestly, I wasn't looking forward to going back on the road, but I was prepared to if that's what you'd decided. This—staying here—sounds like the best plan I can imagine." She glanced back at Hayden. "I'm really thankful you guys are including me."

"You're our family," Audrey told her. "By all means we want you with us."

Everly gave Audrey a questioning look. "You have contractual obligations though?"

"Three tours a year, not long ones. About three weeks at a time. And the other thing…" She told Everly and Hayden her idea about the recording studio.

"That's pure genius," Everly told her.

A phone call from Jericho dinged on her dash. Audrey picked up her phone to take the call without the others hearing. "Hi, Jericho."

"I picked up the papers and am holding the envelope now. Can you meet me on the south side of Brook Park in an hour?"

Nerves jangled in Audrey's belly. "I'll be there."

She thumbed off the call, hoping to sound nonchalant.

"I'm meeting Jericho for coffee. Hayden, will you help Everly unpack and get settled until I return?"

"Sure, Mom. Bring us lemon pie if you go to Pearl's."

"Will do."

His voice had given nothing away. She didn't know if he'd already looked at the results or if he was waiting for her. Less than an hour, and she'd know the truth...if not her future.

# CHAPTER FIFTEEN

*a*udrey pulled in beside Jericho's slate gray Silverado Trail Boss, which was running. He got out carrying a manilla envelope, and she unlocked her passenger door so he could get in. His woody sandalwood scent carried to her, adding another layer of tension to her already turbulent emotions. "Did you look?" she asked.

"No. I waited." He held the envelope between them.

"Open it," she prompted.

He turned it over, his long fingers steady and competent, pinched the brad and opened the flap. He paused fractionally, revealing he wasn't as calm as he appeared, then slid out the papers.

A header stated the name of the laboratory and its address, beneath it a chart. Audrey leaned toward him to get a closer look. The columns were divided into two sections labeled 'child' and 'alleged father'. On the left was a list of numbers, apparently codes for DNA strands or something, and in the 'child' and 'alleged father' columns were two-digit numbers. Red circles were drawn around matching numbers.

To the far right was a column of green checkmarks on every single line.

Audrey's heart beat so hard and fast Jericho had to have heard it.

At the bottom she read:

Combined Paternity Index: 533, 475
Probability of Paternity: 99.9998%

Jericho read the rest of the interpretation of the genetic testing without comprehending much more than the 99.9998% assurance that Hayden was his daughter. He laid the papers on the console and stared out the side window. The snow had melted, but the ground was frozen, the park a bleak shadow of its summer lushness. None of it was dead however. The plant life lay dormant, waiting for a resuscitating breath of Spring, for life-giving sun and rain. In a few months the grass would grow in green, the bushes renew themselves with buds. Seasons passed and there was always the promise of what lay ahead. Maybe he'd been dormant, too, life just under the surface, too afraid to feel.

Hayden was his child. Did he dare feel this? There was no guarantee they were staying.

He looked over at Audrey.

Her deep blue-grey eyes held an uncertainty that pained him. He felt her regret. Shared it.

"Now we know." Her voice was barely above a whisper.

"Now we know," he agreed.

She pursed her lips for a second. "There's nothing I can say."

"You don't have to say anything. You've said it all. I'm—I'm struggling to know what to feel."

"Are you angry with me? Disappointed?"

He gave a negative shake of his head. "No. I'm just…"

*Terrified. Scared I'll open my heart to love you both and lose you.*
"I'm not mad at you, Audrey."

She reached for his hand where it rested on his thigh, and
her fingers were surprisingly cold. He glanced at her dash
and turned the temperature higher, then engulfed both of
her hands in his, rubbed them, brought them to his lips and
exhaled warm breath. She was scared too. Scared he'd blow
up. Maybe scared about their families' reactions. Maybe
scared to tell Hayden.

She withdrew her hands to lean over and wrap her arms
around his neck. The embrace was awkward because of their
coats and the console between them, but her cheek against
his, the scent of her hair comforted him. He was a grown-ass
man afraid of being hurt by this woman who'd been in his
blood since he was old enough to know the difference
between boys and girls.

Jericho bracketed her head with both hands and kissed
her hard. She expelled sharp breath in a half-groan, half sob
that instantly burned up against his lips. He had enough
sense to dial back the heat and finesse a string of kisses
across her lips and chin, along her jaw until reaching her ear
and whispering *"'Your eyes say one more kiss. What I want is one
more kiss.'"*

She drew back and met his eyes with a smile. "It was
always good between us. I made it awkward, and I didn't
mean to."

"I know." He kissed her tenderly. "You did something you
loved. Followed through. A lot of people go through life
without the courage to go for their dream. You made your
dream happen and I've always been proud of you."

When she placed her fingertips along his jaw, they had
warmed. "And you? Have you been happy with the ranch and
your deputy job? That was what you wanted."

"Living and working on the ranch has been satisfying. My

position in the RCSD is rewarding. It's what I wanted to do."
Having her *and* those things hadn't been possible, but he
didn't have regrets.

She laced their fingers together. "Maybe we can have it all
now."

"Maybe." Until she needed more. "Are you going to tell
Hayden?"

"I've stayed awake nights thinking about that. We can't
not tell her. Do you think we should do it together?"

"Whatever you think is best for her," he replied.

She nodded. "Let's give ourselves a few days to think
on it."

"Okay."

She leaned in for a parting kiss.

Jericho left the manilla envelope on the seat when he got
out of the Escalade. He got into his truck, which was still
running and raised a hand in farewell. Things were okay
between them. Not settled, but okay. There was an ocean of
feeling, none of it defined or declared. He had no idea how
this was going to play out.

But he wasn't going to make the same mistake twice.

The Winter Festival had been underway since the first week
in December, an event locals and tourists alike enjoyed.
Dorris agreed to join Audrey, Everly and Hayden, so they
bundled in warm coats, hats and mittens and met the
Tanners at the entrance to the fairgrounds. Christine was
insistent they first see the snow sculptures, so they made
their way through the crowd toward the pavilions which
held food vendors. An enormous area beside the tents and

small buildings featured row after row of gigantic sculptures, each cordoned off with a low metal fence.

"I had no idea they'd be so big!" Audrey stared in awe at a twenty-foot sparkling white gorilla seated on a rock, reaching down to pull up her baby.

"Aren't they wonderful?" Christine wore dark sunglasses, and Audrey immediately drew hers from her bag to prevent glare. "Many of the same competitors enter each year, but the sculptures are always new and ingenious."

Atwood had his phone in hand. He and Christine had been lavishing attention on their newfound granddaughter. "Hayden, stand in front of the fence so I can get a picture of you."

Hayden grinned, her cheeks already pink from the cold, her joy obvious as she posed in her striped stocking hat and puffy pink coat.

Audrey's throat tightened with emotion. She glanced at Jericho and caught barely revealed pride and pleasure in his expression.

"Let's get a photo of all the girls in front of this whale." Bethel pointed with a fuzzy blue mitten.

The whale had been sculpted with its mouth gaping wide, and deep in its belly was a rowboat with a fisherman in a hat and life jacket. "This sculpture looked so simple at first glance," Audrey commented. "But look at the amazing detail —even the man's surprised face. How in the world did they get the fisherman and boat inside?"

"Probably made it first and then sculpted the whale around it," Atwood said.

She gave him a sheepish glance. "Well, duh."

Audrey and the other females stood where it appeared the whale was swallowing them. Even Jericho had his phone out for that shot. He showed it to Hayden, and she grinned up at him.

A minute later, Hayden spotted Brinlee and her parents, and the two girls hugged delightedly. Audrey hadn't met Brinlee's dad, so she introduced herself, and chatted a minute.

She caught up with the others who had moved on along the row of sculptures.

"Just like a local," Jericho commented with a grin. "Running into friends."

His remark pleased her immeasurably. A few months ago, she'd set out determined to blend herself into the community, and it seemed she'd made headway.

Later however, as they stood in front of a food truck, waiting for hotdogs, two twenty-something girls spotted Audrey and asked for selfies. She gave Jericho a shrug and stood between the young women with a smile as they attempted to get the three of them in the pic.

"May I?" Jericho reached for one of the girls' phones and snapped a couple pics for them.

"You're the best!" The two thanked them and moved on.

"They recognize you even in sunglasses," Dorris said.

Jericho gave a shrug. "It's gonna happen."

Audrey nodded. "It's okay. No one I've met in Spencer has been pushy or rude. It's part of the job."

Dorris bought Hayden a funnel cake and watched her granddaughter try it. Her face lit up at the child's enjoyment. So many people loved Hayden. Audrey had been making the right choices. Bringing her here had absolutely been the best thing she could have done for her daughter.

Dorris' gaze traveled to Atwood and Christine, where they stood together sipping hot chocolate. Her expression changed swiftly, and she looked away.

Perhaps seeing the couple together reminded her of what she'd lost. Audrey experienced a moment of sympathy. Her mom was often critical and difficult, but her behavior must come from a place of unhappiness. Unhappy people made others unhappy.

"There are Paralympic competitions to watch," Bethel commented. The fellow from Puppy Love Dog Rescue is competing in a torch relay that should be starting in a few minutes. Is it okay if Hayden and Everly and I go check that out?"

"Sure," Audrey responded with a quick smile. "We'll find you later."

Dorris walked ahead with Judah and his parents. Jericho glanced around and took Audrey's mittened hand.

"It's okay if someone sees us," she said. "I'm not hiding anything."

"Neither am I."

"I'm organizing a Christmas party at the senior center this coming week if you want to come by."

"Need the law to keep residents from partying too hard?" he asked.

She bumped his shoulder with hers. "Not in an official capacity, dork."

He laughed.

She turned his wrist and slid back his coat sleeve to look at his watch. "The Madrigals from Spencer High are going to perform at two if you want to see that."

"I wouldn't miss it." He leaned down to give her a quick kiss.

"I saw that!" Bethel called, waving from where she stood on a bench fifty feet away. "I'm selling the pic to the *Enquirer*!"

He gave her a dismissive wave in return. "Just so she doesn't sell it to Edith. I have a hard enough time going into Pearl's without catcalls these days."

Alone together he and Audrey enjoyed the activities and met up with the family again later that afternoon. His folks went to find coffee, and Judah and Bethel wanted to watch more of the competitions.

Hayden took Audrey's hand. "Look, there's a cupcake booth inside!"

"That's Cookie's Cupcakes," Jericho told her. The two of them followed her lead toward the booth where a sign read 'buche de noel cupcakes.' They were cream-filled chocolate cupcakes with a mini frosting log on top.

There were a few benches, so they sat and enjoyed their confections. The three of them felt very much like a family today, and Jericho liked the feeling. Seeing Hayden enjoy herself gave him pleasure.

After purchasing cupcakes, a couple with a baby in a stroller pushed the infant a few feet away, still under the protection of the tent. Dressed like everyone else in a warm coat and stocking cap, the dad fed the baby a taste of frosting on his finger. Both parents laughed when the baby's eyes widened and she smacked her lips.

Watching them, Jericho's pleasure dimmed for a moment. He'd missed all the firsts with Hayden. Holding a newborn, changing diapers, walking the floor at night, things parents didn't appreciate at the time, but treasured forever.

Hayden's voice cut through his thoughts. "Would you rather have one giant birthday cake or a hundred cupcakes shaped into a cake?"

He licked frosting from his lip and glanced at Audrey. Had she seen his reaction to the couple with the baby? She wiped her fingers on a napkin.

"That's a really difficult choice," he said. "I like cake and I like cupcakes. But with cupcakes there's a lot of peeling off the paper and I'd have to eat two or three to get my fill. A cupcake is perfect for a day like this, but for my birthday, I'd for sure take a giant cake."

"Me too," Hayden said. "Good choice."

He remembered his mom's words about looking ahead and not behind. He'd missed the beginning of her life, but he was here with Hayden now, and he wanted to be here for her in the years to come. Of course, nothing was certain about how she'd react or how he and Audrey would work things out between them.

Snow fell the day of the party at the senior center. Audrey packed their baked goods in the back of her vehicle and ushered Hayden, her mom and Everly through the falling flakes to buckle in for the ride to town.

The social director was waiting for them, having prepared the dining room by arranging tables and chairs and lining additional folding tables draped with red plastic along the wall. Other helpers brought the piano from the music room while Everly and Hayden hung paper snowflake streamers from the ceiling.

Audrey had ordered enough poinsettias for each resident and staff member to take one after the party. A dozen family members showed up to help with decorations and games, and before two o'clock Jericho and Sheriff Cavanaugh joined them in uniform. Joe and Ben Rumford were long-time acquaintances, and the two engaged a table of seniors with their fishing stories.

Thelma Beardsley latched onto Jericho and told him all about her granddaughter, Francie, who was now engaged and would be coming to visit over the holiday. She had a photo of Francie in the pocket of her wheelchair, and proudly showed it to anyone who would stop and chat.

While the gathering enjoyed their treats and hot chocolate, Jericho surprised Audrey by producing his guitar and accompanying Peggy who played and sang carols on the unexpectedly well-tuned upright piano. It had been a long time since Audrey had joined in an impromptu sing-along, and it pleased her immeasurably that the others treated her as though she was another amateur simply here for the fun and enjoyment.

Dorris had joined two ladies and their visitors putting together a jigsaw puzzle, and seeing her mom participating warmed Audrey's heart.

Sometime later, Audrey sat with Buddy and Ben Rumford, while they reminisced about old times. "You and Jericho aren't the only talent in Spencer. Ben here played mighty fine tunes on his fiddle back in the day," Buddy told her, jabbing a thumb toward his friend.

Ben grinned. "Me 'n some of the other fellas used to play for Saturday night dances," he said.

"I wish I could've heard you play," Audrey said. "What kind of songs were your favorites?"

"Oh, we played Sam Cooke, Bobby Daren, Everly Brothers. I had a solo in *All I Have to Do is Dream*."

"I love that song," Audrey said.

"So did your mama," Buddy said. "She and Atwood always requested that one for the last song of the night."

"You must mean my daddy, Charlie," Audrey corrected. Buddy must still get confused sometimes.

"No, not back then," Buddy said. "Your mama and Atwood were always together."

Ben nodded. "Since high school," he agreed.

Audrey sat back and let their confident agreement sink into her thinking. "What about my daddy?"

"Dorris married Charlie maybe a year after that," Ben said and looked to Buddy for confirmation. He winked. "I reckon parents don't tell their youngin's about old beaus."

"I reckon not." If one of the paper snowflakes overhead fell on her, she'd be knocked off her chair. Her mother and Atwood Tanner? She tried to imagine that, but couldn't. Neither she or Jericho would even exist if those two had married each other.

Sandwiches were served, and Audrey sat between Thelma and another woman, deliberately not thinking of her mother with Jericho's father. Hayden and a girl of about twelve carried trays and gave the seniors their choices of cookies.

She joined the staff in pouring coffee and seeing that the residents had cream or sugar. Jericho was seated with two silver-haired ladies who were asking him all about the television show he was on. His ruddy complexion showed his discomfort, and Audrey rescued him by asking him to help her gather trash.

In the kitchen, she faced him. "Have you ever heard anyone say that your father and my mother were a thing in high school?"

He emptied paper cups from a tray into a plastic trash can. "Seems I remember seeing prom pictures in one of my parents' year books. I'd forgotten about it."

"Seriously? You didn't think it was weird?"

"I guess not. It was never a secret. Nearly everyone dates other people before they find the one they marry. You went to prom with Kipp Hudson."

"Because we were friends and agreed to go together so we didn't have to go alone. It wasn't romantic."

He shrugged and rinsed off the tray in an enormous stainless-steel sink.

She filled an air pot with fresh coffee. "Who did you go to prom with?"

"LeAnn Abbott."

"The *mortuary* girl?"

"The Abbots own a funeral home. She's not a mortuary girl."

"Were you dating her?"

"No. We just went to prom together."

"Oh."

"You're thrown because your folks dated other people?"

"I don't know. I guess it bothers me that I never knew before."

"Yeah, not knowing stuff sucks."

She stopped wiping off the air pot to look at him.

"I didn't mean it that way," he said.

"I know. Forget I said anything."

They joined the gathering again. The social director thanked them for the best Christmas party ever, and they helped clean up while the residents were taken to the common area for the rest of the afternoon.

"A day like this makes a big difference for our residents," the director told them.

Dorris showed up with their empty plastic containers, so Audrey and Hayden said their goodbyes to Jericho, and headed home.

That evening after Dorris had gone to bed, Audrey searched the cabinet with the photo albums to find high school yearbooks. She came across hers first, then her parents'. She carried a couple into the kitchen and sat at the table with a glass of wine. Using the student index in the back, she found her mother's maiden name and a few page numbers.

Her mom was indeed a beauty, with long blond hair, winged brows and a beautiful smile. Audrey had seen the graduation photo many times. The same one sat in a frame on her father's desk. In the prom photos, as Buddy had said, was a picture of Dorris and Atwood. Dorris wore a spaghetti strap formal with layers of ruffles, her feet in pointy-toed heels. Dressed in a tux, Atwood had jet black hair and a youthful hundred-watt smile. They posed for the camera with their cheeks pressed together. She stared at the photo.

More curious than ever, Audrey flipped, not finding her father. He'd been a year older, she remembered, so she located him in a different book. Her heart ached at the images of her beloved father, smiling, looking young and so very alive. His prom date was someone she didn't recognize, pretty enough, but not Dorris.

After briefly perusing the yearbooks, she put them away and got out the album of her parents' wedding photos. All the typical poses, bride and groom with their parents, with the wedding party, a shot of their hands and the wedding rings. She only recognized a few people. Like Jericho had said, it wasn't unusual for anyone to date several people before marrying, so why did the thought of her mother with Atwood bug her so much?

After breakfast the following morning while Hayden practiced guitar in her room, Audrey brought up the subject with her mom.

"Yes, we were together in high school," Dorris said.

"I'm curious, Mom, because I never knew that before."

Dorris rinsed out the coffee pot. "Well, it doesn't matter now. Shall I start another pot?"

"Let's do decaf this time," Audrey answered.

Her mom filled the pot and measured grounds. While the coffee brewed, she came to the table where Audrey sat and took a chair. "How well do you remember your grandparents? Not your father's parents, but mine."

Surprised at the question, Audrey replied, "They lived in Glen Haven before they lived here."

"That's right. My father was the postmaster in Glen Haven until we moved to Spencer just before I went to high school. We didn't have much, and I didn't dress nice like the other girls. Your grandpa was a stern man and ruled our house. My mother never questioned his authority, and I learned not to."

Audrey got up and poured coffee. It was uncharacteristic for her mother to speak so openly. "That must have been hard."

"I met Atwood at school when I was in tenth grade. I didn't tell my parents because my father wouldn't have approved. I'd never met anyone like him. I don't remember him ever saying an unkind word or being a smart aleck like the other boys in our classes. His folks had the *Double T*, but it wasn't as big as it is now. Atwood had aspirations for law enforcement."

"And he became sheriff," Audrey said.

"Back then, *Big Pine Ridge* was the largest ranch in the county—probably in several counties, and Grandpa Monroe was the richest rancher, had the most stock and the best land. Your father was heir to all that."

Audrey nodded, wondering where this was going.

"My father found out I'd gone to dinner and prom with Atwood, and he forbade me to see him again."

Having had the kindest father imaginable, Audrey had trouble comprehending an edict like that. "What would have happened if you'd defied him?"

"I tried it once. He locked me in my room and hit my mother because she hadn't been keeping watch over me."

Stunned, Audrey stared at the woman sitting across from her. Her father's treatment sounded barbaric, like a villain in a suspense movie. "Oh, Mom."

Dorris looked away and straightened the front of her cardigan, drawing in a breath. "I was ashamed. And I was eighteen. My choices were limited. Run away and have him come after me—or worse, hurt my mother...or end it with Atwood. Which is what I did."

"But your father let you see Daddy?"

Dorris' expression showed her reluctance to go on.

Audrey placed her hand over her mother's. "It's okay. You can tell me."

"The Monroes were the wealthiest ranchers in the area, and your Grandpa Monroe was respected. On the city council, head of the rancher's association. My father told me to do whatever it took to get Charlie to marry me."

Audrey let this story soak in. It explained so much. And yet raised even more questions. "Daddy was a kind man too."

"Yes, he was."

"He loved you very much."

"Yes, he did."

"He was the safe choice...for you and your mom." Audrey swallowed hard. "Did you ever love him?"

Dorris' hand trembled under hers. She pursed her lips before speaking. "He earned every bit of my respect. In so many ways. He even helped out my parents, which of course was what my father was gunning for all along. Your father was a big man. Big in character, big of heart, reliable, determined...forgiving."

"I've never heard you say anything bad about him."

She shook her head. "He gave me everything he could. He wanted to make me happy."

"Did he?"

Dorris took a minute before replying. "I don't think I ever realized what I had, because I was so resentful about what I didn't have."

"You said before I had more choices than you had," Audrey remembered.

"You were your father's darling girl. Whatever made you happy, whatever you wanted, he wanted for you."

Audrey's eyes stung with tears. So why hadn't her mother been happy about that? Audrey always felt as though Dorris resented her father's love for her. Hadn't she wanted better for Audrey than she'd had herself? This story explained everything except that.

*We don't always get what we want. We all do things we don't want to do.* All the cryptic things her mother had said over the years made sense now.

For whatever reason, Wyatt had been her favorite, and his death had aggravated her criticism of Audrey.

This was the most honest her mother had ever been with her. She needed more, but she wasn't going to push Dorris beyond what she was prepared to say. "Thank you for telling me."

Dorris nodded.

Audrey had something huge to tell her daughter too. The longer she waited, the more problematic it would become. She should tell her mom now while the atmosphere was clear between them.

"I have something to tell you too, Mom."

# CHAPTER SIXTEEN

*I want pictures,* Jericho had texted her that afternoon. She'd known exactly what he meant, so she unpacked a couple of Hayden's baby books and put them in an oversized handbag. She and Hayden were going to Jericho's for supper.

*"I always wanted you to choose him,"* her mother had said upon learning the news the day before. But unlike her own father, Dorris had left Audrey to her own decisions.

Hayden brought along her guitar case, obviously planning some learning time. Maybe they'd get to that.

Jericho met them at the door. Sully stood behind him, tail wagging. The cabin smelled of the garlic bread and pasta sauce he'd prepared.

"This is your dog?" Hayden asked.

"That's Sully. Sully, high five."

The dog sat and raised a paw.

Grinning, Hayden touched his paw, then petted his head. "He sure is smart."

"He'll show you more tricks later, okay?"

"Sure." She stood and looked around. I love your cabin!" she squealed. "Did you build this by yourself?"

"Not entirely by myself. I had a lot of help, but I designed it."

"It's so cool." She set her guitar case on the floor under where his row of instruments hung and went to kneel before the crackling fire. "Where did you get all these rocks?"

"I dug several out of the ground while excavating, but I bought the rest. You like the fireplace?"

"I love it. I would bring a sleeping bag and sleep right here."

He grinned. "I admit I've fallen asleep on the sofa here a few times."

Audrey conjured up an image of Jericho casually napping on the sofa in his comfortable home and smiled.

"Dinner's ready," he said, and gestured for them to take seats. There had only been two chairs in the kitchen last time, but a third had been placed at the table.

"I didn't know you could cook," Hayden said, opening her napkin in her lap.

"I'm adequate," he said. "I eat meals with my folks a couple of times a week, and sometimes I grab food in town on my way home. I usually eat breakfast or lunch at Pearl's."

"I love Pearl's," Hayden said.

"It's the place to hear what's going on in town, but better than that is the great food," he agreed. "Edith makes an unrivaled Swiss steak. And Marty's chili?" He rolled his eyes skyward, took individual salads from the refrigerator then dished up flat bowls of spaghetti and meatballs.

Hayden immediately picked up her fork. "This is my favorite."

Audrey's child dug in, and Audrey observed the pleasure on Jericho's face. She'd provided meals for Hayden since her birth, but cooking for his daughter was a big deal for him. The pasta was mouthwateringly delicious.

"We all eat garlic bread," Jericho insisted, holding out the basket.

Audrey gave a half laugh, took a slice and bit into the crusty bread.

Once they'd finished and cleared the dishes, her heart skipped a few beats. She met Jericho's eyes, and he nodded. He pointed to the living room.

It seemed fitting that they tell Hayden in the same place where she'd told him.

"Don't you have a TV?" Hayden asked.

"It comes up out of that cabinet," he replied.

"Can I see?"

"Let's talk first," Audrey suggested. We have something important to tell you."

"Okay." Hayden took a seat on the sofa and glanced from one of them to the other, waiting. "You both look serious. Is anything wrong?"

"No, honey. You know Jericho and I were friends for a long time," Audrey began.

"Yep. He played his guitar for you at fairs and stuff."

"Right. And then I left for Nashville and came back to visit a few times. There's something I didn't know until only a week ago."

Hayden's wide blue eyes showed curiosity and more than a hint of concern. "What?"

Audrey's stomach lurched. She worked to keep her voice even. "Jericho is your father. Your biological father."

Hayden blinked. Then frowned. "But what about Daddy?"

"I believed all along he was your father," Audrey told her. "But when we got here, and I saw Jericho again, along with his sister and family, I realized you looked like them. So, remember the day we went to Dr, Ewing's office, and he rubbed a cotton swab inside your cheek?"

Hayden nodded.

"That was a DNA test. When the laboratory compared it to Jericho's DNA, it showed you are his child."

Hayden looked from her mom to Jericho. Her eyes filled with tears. "So, Daddy didn't know either?"

"None of us did. It wasn't a we kept secret from you," Audrey said. "I made a big mistake."

"And I'm not upset at all," Jericho said. "In fact, I'm really happy—and proud too."

Silent tears ran down Hayden cheeks. Leaning forward, she put her hands over her face and sobbed.

"Baby, it's okay." Audrey slid to her knees and wrapped an arm around Hayden's shoulders. This was a shock and the unexpected changes in Hayden's reality must be frightening. "I'm sorry this is such a big surprise. I never meant to hurt you—or to hurt anyone. I really didn't know."

Glancing up, she read Jericho's distress. He obviously felt helpless to do anything, and Hayden's anguish was all her doing.

Raising her head, Hayden lowered her hands from her face. "I-I'm not hurt," she said, her voice catching. "I'm n-not mad a-at a-anybody."

"Baby, you're crying so hard," Audrey said on a sob of her own.

"I'm h-happy," Hayden managed. "My wish i-in the f-fountain that day you gave me the pennies…" She looked up at Audrey, then over at Jericho. "I wished for a—for a family —and a dad." She reached for Jericho.

He took her hand and immediately moved to perch beside her. Hayden climbed onto his lap and curled up like a baby.

He smoothed her fair hair, pressed his lips to the top of

her head, and his eyes met Audrey's. She could barely see him through her tears, so she swiped them with her sleeve and only then made out the stream of tears on his cheeks.

"I have a dad," Hayden said softly against his chest. Then she pulled back and looked up at him. "Are you happy I'm your kid?"

He looked into her eyes and gave her an adoring smile. "I couldn't be any happier or prouder that you're my kid."

Once Hayden had calmed and they'd all dried their tears, Audrey did her best to clarify things in terms an eight-year-old would understand. Hayden seemed satisfied with the explanation.

Audrey took the baby book and photo album from her bag, and the three of them sat together and talked about all the memories and milestones Audrey had recorded.

"Thank you for having these," Jericho said.

Determined not to cry again, she gave him a watery smile. "You're welcome. And I want you to have them now."

"But they're yours," he said.

"I have the memories. The least I can offer you are these. Someday you'll give them to Hayden."

"Thank you." His voice was thick and he cleared his throat. He rubbed the cover of the album with a palm, then glanced up. "What did you bring that guitar for?" He spoke to Hayden. "We gonna sit here blubbering all night or play some music? Let's celebrate."

She grinned. "Play some music!"

The next few days Jericho used every opportunity to spend time with Hayden. He took her to breakfast on his day off and coached her guitar playing in the evenings. Last night he'd been at their place to tell her goodnight. Hayden's delight was obvious. She had the love and attention of a father for the first time.

The next day, a courier brought papers for Audrey to sign and return. The Nashville house was sold. The attorney had sold her car as well. Her belongings had been delivered to a climate-controlled storage facility in Spencer. She called Jericho to tell him the news.

"So, it's done," he said.

"It's official," she answered. "I don't live in Tennessee anymore."

"Now what?" he asked.

She sensed he was holding back. "Now, I guess I'd better call Sidney and see what he's figured out about a studio. Who shall I call about building construction?"

"Dagleish Construction. I'll text you the phone number. Are you talking a house or the studio?"

"I was talking about the studio. I don't want to rush into the house." Things had been a little strained between the two of them, which was probably normal, considering the tense situations they'd been through recently. Things were great between him and their daughter, but they hadn't talked about what was next for them. If anything.

"I was going to call you," he said.

"About what?"

"There's a Christmas party at the Wild Card. Will you go with me?"

Her heart lifted. "Like a date?" she asked.

"Like a date."

"I'd love to," she answered. "When is it?"

"The twentieth."

"Looking forward to it."

"Okay," he said. "I'll talk to you later."

"Bye." She touched off the call with her thumb.

She allowed herself a twinge of excitement and was glad she'd let Gianna talk her into sending a trunk of dresses and boots to the ranch. She'd packed a red dress that would be perfect.

She found Hayden in her room, where she had everything that had been in her drawers stacked on the bed. She was wearing a pink T-shirt tucked into a floral skirt with knee socks and no shoes.

"That's cute. What are you doing?"

"I'll be starting school after Christmas break, so I'm looking at all my clothes."

"Want to show me?"

"Okay." Hayden used the bathroom as a changing room and emerged time after time in a different outfit. A long-sleeved black T-shirt and short pleated houndstooth skirt was Audrey's favorite, buy Hayden didn't seem pleased. "Which shoes will you wear with that?"

Hayden produced black loafer-like shoes with a gold chain across the top.

"I don't remember those."

"I've had them, but they were too big. Now they fit."

Hayden sat on the side of the bed, her expression showing concern. "I just want everybody to like me."

"They're not going to like you because of your clothes," Audrey told her. "Annabelle and June and Brinlee like you because you're fun to hang out with. Because you're smart and funny. They would like you if you wore a potato sack."

"Like a potato chip bag? Eww."

"No, like a feed sack. Burlap, like—never mind. Wear what makes you happy and what you feel comfortable in."

"Annabelle wears jeans sometimes."

"I wear jeans all the time."

"Yeah, but yours are…" She stopped and looked sheepishly at her mom.

Audrey figured out what Hayden was stressing over. The other girls probably had nice clothes, but most likely wore less expensive outfits. "I get it. We'll buy you some jeans at one of the stores in Spencer. Go on a little shipping trip. How would that be?"

"Can Everly come?"

"Of course."

"I can wear my leggings for school."

"Okay."

"Maybe I could get some tie-dye shirts."

"Sure. Or we could make some."

"You can make them?"

Audrey laughed. "They're called tie-dye because you fasten knots with rubber hands and dip them in dye."

"Oh my gosh, that sounds so cool." Hayden hopped up and ran to the doorway. "Everly!"

Her nanny showed up with ear buds dangling around her neck. "Need something?"

"We're going to tie-dye shirts!"

"That sounds like fun."

Audrey left them chattering and found her mom putting away laundry in her room. She sat in an upholstered swivel chair and glanced around. The room looked much as it always had. On Dorris' dresser was a photograph of a black-haired teen, and for a minute Audrey wondered why her mom had a picture of Jericho.

She got up slowly, and as she neared realized the image was obviously of Wyatt. Audrey picked it up and touched the glass with a fingertip, remembering his teasing smile, his laugh. She smiled.

No wonder so many people had asked if they were brothers. Both had that thick black hair that curled around their ears when it got too long. Both had bright blue eyes that sparkled with mischief. Both resembled...

Audrey turned and looked at her mother. Dorris met Audrey's gaze with obvious discomfort. And there it was... the truth. She'd always been a little too quick to say, 'he looks like my father' when anyone had mentioned the resemblance. But did Wyatt look like Dorris' father? Not that Audrey could remember. And him looking like her maternal grandfather should have been a problem with as many issues as Dorris had with the man.

But Wyatt had been the apple of her eye. She'd lavished him with attention and always spoken encouragingly to him and kindly about him. He hadn't been on the receiving end of criticism or harsh tones. Wyatt had been...her love child.

# CHAPTER SEVENTEEN

*W*yatt had been born two years after Audrey. Dorris sat on the bed.

"Did Daddy know?" Audrey asked. If her mother was going to deny it, this would be another horrible conversation.

"We never spoke of it."

Dorris' admission in those few words came as a relief. "But he had to have known."

"If he did, he didn't want to talk about it."

"And you didn't apologize." She'd never heard an apology from her mother. In some warped way she understood her mother's motivation now though. She'd loved Atwood. He'd been the man she couldn't have. "What about Atwood? Did he know?"

"He asked me once. I was too angry with him, too hurt to give him the satisfaction of an answer."

"How did it happen?"

"It was me. I went to him. But then he said he'd made a terrible mistake. He loved Christine. He begged her forgiveness and she forgave him. They already had Judah. I found out I was pregnant about the same time they learned she was pregnant with Jericho."

So Christine knew what had happened. She must have suspected Wyatt was Atwood's. Or she'd been certain, seeing as how she'd intuitively recognized Hayden's parentage right off.

"And our two families stayed close all those years? Holidays and barbecues. That had to have been awkward."

"You know Christine."

"I do."

"She had Atwood. He loved her. Maybe she knew how lucky she was. Maybe she knew Wyatt was his and wanted her husband to see him. I don't know. But she never treated me poorly."

Surprisingly, Audrey felt no anger. Only a deep sadness for her mother—for her dad as well. His love for Dorris had been obvious. Maybe her mom would answer this time. "Did you ever love Daddy?"

She looked up. "I loved him."

But she hadn't been in love with him. "I can almost understand," Audrey told her. "Grandpa made you marry a man you didn't love. You messed up, but I guess you made the best of it. At least I know why you loved Wyatt more than me."

Dorris leaned forward as though in pain. and her shoulders shook. She reached for a box of tissues on her nightstand. "It's not that I didn't love you, Audrey." She met her daughter's eyes. "I know I was hard on you. But I wanted more for you. I wanted you to marry someone you loved. I always thought that person would be Jericho."

Atwood's son. Had that been a factor in wanting Audrey to marry him? "If I ever felt that way about him, I probably denied it because we were friends, because he was Wyatt's friend." *Brother actually.*

"I was angry with myself. I was manipulated into a marriage I didn't want."

"And I was the result."

"I love you, Audrey. I wasn't a perfect mother, but I'm proud of you. You did it all in spite of me."

Well, that part was true. "You've never said that before."

"You were brave enough to move away from home and go after what you wanted. I wasn't that brave."

"I had more choices, remember? Daddy supported me."

"But it was brave. I was never brave. You made your own way, earned your own money. Look at you."

"You earned your share of the ranch, Mom. I remember you helping cut hay and cooking for crews. I remember you as Daddy's right hand. We own this land together."

"That's how you remember your childhood?"

Well, that and her father supporting her 4-H projects and coming to hear her sing, while Dorris only attended swim and track meets. "Some of it."

"I'm sorry I disappointed you," Dorris said. "I know I did. Charlie was right to love you so much. You deserved all the love."

Audrey's throat tightened with conflicting emotions: Grief, rejection, sympathy, regret. She swallowed hard and inhaled deeply. "I forgive you. For all of it."

Dorris stood and Audrey met her in a conciliatory embrace. A few minutes later, her mother leaned away and wiped Audrey's cheek with her thumb. "Thank you."

Audrey smiled at her. "Thank you. For helping me understand."

Dorris took a step toward her laundry basket. "I've been thinking about what I want. When you and Hayden talked about building your own house, you took me into consideration. I know what I want though."

"What is it?" Audrey asked.

"I want to stay here on my own. I'd like to start riding again. I haven't ridden for years. And I'd like to get a dog."

"Well, that all sounds very easy to accommodate," Audrey told her. "You're not even sixty yet. There are a lot of things you can do. You could make friends, play cards or scrapbook or travel."

"One thing at a time." Dorris actually grinned.

"I've run an ad and have been interviewing for a financial manager for the ranch. We talked about that."

Dorris nodded, hopefully conceding a last. "Anyone promising?"

"Yes, one is very promising but I need to run him passed you."

"Okay."

"Judah Tanner."

Her mom looked at her with surprise. "Judah?"

"He's perfect, actually. He has handled *Double T* finances with Atwood for nearly ten years. He's close, trustworthy… he's like family."

"If I recall he has some sort of business degree," Dorris said.

Audrey nodded. "And knows all the workings of a ranch, his contacts are almost all the same as ours, knows the suppliers, breeders. I think with his help and by hiring several hands, we could have *Big Pine* operating the way it used to within a year."

"Your father would be very happy and proud of this decision," Dorris said, then added, "I am."

Her response surprised and pleased Audrey. It seemed she really was changing her attitude. Now that the air was cleared and everything out in the open, they could move forward like a family.

"I've heard about a rescue called Puppy Love that's not

far," Audrey told her. "We'll drive out there and find you a dog. Do you want a puppy or an older dog?"

It was hard to collect all her thoughts about her last few conversations with her mother. Learning about Wyatt hadn't been shocking, as much as it had been a revelation and the answer to many questions. The air was clear between them, but now she had another quandary to deal with.

Whether or not to tell Jericho.

He'd called and told her what time he'd pick her up, and met her on the back porch. She wore a puffy white coat, nothing different than anyone else in Spencer wore. He opened the truck door and she reached for the hand grip to climb in. She wore black leather-tooled boots with rhinestone designs. There would be no one photographing her arrival, no one to comment on which coat she'd chosen or the designer of her dress. America's country sweetheart was arriving at a local bar in his Silverado.

Jericho got in and glanced over. Audrey was stunning as always, but tonight she wore a contagious smile. "You're happy tonight."

"Yes, I am." She looked at him. "This is a real date."

She still confounded him. "Didn't you want it to be?"

"Yes."

He reached over and took her gloved hand. "So did I."

He headed for the highway.

"I met with your brother today," she said.

"Yeah?"

"He's *Big Pine's* new financial manager."

"He told me he really wanted the position. He'll do a fine

job for you."

"That takes a lot of worry off my plate," she said. "One of
the first things we're going to implement will be wages for
Lane and Dana. They do a lot, and they have the little house,
but *Big Pine* needs employees in order to flourish again."

"Good decision."

"I've made a lot of changes the past several weeks. Had a
lot to work through. But I feel a thousand times lighter."

He could tell that was true by how relaxed she seemed, by
the tone of her voice and the way she smiled. He didn't want
to think her newfound happiness frightened him, but he still
had an unease he couldn't shake. Audrey's return, their
growing relationship, had weakened his defenses and let in
hope.

He loved her unreservedly. After all these years, she was
still the only one he wanted. Seeing her hurting had been
unbearable. It had been years since he'd considered more,
even remotely thought about a loving, committed relationship. He hadn't been sure he was capable of the vulnerability
it would take to open his heart and trust. But everything had
changed. He wanted to be with her, wanted to be part of her
life.

The evening was bitterly cold, so he dropped her off
under the awning at the back entrance and parked the truck.
She hadn't gone in, but was still waiting for him when he
jogged to the door. She faced him and looked up. The music
from inside was muted, but he knew the song.

He quite naturally framed her face with both hands and
touched his nose to hers. "I want to kiss you, but I don't want
to mess up your lipstick."

"I'll slip into the bathroom and fix it. Wait." She took a
tissue from her coat pocket and blotted it against her lips.
"Kiss me."

He didn't need another invitation. He covered her lips

with his. By now their noses were cold, and their breath was visible, but her lips were soft and warm. He loved everything about this woman. Wanted to kiss her like this every night and day for the rest of his life. Sometimes it still felt unreal to have her undivided attention, to think she wanted him like this.

The back door opened, light pouring out, sounds of music and laughter reaching them. "Oh, sorry," a young man said. "Just getting something from my car."

"Sorry," Jericho said and moved around the guy to usher Audrey into the building.

"I'll be right back." She disappeared into the women's restroom and returned a minute later.

He led her along the hall past the bar and into the main room. Sparkling lights draped across the windows and walls and white poinsettias decorated the bar and tables.

Kipp and Ronnie Hudson automatically waved them over and pulled another table against theirs. Ronnie's wife, Delaney greeted them, and Piper was seated beside Kipp. "Great to see you again," Piper said. "You've been here what, like four months now?"

"Yep," Audrey said. "I'm staying."

Ronnie's eyes widened. "What?"

"Audrey, that's great," Kipp said.

"Great for you, Deputy Tanner," Delaney said.

He grinned and turned to order drinks from the server. "White wine for you?" he asked Audrey.

She responded, then fielded a dozen questions about her plans.

"A recording studio?" Ronnie said. "That's awesome. Maybe you and Jericho can record something together."

"Well, we did write a song together already." She tilted her head toward him. "The one we sang at the showcase."

Jericho shrugged. "Maybe."

The band had taken a brief break and were back on the platform. The intro of a song played, and he took her hand. "Let's dance."

This was all new. Though he knew her better than he knew anyone, they'd never had this kind of relationship. Holding her, touching her, dancing with her, none of it was awkward. It felt right. He waved away an invitation to sing, as did she, and they focused on each other. They visited with friends, but for the most part they stayed on the dance floor. A couple of hours felt like no time at all when she asked if he was ready to leave.

He'd started the truck from inside, so it was warm when they got in.

"You never drink much," Audrey said.

"Nah. Never know when I might get a work call. Two is my limit."

"Well, I had too many glasses of wine. Everybody bought me one."

"Come home with me," he suggested. "I'll make you some coffee."

"That sounds like a perfect idea."

And a perfect evening became a perfect night.

Early the next morning, he checked stock and came back with a breakfast casserole his mom had sent, and heated it in the oven while aromatic fresh coffee dripped.

"You were up early." Audrey wrapped her arms around him from behind. He turned to fold her into his arms. The scent of her hair under his nose was as arousing as everything else about her. He ran his palm down the back of his shirt she'd pulled around herself, his mind wandering to the previous night.

"You made breakfast?"

"No, my mom texted me to come get it."

She leaned away and he released her. She poured herself a

cup of coffee that had just finished brewing. She leaned back against the counter and put one foot on top of the other. She'd found a clean pair of his white socks. She was adorable.

"I need to tell you something."

His thoughts were sidelined. "Do I want to hear it?"

She shrugged.

He took a deep breath. "Hit me."

"Wow, I really don't want to say this now."

"Sorry. The last time you said you had something to tell me, my world tipped over."

"I know."

"I started a fire before I went out. Let's get comfortable."

They went into the other room, and he handed her a throw to cover her legs.

She settled and took a sip of her coffee. "I've had some interesting and good talks with my mom, you know. Revealing. She was in love with your dad. For years and years."

He listened as she explained Dorris' story and how her father had forced her to lure and marry Charlie Monroe. It seemed unfathomable in today's world, but there were still plenty of abusive and controlling men. He'd seen the results firsthand. Audrey told him the whole story as she knew it, revealing her brother Wyatt, his friend, had been his half-brother.

"I feel like I'm in some alternate universe where things we thought were true are something else," he said finally. He considered his own father making such a big mistake and then coming to regret it. His mother had forgiven him and moved on—because she loved him. He obviously loved her. They were happy together, clearly still in love after all these years. His dad's indiscretion hadn't torn them apart. That was impressive. "I'm torn. I wish I didn't know, but it's a good thing we both know. Now I wonder how we didn't realize it before."

"I didn't want to tell you," she said. "It's painful to learn things about your parents. But I'm glad I know because it explains so much. It explains my mom's anger and unhappiness, her favoritism."

"Still wrong," he told her.

"She apologized. She told me she loved me and was proud of me. She admires me for being braver than she was."

"I always admired you."

She gave him an uncertain smile. "Are you okay? Are you angry?"

"No. I'm sad. Knowing why so many people asked if Wyatt and I were brothers makes sense. We were."

She scooted closer and snuggled into his embrace. He kissed her and she moved into his lap where they held each other.

"Will you say anything to your parents?" she asked.

"Apparently, they both know what happened and have put it behind them. If my dad doesn't know about Wyatt, it's not my place to tell him. I'd wager they both know though. They're happy. My mom has kept a relationship with yours all these years, despite what happened. I'm not going to rock that boat."

"Everything is out in the open between us though," she said.

The facts anyway. "Audrey?"

"Mmm?"

"Can I sing you a song?"

She tilted her head. "Any time."

He released and covered her with the throw to go take his guitar from the wall. In his oldest guitar case were several notebooks filled with songs he'd written. He flipped through one and found what he was looking for. The song that conveyed his feelings better than words.

He'd vowed he wouldn't make the same mistake twice.

But his mistake hadn't been loving her or letting himself care. His mistake had been not telling her how he felt. She'd wanted to leave and he'd wanted to stay, but if he'd spoken up, they might have been able to work something out. All this time he'd hung back, remaining uncommitted for fear of getting burned.

The handwritten song was the early version, before he'd copied it over neatly and mailed it to her. He played the first few chords and sang. *"Like a shooting star you shine bright, brighter than all the others. Your love is sweet and your love is big, bigger than other lovers. We all have to play our parts, but if tomorrow you look back—if you wake up and think your good sense is gone...I'll still be here, because baby, maybe I'm the one."*

Eyes shining with tears, Audrey sat on the edge of the sofa. He had to stop holding back the love and desire, stop fearing his need for her and for a family. He thought he'd protected himself, but he'd shut himself off from any possibility of a future.

*Maybe I'm the One* was a love song, not the pop single her manager husband had turned it into. The song held his hopes and dreams. Could she tell now?

"It's beautiful," she said. "Hearing it the way you wrote it —for me, it means everything."

"Maybe I *am* the one, Audrey," he said.

"You have no reason to trust me," she answered. "I didn't mean to, but I let you down. Can you trust me from now on? I'm going to make a life right here in Spencer. I couldn't have done it before, but I can now. I don't want to lose any more time with you." She gave him a tremulous smile. "I want us to be together."

He laid his guitar on the other sofa and knelt at her feet. "I love you, Audrey. I've always loved you. I loved you when you were ten and sang your heart out on a haybale in your daddy's barn. I loved you when you were fifteen and threw up on my boots backstage before that performance at Cade County fair."

"I forgot about that."

"I felt it every time I heard your voice on the radio and every time I saw you on a magazine or your pictures on the wall at Pearl's. I was afraid of feeling it, but I'm done hiding it. You're my one. You—and now Hayden—have my heart. I *am* still here. I just need you to say I'm the one too."

She framed his face and kissed him so sweetly it hurt. "You're the one, Jericho Tanner."

"This isn't a glamorous setting, and I'm wearing my work clothes."

"I'm wearing your good shirt," she teased.

He took her hands. "I don't have a ring yet so this probably isn't the best time, but...will you marry me?"

She smiled through tears. "Oh, this is the best time." She kissed him. "I will gleefully, joyfully marry you. I love you."

Christmas had been a whirlwind, sharing their news, spending the holiday with their combined families. They'd gone to the Tanners on Christmas Eve to watch Audrey's Christmas Special, and Christine had invited friends to join them.

Audrey hadn't sung *O Holy Night* on the special this year, so she sang it for Edith while Jericho accompanied.

On Christmas Day the families enjoyed brunch at Jericho's cabin and exchanged gifts. Audrey knew what her gift from Jericho was, because they'd selected it together, but he'd picked it up and wrapped it. She opened the white leather box and he slid the sparkling engagement ring on her finger.

"I love you," he said.

Somewhere deep inside she'd known all along. Known she loved him in this deep and abiding way. "I love you."

Their loved ones clapped and gave them tearful hugs.

"I can't tell you how happy I am to have another daughter and my first granddaughter." Christine lifted her mimosa for a toast.

"What shall I call you?" Hayden asked.

Christine sat on a chair more level with Hayden's gaze. "Well, I don't know. You call your other grandmother Gramma. You could call me Grammy or Nana or whatever you like."

Both Christine and Hayden looked at Dorris. She'd worn a festive red sweater and several of the plastic loop bracelets Hayden had made her. She seemed less standoffish than previously, and offered Christine a hesitant smile before giving Hayden her attention. "I heard Annabelle call her grandmother Nana."

"I like Nana," Hayden said.

"Then I like it too." Christine hugged her and gave Dorris a nod.

Audrey experienced joy knowing her daughter had a father and grandparents who were going to show her love and acceptance.

"Audrey and Hayden have decided to live here after the wedding," Jericho told them. "At least until the studio is built and operating. After that we'll decide if we want to build another home."

"Can I have your place if you move?" Bethel asked.

The others chuckled.

"To be decided," her brother replied.

Audrey hugged Jericho. "I still have your gift."

She went to the dwindling pile under the tree, took out a wrapped square package and handed it to him.

"It's heavy." He set it on the coffee table to untie the ribbon and peel away the paper. He opened the lid, finding molded cardboard that protected the contents. He removed that and lifted out the trophy. She knew the instant he recognized it.

"What is this?" he asked.

He read the inscription on the plate and turned it so the others could see.

National Academy of Recording Arts & Sciences

Jericho Tanner/Audrey Knox
Songwriter/Artist

BEST SINGLE OF THE YEAR
MAYBE I'M THE ONE

"You have credit with the Recording Academy. This Grammy is now registered to both of us. The man who makes them lives in California, so I was thrilled he was able to engrave the plate in time for Christmas." She waited for a reaction.

Finally, after staring at the Grammy another minute, he looked at her. "I don't know what to say, Audrey. Thank you."

"You deserve it," she said. "It's your song. And eventually, maybe on my next album, I want to record it the way it was intended. Together."

He nodded. "Okay."

He hugged her soundly. He wasn't demonstrative, but he obviously felt things deeply. This was important to him, and it had been important for her to give him the credit he rightfully owned.

"I didn't realize the song you told us Jericho wrote had won an award." Atwood stepped closer and took glasses from his shirt pocket to have a better look. "This is a really big deal."

"It's a huge deal," Audrey agreed. "Your son's talent has been recognized by the industry and peers."

Jericho gave her a proud glance. "Audrey has won several, Dad."

"Does Ariana Grande have one?" Atwood asked.

Judah and Bethel broke into laughter.

Atwood turned to look at them. "What?"

"She has over a dozen," Hayden supplied.

Christine took her husband's arm and gazed fondly at the couple. "You're like Tim and Faith now."

Jericho shook his head. "Not quite."

"When is the wedding anyway?" his mom asked.

"Valentine's Day," Audrey announced. "We're not waiting any longer than that."

That news was met with more appreciation and another toast.

Jericho set the Grammy on the mantle, studied it a moment and returned to envelop her in his embrace. "Valentine's Day can't come too soon," he whispered.

Audrey had achieved the success she'd dreamed of with her career, but dreaming big wasn't over. Now she had someone to share her life and dreams. She and Jericho had the hope and promise of building the rest of their lives here on the land their families had owned for generations. She had a feeling the best was yet to come.

If you enjoyed *Maybe I'm the One*, please leave a review.

With today's world of vast reading choices, word of mouth is the best advertising. So please let others know about this book. Tell your friends, relatives, acquaintances, the book reading stranger on the bus. By sharing a good book, you may discover a new friend.

Reviews help readers discover and connect with new authors. Every review is important to us and is greatly appreciated. Please consider leaving an honest review of this book at your favorite review sites or at any or all of these places.

Store link

Goodreads

Bookbub

NEXT IN THE SERIES

**Just My Imagination** Aspen Gold Series 18

(Friends to lovers Forced Proximity Family Saga Fantasy Romance)

*lizzie starr

*Will his magic heal her reality?*

A son of Faerie, Konnor owns the Keltic Ranch, a gift shop in Spencer's Olde Town, specializing in Celtic and fantasy art and jewelry. Oh, and there's also a cranky fairy pony kids love to visit and pet. Keeping his heritage hidden hasn't been a problem, in fact, he often ignores his magical side.

Bonnie Zhang comes to Spencer with secrets of her own. Leaving her bitter mother and her broken past behind, Bonnie and her pair of therapy doxies need a place to belong and friends who care. But the knowledge she keeps secret could change that acceptance in the time it takes to speak a few words.

Can they trust each other with their truths to discover the love they've both searched for?

# DEAR READER

Once upon a time a group of writer friends got the grandiose idea to create a continuity series. We threw ourselves into developing characters, fashioning families, dynamics and a setting, which evolved from one member's love of all things Colorado. We created character profiles, detailed maps, brainstormed titles and themes. We collected photos and researched. We proposed our idea to a few publishers and got no traction. So, after a time the contracted books came first, members came and went, and the project was set aside.

Years after the initial idea, we rallied again to write the stories, now hoping readers will feel the same intensity and appreciation for this project as we do. We welcome you to join these families, laugh in their good times and cry in their sad times, follow them as they solve mysteries, expose secrets, recover from their pasts, reach for their goals and, most importantly, as the residents of Spencer Colorado fall in love.

Thank you for reading. Telling stories is one of our greatest delights and we hope you enjoyed your time in

Spencer. Readers like you spark the energy needed to tell these tales.

These Aspen Gold books are independently published by the authors. We thank you for your support, and we take pride in giving you quality books and excellent stories. We're thankful you've chosen to follow us and be part of the AG community.

Again, thank you.

# The Aspen Gold Authors

Want to know more about Spencer, Colorado, and the Aspen Gold Series? Sign up for our email messages which include the monthly *Rocky Mountain Rumors*, new book announcements, and fun surprises. Your email is safe with us, will never be shared, and you can, of course, unsubscribe at any time. You can find the link on the Aspen Gold Series website www.aspengoldseries.com

**Be sure to follow all the Aspen Gold Series updates at:**

Aspen Gold: The Series Website
https://www.aspengoldseries.com/
Aspen Gold Twitter
https://twitter.com/@gold_aspen
Aspen Gold: The Series on Facebook
https://www.facebook.com/AspenGoldSeries/

*Rocky Mountain Rumors*, the newsletter
https://www.subscribepage.com/n9n7p3

# THE ASPEN GOLD BOOKS

**Dancing In The Dark** Aspen Gold Series 1
(Second Chance Small Town Family Saga Romance)
Cheryl St.John
*He had everything a man could want--except her forgiveness...*

~

**Call Me Mandy** Aspen Gold Series 2
(Second Chance Small Town Romance)
Debra Hines
*The last man she loved took everything from her...*

~

**Ryder's Heart** Aspen Gold Series 3
(Homecoming Forced Proximity Psychic Small Town
Romance)
*lizzie starr
*She can't allow secrets to steal love from her...*

~

**For Keeps** Aspen Gold Series 4
(Secret Baby First Love Family Saga Small Town)
Barbara Gwen & *lizzie starr
*Hiding the truth is like denying the sun...*

~

**Second Chances** Aspen Gold Series 5
(Second Chance Small Town Single Mom Romance)
Donna Kaye
*She tried the fairy tale and the fairy tale didn't work...*

~

**Sleepin' Alone** Aspen Gold Series 6
(Protective Hero Romantic Suspense Small Town Enemies to
Lovers)
Bernadette Jones
*Every man is guilty of the good he did not do...*

~

**Stay A Little Longer** Aspen Gold Series 7
(Protective Hero Romantic Suspense Small Town Second
Chance)
Bernadette Jones
*Death wasn't frightening. Living scared the hell out of him...*

~

**Speechless** Aspen Gold Series 8
(Small Town Wedding Romance Short Story)
*lizzie starr
*How many peonies does it take to get married?*

~

**Close to the Heart** Aspen Gold Series 9
(Friends to Lovers Small Town Seasoned Romance)

Debra Hines
*He'd raised her child as his own...*

~

**Finding Hope** Aspen Gold Series 10
(Cowboy Former Military Small Town Romance)
Donna Kaye
*Is the peace he's found too good to be true?*

~

**Fortunate Cookie** Aspen Gold Series 11
(Friends to Lovers Small Town Bakery Romance)
*lizzie starr
*This woman... wearing frosting... and nothing else...*

~

**Lonely Eyes** Aspen Gold Series 12
(Protective Hero Romantic Suspense Small Town Forced
Proximity Age Gap)
Bernadette Jones
*She'd come to the right place. He was the monster hunter.*

~

**Whisper My Name** Aspen Gold Series 13
(Secret Identity Small Town Sheriff Next Door Romance)
Cheryl St.John
*She was the girl behind the headlines*

~

**Gorgeous Scars** Aspen Gold Series 14
(Contemporary Romantic Suspense Rodeo Cowboy Heroine
in Peril)
M.A. Jewell
*The rodeo never prepared this cowboy for bodyguard duty.*

~

**Another Night Alone** Aspen Gold Series 15
(Protective Hero Romantic Suspense Small Town
Older Man)
Bernadette Jones
*She'd had the courage to save her child. Can she do the same for
herself?*

~

**Yesterday's Promise** Aspen Gold Series 16
(Anthology Short Stories Romance Collection)
*Romantic short stories from the Aspen Gold Authors*

~

**Maybe I'm the One** Aspen Gold Series 17
(Friends to Lovers Second Chance Small Town Deputy
Romance)
Cheryl St.John
*While adored by millions, her world has become very small*

~

*Aspen Gold books coming in early 2022*

**Just My Imagination** Aspen Gold Series 18
(Friends to lovers Forced Proximity Family Saga Fantasy
Romance)
*lizzie starr
*Will his magic heal her reality?*

~

**A Better Man** Aspen Gold Series 19
(Protective Hero Romantic Suspense Forced Proximity
Bounty Hunter)
Bernadette Jones
*Loving her made him a better man. Can he keep her alive long
enough to tell her?*

~

**Trust Me** Aspen Gold Series 20
Donna Kaye

# CHERYL'S ASPEN GOLD BOOKS

**Dancing In The Dark** Aspen Gold Series 1
(Second Chance Small Town Family
Saga Romance)

*He had everything a man could want--
except her forgiveness...*

**She'd wanted to dance, get
married and have babies... all she had
left was dance.**

**He had everything a man could
want--except her forgiveness**

Kendra Price had never wanted to be rich, but wanted to be
comfortable, which she was. She'd never wanted fame, but to
live her passion to the fullest and dance, which she did. She'd
wanted to marry Dusty, have babies and live happily ever
after. Which would never happen.

Dusty Cavanaugh has loved Kendra since she walked into the
school cafeteria and captured a dozen boyish hearts with the
sweep of her stormy gray-green gaze and the lift of her chin.

College, marriage, and children had been the plan. Then their dreams vanished like morning fog. He'd had his own baby. Without her.

There had been no roadmap for life apart. Will love be enough to guide them back?

**Whisper My Name** Aspen Gold Series 13
(Secret Identity Small Town Sheriff Next Door Romance)

*She was the girl behind the headlines*

Laurel Whitaker has been her name for fifteen years. Anyone hearing her real identity would know who she was, and she's had enough of cameras, questions and stares. Spencer, Colorado is a great place to remain indistinguishable among the tourists. Unwanted attention comes in the worst possible form—a tough, perceptive, and all too determined lawman.

Sheriff Joe Cavanaugh is accustomed to looking out for people—his large loving family, his teenage daughter, anyone in his county who needs him. But the mistrustful young woman staying in the lake house beside his property goes out of her way to avoid his help, and that's suspicious. Instinct tells him she's hiding something…and attraction motivates him to uncover her secrets.

Will Laurel's truth be his undoing…or hers?

*Rescue Me* is a short story included in: **Yesterday's Promise: Aspen Gold Series Book 16**

A high-stakes poker game, first meets, a dog rescue, loves lost and rekindled, and life-altering choices fill the history of Spencer, Colorado. Discover the challenges faced in these heartwarming stories crafted by the multi-author group who brings you romantic fiction at its finest in The Aspen Gold Series.

This collection includes:
The Card Game~~ M.A.Jewell
Some Days Are Diamonds~~ *lizzie starr
Ah, Venice ~~ Debra Hines
First Chance ~~ Donna Kaye
Racing Hearts~~ Bernadette Jones
Rescue Me ~~ Cheryl St.John

**Maybe I'm The One** Aspen Gold Series 17
*Nashville* meets *Virgin River* when a beloved country singer returns to her roots and encounters the cowboy whose song she unknowingly stole.
*A woman with ambition*
Country singer Audrey Knox has

traveled the world, followed her heart, and seen her dreams come true by becoming a worldwide fan favorite. Her face is on every magazine stand, and her songs are played all over the world. However, in achieving success, her world has become very small.

*A man who's been burned*

For Deputy Jericho Tanner, playing the guitar and singing was all about the music—and about spending time with the girl he secretly adored. His aspirations are to uphold the law and help run the family ranch he'll inherit. He learned early on that love is a weakness.

When Audrey returns to Spencer seeking acceptance, will Jericho allow pride to cost him happiness?

# JOE'S WIFE

*American Western Historical*

*Meg's dead husband could do no wrong*

*Tye Hatcher did everything wrong.... except win Meg Telford's heart*

After Meg Telford's husband dies in the war and is lauded as a hero, she must face the fact that she can't keep the ranch without a man to shoulder the workload. Nothing will stop her from saving Joe's dream. The war has taken nearly all the able-bodied men--and a devilishly handsome bad boy seems her only choice.

Town pariah, Tye Hatcher has a reputation as a hell-raiser, but he's looking to prove himself and has his own plans for the land. Meg's proposal might be too good to be true, but he's willing to take the risk, even if the risk is his heart. Struggling with guilt and the rejection of the townspeople, Meg must learn that her convenient husband is a man who takes risks and does what's right for the sake of others.

Her vulnerable dreams and their hard work will be for naught unless she and Tye reveal their secrets and face what they're both coming to understand--they can't change the past, but the future is in their hands.

# SAINT OR SINNER

*American Western Historical*

In this heartwarming tale of redemption, Joshua McBride returns
from the war a changed man, ready to put down roots and plant his
feet in the community. Prim and uptight Miss Adelaide Stapleton,
leader of the Dorcas Society, doesn't believe he's changed—people
are never what they seem. But she has plenty of secrets of her own—
among them the inescapable fact that Joshua sets her heart to
pounding and makes her long for his disturbing kisses. How long
can she keep her own past hidden—and resist temptation?

# LAND OF DREAMS

In this tale of hope and love, too-tall spinster Thea Coulson wants to be a mother to a child who arrives in Nebraska on an orphan train. When Booker Hayes shows up to take his niece, a marriage of convenience suits them both. Thea's nights are filled with dreams of the tall, dark army major, but she guards her heart. Booker's first taste of home and hearth has him longing for more, but first he must win the trust of his niece…and the heart of the sun-kissed farmer's daughter.

HEAVEN CAN WAIT

*American Western Historical*

Dutch Country Bride Book 1

Raised within the confines of a strict religious community, Lydia
Beker longs for a simple touch, dreams of seeing more of the world.
When handsome farmer, Jakob Neubauer and his family visit the
bakery where she works, she is fascinated, but Outsiders are
forbidden to her. Jakob is attracted to Lydia, as well, and she makes
the difficult decision to leave everything she knows behind to marry
him. He offers love and passion, but will she ever fit into his world?

# RAIN SHADOW

Dutch Country Brides Book 2

*American Western Historical*

Raised by the Lakota Sioux and having traveled with the Wild West Show for many years, Rain Shadow is unprepared for a forced stay at the home of Anton Neubauer while her son recuperates. He is a rock, a man who has lived on and farmed the same several hundred acres since he was young.

Anton needs a mother for his son, but he needs someone domestic and ladylike, not the Smith & Wesson toting female who sets up her teepee in his front yard and whose target practice wakes him at the crack of dawn. But fate, two little boys and two old men conspire to keep them together, and it's too late to deny their passion once love is part of the equation.

# HOMETOWN GIRL

Sweet romance

Small-town life was never enough for rodeo champion, Justin Cooper, but when he returns to Oklahoma to recover from an injury, Stevie Marshall catches his attention all over again. She's still the prettiest girl in town, still rooted to the community, and still doesn't share his passion for adventure.

Resistant to change, Stevie has never fallen in love with another, and she's not about to fall for this handsome cowboy all over again. Her heart has taken too much of a beating to make the same mistake twice. This life wasn't good enough for him last time. Justin thought he'd rather fall off a bucking bull than face his feelings, but their close proximity challenges his thinking. Can blue ribbons and trophies stack up to a life with the hometown girl he loves? This time the cowboy is going to hold on tighter than ever.

***Opposites attract in this first love reunion story.***

# A HUSBAND BY ANY OTHER NAME

Caught in a lie….

Fourteen years ago Dan Beckett's identical twin took off without a word to his pregnant young fiancé or their father. Having secretly loved Lorraine for years, Dan assumes his twin's identity as the first-born son, as Lorraine's husband and father of the baby she carried. Around the lie, he created the perfect life.

But now his greatest fear is coming true. His long-lost brother is coming home—with amnesia. Dan is about to lose his tenuous hold on this masquerade, and he must tell Lorraine the truth before Tom remembers his true identity.

Lorrie built a life with Tom Beckett, the man she loves, the father of her children—or so she believed. Her first reaction to his confession is disbelief…and then anger and hurt. Her whole married life has been a lie. But Lorrie has a secret of her own—a secret that never seemed important until now.

Will the truth unravel the love they once shared? What will become of their family, their children…their marriage when everyone learns the truth?

## ALL ABOUT THE BUNDT: BUNDT CAKE RECIPES

After years of being asked for recipes, Cheryl St.John spent a summer writing down ingredients and baking times, baking and asking for beta testers in order to put together this collection of mouthwatering recipes for Bundt cakes.

Many of the recipes are labeled NO SKILL REQUIRED, indicating exceptional ease of preparation. If you don't consider yourself a baker or if you're an accomplished baker and simply want a quick recipe, you will find these cakes using box mixes are convenient and delicious. You don't have to tell anyone you started with a mix—the cakes are so good that no one will guess preparation didn't take hours. Bake with ease and enjoy serving a beautiful cake to family and friends.

Cheryl's philosophy: Eat cake! It's someone's birthday somewhere.

# ABOUT THE AUTHOR

Cheryl has always loved the
exciting and diverse worlds
available between the covers of
books. As a child she wrote
stories & drew covers, then
stapled them into little books.
She cut all the tiny images from
the book club advertisements in
the Sunday newspaper & glued

them to bits of cardboard so Barbie® had a full library.

Cheryl is the married author of more than fifty books, both
historical and contemporary. Her stories have earned
numerous RITA nominations, Romantic Times awards & are
published in over a dozen languages. One thing all reviewers
& readers agree on regarding Cheryl's work is the degree of
emotion & believability. In describing her stories of second
chances & redemption, readers & reviewers use words like,
"emotional punch, hometown feel, core values, believable
characters & real-life situations." Reader reviews show her
popularity with readers.

The author lives in the Midwest, USA. When she's not
writing or spending time with her family, she's checking out
garage sales, flea markets & antique malls. Among her collec-
tions are teacups & teapots, roosters, chicken kitchen timers,
vintage spice tins, wooden recipe boxes, Barbies®, charm

bracelets, vintage jewelry, Kokeshi dolls, white stoneware, Delftware, souvenir spoons, Goebel birds, Royal Copley planters, vintage hankies & BOOKS. Cheryl admits she's a bargain hunter with the heart of a hoarder, trying to live as a minimalist. The struggle is real.

Check out Cheryl's website to see an entire listing of all of her books.
Cheryl's Newsletter Sign up:
http://eepurl.com/bqCji9
Aspen Gold Newsletter:
https://www.subscribepage.com/n9n7p3
email Cheryl at: SaintJohn@aol.com

Visit her on the web:
http://www.cherylstjohn.net/

facebook.com/CherylStJ
twitter.com/_CherylStJohn_
instagram.com/cherylstjohn
bookbub.com/profile/cheryl-st-john
amazon.com/Cheryl-St-John/e/B001IXM9IE
pinterest.com/cheryl_stjohn